The Unsinkable Herr Goering

by
Ian Cassidy

Copyright © 2012 by Cassowary Press. All rights reserved

Published by Cassowary Press

No part of this publication may be reproduced in whole or in part, or stored in a retrieval system, or transmitted in any form or by any means, electronic, mechanical, photocopying, recording, or otherwise, without written permission of the publisher. For information regarding permission, write to Cassowary Press.

All characters in this publication are fictitious and any resemblance to real persons, living or dead, is purely coincidental.

The Unsinkable Herr Goering / Ian Cassidy
First Edition Paperback: March 2013
ISBN 978-0-9849644-0-6

Published by Cassowary Press

Printed in the USA

I have not necessarily
kept to the truth;
all mistakes are my own.

foreword

What follows is the true story of how Reich Marshal Hermann Goering, Nazi, Commander-in-Chief of the Lufftwaffe and the second most powerful man in the Third Reich came to miss his appointment with US Army Master Sergeant John C. Woods in the gymnasium at Nuremberg on the 16th October 1946.

He did not leave this world courtesy of a cyanide tablet secreted in the heel of his jackboot minutes before his scheduled execution. The truth is far more bizarre.

one
21st March, 1938

11.46am. Frittenden, Kent. Goering was beginning to regret his choice of underwear. The black lace suspender belt and silk stockings he had chosen that morning were chafing his thighs. He fidgeted in the back seat of his Mercedes as the chauffeur motored through the English countryside.

He wiped the first traces of sweat from his brow and tapped on the screen. The chauffeur lowered the screen and asked: "Yes, Herr Reich Marshal."

"How much further?" Goering barked.

"Not far, Herr Reich Marshal, at the current rate of progress we should reach the Ambassador's Residence in about twenty minutes."

Goering grunted and sat back in his seat. He motioned to the chauffeur to raise the screen and reached for his briefcase.

He took out the papers that required Von Ribbentrop's signature and frowned. What was Hitler thinking of, sending him on this piffling errand. He was Hermann Goering, hero of the Lufftwaffe, scourge of the Royal Flying Corps, Reich Marshal of Germany, and not a messenger boy. There must be a reason why Hitler had not chosen that senile old fool Ludendorf or his educationally sub-normal lapdog Hess for the job but Goering could not think of one. He racked his brains in a vain attempt to decipher the Führer's motives but his attention once again wandered to the suspender belt that seemed to be crawling all over his bloated midriff.

The Unsinkable Herr Goering

Goering wound down the window and spat. And why had that pretentious ass Von Ribbentrop refused to cut short his shooting weekend? Why was he forced to make this ridiculous trip to wilds of Kent? And more to the point why hadn't Ribbentrop returned to Berlin? Almost a month had passed since The Führer had appointed him Foreign Minister and winding up his affairs in Britain couldn't take so long, could they?

The answers to these questions eluded Goering and sulkily he tugged at the suspender strap through his uniform breeches and motioned to the chauffeur to step on it. He brooded as the Kent countryside swept by.

His mood had not improved fifteen minutes later when the chauffeur slowed the limousine and made a left turn. The gatehouse guard hastily swallowed his coffee and rushed out towards the car. On seeing the Reich Marshal's insignia flying on the fenders of the Mercedes, the guard switched direction and headed for the barrier. He raised it soundlessly and waved the car through, saluting as it passed.

The chauffeur gunned the heavy car along the tree-lined driveway. As the car bumped along the untreated drive, Goring grumbled. *Just like that Anglophile fop, to leave the drive potholed.* Asphalt would destroy the drive's authenticity, rob it of its essential Englishness. Goering snorted and gripped tightly on the door handle but try as he might he could not stop the metal clip at the back of his suspender belt digging into his ample buttocks every time the car crashed over a pothole.

To take his mind off the ordeal he looked out of the window. The rhododendrons were in bloom all along the drive and Goering thought of the many thousands of man-hours that must be expended by the army of gardeners in dead heading the pink flowers.

Presently the car came to the top of the drive and from here Goering could see the Ambassador's house and gardens in all their splendour. In front of him was the newly acquired German Ambassador's Official country residence, paid for from the Reich's coffers in Berlin. Of course Ribbentrop had purchased his own suburban atrocity, in Pinner Hill of all places, a bungalow with views over the golf course! Goering snorted. Shocking middle class upstart but he was secretly relieved that he was not forced to visit the damned wine merchant in his natural habitat. Goering

Ian Cassidy

grunted and wriggled in his seat, his twenty stone of congeniality or brutality, whichever the occasion demanded, leaning decidedly towards brutality.

The first sight to catch his eye was the folly. He snorted, *This is too much, and the Volk is paying for all this.* His face faded to a more subtle shade of puce when he remembered that the grounds had been in their current state when his government had purchased the house. At least the folly had not been erected on one of Von Ribbentrop's whims, but the upkeep, oh the upkeep.

He poked his head out the window and took a deep breath. From this position, filling his lungs with calming azalea-scented air, he had no choice but to study the folly more closely.

It was an ornamental bridge in the Adam style, made from stately grey stone. Five arched spans bridged the lake, all this surmounted by a Palladian style balustrade with classical urns fronting columns at regular intervals. All very attractive and fairly standard for the park of a fine English country house. It was when you looked above the balustrade that you were confronted by the folly in its entirety. The bridge was covered, roofed over and the grey-green of the lead twinkled in the sunlight. *I bet that's new*, Goering said to himself. The central portion of the roof was supported with two rows of classical Doric columns. At each end of the central portion was a larger Palladian arch, again supported by Doric columns and topped with carved friezes beneath unbroken pediments. Goering pulled his head back inside the Mercedes and turned away.

His gaze took him away from the park, over the immaculate lawns and the haha to the house itself. Up till now he had only seen photographs.

Beyond the sweeping gravel driveway with just a single fountain were a series of terraces and steps leading up to a two-storey house built from Cheshire stone. At the top of the steps was a grand four column portico with an unbroken pediment top, matching those of the folly. The main door was flanked on each side by two floor-to-ceiling casements. These in turn were flanked by two wings each with a large arched window, providing access to the terrace. The roof had a low sloping pitch and even to Goering's untrained eye, it looked newly repaired. *The stonework has been cleaned as well*, he said to himself through clenched teeth.

The Unsinkable Herr Goering

Goering grumbled about the running costs of such a place as the chauffeur brought the car to a halt at the bottom of the steps.

The chauffeur opened his door and helped the Reich Marshal from the car. Goering said a prayer of thanks for the tradition of boot-wearing among Lufftwaffe officers. His counterparts in the RAF would be wearing shoes and shoes would risk revealing a glimpse of stocking.

He straightened his uniform, attempted to surreptitiously adjust his suspender belt and waved the chauffeur to the servant's quarters at the back of the house before commencing his assault on the vertiginous stone staircase. He shambled up the steps resting at regular intervals. On reaching the top he stopped and took several deep breaths, his hand resting on a carved stone lion's head. One of four, lining the top of the terrace. *No one to greet me.* This time he ground his teeth. He walked to front door and as if by magic the door swung open. A footman bowed and snapped his heels together:

"Herr Reich Marshal. The ambassador will be with you shortly."

Goering was incandescent; he thrust his case into the footman's chest and barged into the hall. *He hasn't even the decency to welcome me himself.* He swore. *This will have to be noted.*

Barely able to contain his anger, Goering stood in the hallway and looked around.

The marble floor of the vestibule was disappointingly plain but the rest of the room was a profusion of gilt and ormolu. The ornate plaster ceiling was heightened in gold and contained a series of hand-painted panels showing classical scenes of Diana and Cupid and other deities. Goering studied the ceiling and despite rapidly calculating the restoration costs, he found that his mood was improving. The ceiling was just so beautiful.

He brought his eyes down to the walls, below a gilt frieze the walls were lined with domed recesses, each containing a white marble statue of obvious antiquity. The windows too were domed and flanked with gilded Doric columns.

His eyes came to rest on the obligatory portrait of the Führer in SS uniform. He moved quickly on to the other paintings, scenes by Bosch, Durer and Caspar David Freidrich, showing Frederick Barbarossa and Charlemagne and Parsifal and Siegfried.

Ian Cassidy

He looked towards the door; it did not open so he studied it. It was large and impressively panelled. Cuban mahogany, in a gilt doorframe and architrave, with a broken pediment top, flanked by two gilt wood and marble topped console tables.

Goering looked at the corner of the room towards the glorious flowing staircase, covered in a lavish red carpet, with just a hint of dark green marble poking out at the side. The rich mahogany banister was supported by lyre-shaped gilt balustrades and the walls were lined with massive paintings of battle scenes. Goering tapped his foot impatiently and looked from the staircase to the door and then back again to the staircase. Which one would Von Ribbentrop choose for his grand entrance?

Finally the door opened. Von Ribbentrop sauntered through and saluted. Goering returned a perfunctory "Heil Hitler." And sniped: "I do hope you're comfortable here, Joachim."

"Splendid isn't it," smiled Von Ribbentrop, deliberately ignoring the irony.

"I must say that I am very impressed." Goering was about to go further and suggest that the massive expenditure may even have been worth it. German prestige on the world stage was a worthwhile investment. He stopped himself; the ridiculous poltroon was puffed up enough without further compliments from him.

"The restorers have done a magnificent job, shall I give you the grand tour?" asked Von Ribbentrop.

Goering's first instinct was to say no, he had to get back to London, conduct some business there and then rush to Croydon in time for the night flight to Berlin. He changed his mind, he wanted to see more of the house, more of the Reich's expenditure: "Lead on," he grunted.

Von Ribbentrop held open the door and ushered Goering into the small salon. His boots clicking on the parquetry floor, Goering studied the room. The walls were of muted eggshell blue, with a low gilt dado and off-white panelling beneath. He was almost reluctant to walk across the highly polished floor but as from his current position all he could see was another portrait of Hitler, this time in a cheesy classical style uniform, he reluctantly barged across. Once again Hitler's portrait was surrounded by classical pictures from the hands of German masters but was curiously framed by two blackamoor figures. *An odd juxtaposition*,

The Unsinkable Herr Goering

Goering thought, reluctantly smiling at Von Ribbentrop's sense of humour.

The room was filled with Louis Quinze furniture throughout. A cream and gilt wood salon suite, with eggshell blue Regency striped upholstery lining the walls, whilst the centre of the room was filled with elegant bijouterie tables fashioned from kingwood and decorated with ormolu mounts.

"It's a wonderful room, Joachim."

"Yes the work of very talented English craftsmen."

"Surely there's nothing of English manufacture in here," snapped Goering.

"True, true but as a whole don't you think there's something quintessentially English about the room."

Goering made a vague gesture of agreeing with the Ambassador; he did not want to get into a discussion of aesthetics with the man. That was almost as foolhardy as talking politics with Hitler.

Von Ribbentrop continued: "In any event I was not referring to the cabinet makers but to the restorers, they were English."

"I see," said Goering who was hardly listening and already striding towards the next room.

The two Nazis found themselves in the Grand Salon. The parquetry floor ran seamlessly into this magnificently muted green room, although it was obscured by an enormous Persian carpet. Goering marvelled at the size, and could not conceive of a loom big enough to weave it. Feeling more comfortable on the thick pile, he strode across the carpet and stood in the centre of the room. He looked first at the ceiling; again it was domed and decorated in rich reds and golds, surrounding a series of Pietra Dura panels.

The focal point of the room was a magnificent row of arched windows surmounted by a carved Chippendale pelmet, the wood shaped in an imitation of draped cloth, seamlessly joining the heavy tapestry curtains. Goering looked through the window to the garden, and saw a formal water garden in the French style with gravelled walks surrounding formal ponds, parterres and fountains. There were nine ponds of symmetrical rococo design with curved borders, separated by flowerbeds filled with low growing plants and rows of box mirroring the curving organic edges of the pools. Beyond this were two square pools each with a central fountain and an obelisk at each corner. And beyond these was the Capability Brown inspired "natural garden," a charming landscape of trees, woods and grass.

Goering gave no thought to the army of gardeners needed to maintain such a view and turned back to Von Ribbentrop with a smile on his face.

"Shall we?" he said.

Von Ribbentrop opened the door to the library. A much more muted room with a fitted carpet and an absence of gilt. The high ceiling was decorated in green and pink with white plasterwork but the focal point in the room was the frieze above the bookshelves. All around the room, in imitation of the Portland Vase, classical maidens and warriors besported themselves, in glorious limpid white cameo against a vivid lime green background. Below the frieze were fitted mahogany bookcases filled with impressive Morocco-bound volumes. Goering did not linger over the books; he suspected that most were merely fronts, hiding booze and back copies of Health and Efficiency and The News of the World.

"A very comfortable room, Joachim, but I think I've seen enough, time is pressing."

"Yes of course, my office is this way," said Von Ribbentrop, heading for the door.

He led Goering into the Ambassador's formal reception room. Goering ran his hands over the red hand-painted wallpaper and studied the paintings. Italian masters, Madonnas, Venetian scenes, and the obligatory Hitler. Von Ribbentrop sauntered to his desk, a massive Boule work bureau plat twinkling with highly polished brass and a profusion of even more highly polished tortoiseshell. He sat behind it and offered Goering a seat. Before he sat Goering commented: "They say that for every piece manufactured by Monsieur Boule there is an exact mirror image made from the brass and tortoiseshell that was cut away when making the first piece. In a house as grand as this I would have thought both pieces would be here."

Von Ribbentrop sighed: "Regrettably the other bureau is in Versailles and the French are reluctant to part with it."

"Perhaps one day we will be in a position to persuade them," said Goering.

"One day soon, I hope."

"Perhaps, Perhaps." Goering made his way towards the chair Von Ribbentrop had offered him. He hesitated. It was a delicate cabriole-legged fauteuil and Goering did not think it would hold him. *The bastard planned this*, he said to himself. *Think of the humiliation if the chair gave way.* He thought fast. "I've been thinking, Joachim, our business is not so very formal, perhaps we could adjourn somewhere that is a little less grand, somewhere a bit more business like."

Von Ribbentrop frowned briefly, regretting the failure of his little scheme to embarrass the Reich Marshal. He smiled: "Yes of course, Hermann and I'm glad you suggested we move elsewhere. I've been dying to show someone my private apartments. Now they really are cutting edge. What's been done down here is merely restoration. Just wait until you see what's been done upstairs, it is ultra-modern, really impressive, really top drawer."

Goering said nothing.

Von Ribbentrop rang for the footman, who appeared just seconds later: "Take the Reich Marshal's case to my private office." He turned to Goering: "We'll use the back stairs." He said heading for the door.

Goering shuffled after him snorting. The pair went through another stateroom, of similar grandeur to those that had gone before, and soon came to the back staircase. Less grand than the main staircase but still very impressive, mahogany and gilt with a massive Aubusson tapestry showing Diana the Huntress flanked by Satyrs surrounded by a border of crimson silk highlighted with real ostrich feathers. Goering surveyed all this as he puffed his way to the top. He was resting against the Black Forest bear hall stand when Von Ribbentrop announced: "Prepare yourself, Hermann, what I'm about to show you is truly awe inspiring." With a flourish he flung open the door.

The first things to strike Goering were the blank walls, not even a portrait of Hitler. The anteroom had cream walls and a plain wood-block floor. Against the walls stood a Bugatti suite of blonde and ebony wood, comprising a pair of small tub chairs with high backs, bronze panelled fronts and horsehair tassels hanging from each arm and a curious three seater settee also high backed, bronze panelled and horsehair tasselled.

"Well, don't keep me in suspense," enthused Von Ribbentrop. "What do you think?"

"It's all very modern and not really to my taste," grumbled Goering. "Forgive me but these decorators you were raving about, all they seem to have done is slopped some white paint on the walls and varnished the floor. As for the furniture, well that damned funny Italian stuff looks most uncomfortable."

"Patience, Herman, the best is yet to come," said Von Ribbentrop, pointing out a grille in the wall just above head height. "These for example, what do you think of these?"

Goering looked at the black cast-iron grille, decorated with a stylised leaping stag.

"Very pleasing, I've always been a fan of Herr Brandt's work but I think you could have placed it in a more suitable position, it's simply too high up."

"It needs to be that high up, Herman, for the acoustics, don't you see, it's a radio speaker. I've had one fitted in every room and from a central control panel in my study I can pipe the radio and even the gramophone throughout the apartment."

"Why?" grizzled Goering. "Are you planning to hold dances in here?"

"As a matter of fact I've done some very successful entertaining in here," replied Von Ribbentrop. "But that's not the point, this is what I was so keen to show you. I've got every mod con, every comfort; it's the technology that's important. Sobel made the sound system personally and my 'decorators' as you call them worked with him and fitted it so well that everything works without a hitch."

"Perhaps," mumbled Goering. "But there is more to life than listening to music, Joachim."

"It's not just the music, Hermann, although now I never have to miss a moment of the Führer 's broadcasts. It's the little labour-saving devices If there is time you really must see the bathroom and the kitchen," said Von Ribbentrop, opening the door to his private sitting room. "Shall we?"

"If there's time," muttered Goering as he pushed into the room.

The room was filled with chunky blonde wood furniture in the Beidermier style, functional in design, simple and plain but extremely robust.

"At least the furniture is from the Fatherland," snorted Goering. "Much more to my taste than that weak-kneed Italian stuff."

Von Ribbentrop nodded and pointed to the walls. "It's not just the technical wizardry behind the panelling," he said, pointing at the hand-painted wallpaper. "It's beautiful, isn't it?"

Goering looked at the pattern of rich sienna stylised leaves on a sage green ground and through clenched teeth he agreed. "Yes, it's marvellous piece of work."

"Thank you Herr Reich Marshal." Von Ribbentrop smiled and brought his heels together with a ferocious clash. "And the floor, now you must agree, that is a tour de force."

Goering looked down and his eyes were dazzled by the highly polished black marble floor. He almost jumped to the nearest of the geometrically designed rugs that were dotted seemingly at random around it, subconsciously unwilling to mark it's perfection with his jack boots.

"I only hope the ceiling joists can stand the weight, Joachim," he said, heading for a chair.

"Oh I'm sure they can, I had them…"

Goering interrupted: "You had them specially reinforced by your darling decorators," laughed Goering, anticipating Von Ribbentrop's answer.

"Yes as a matter of fact I did. Do take a seat."

Goering selected the larger of the two armchairs that formed part of the leather upholstered suite that faced the fireplace. He looked around him and noticed a small dining table and four chairs in the bay window.

Von Ribbentrop followed his gaze. "We'll have lunch here a little later. Unless you'd prefer to make use of the State dining room?"

"No, no, here will be fine. I haven't time for anything more than a snack in any event."

No doubt the size of snack favoured by a hungry lion, Von Ribbentrop said to himself. He smiled at Goering. "That is a shame, Herr Reich Marshal, my private chef here is excellent, rather better in fact than the ones at the Embassy."

Goering nodded. There was, he had to admit, something slightly institutional about the meals served at the Embassy.

Von Ribbentrop rang the bell and a footman silently appeared.

"We'll take lunch here." He pointed to the small dining table. "Set two places…" He stopped. "That is if Her Excellency has not returned from her riding?"

"No Sir,." replied the footman. "Your wife left instructions that she was to lunch with friends."

"Very well, two it is then and get the Reich Marshal a sherry."

The footman bowed and opened the drinks cabinet. He poured Goering a generous measure of sherry and presented it to the Reich Marshal on a silver salver.

As he sipped his aperitif, Goering noticed a strangely veneered box in the corner of the room. His eye was drawn to it because it lacked the quality of the pieces surrounding it. Moreover it had a funny little Bakelite label on the front. He strained his eyes trying to decipher the cheap gold letters: "Baird."

A television as well, Goering grumbled, *when does the buffoon find the time to do any work?* "How do you find the British Broadcasting Corporation, Joachim?"

"Enlightening in a way and somewhat limited but the machine itself is an interesting novelty. Despite what that awful American said I'm sure it will catch on."

"Yes, I agree and I hear Goebbels is fully aware of its potential."

"I would expect nothing less of him. Although personally I can't stand the little twerp, the Führer would not have placed him in a position of such responsibility if he was not capable of serving the Reich."

Goering said nothing but took another sip from his drink.

He looked again at the television. On top of it was a Lenci figure depicting a girl dressed as a flapper standing atop a stylised skyscraper holding her skirts down in a typically modish pose. Typical, Goering said to himself, the man is sex mad.

As Goering sulked, Von Ribbentrop made for the door. "Hermann, do you mind stepping into my private office so we can conclude our bit of business? Bring your aperitif with you."

Goering wallowed in the plush cream leather upholstery. *The bas-*

tard's done it again, he swore to himself, ***how am I going to get up without spilling this sherry.*** He angrily snapped his fingers at the footman. "Take my drink," he barked to the servant.

Once relieved of his sherry, Goering stomped after Von Ribbentrop, shouting: "Follow me," to the bewildered footman.

As he wallowed through the door to the office, Goering noticed that Von Ribbentrop was already seated behind a vast macassar veneered Ruhlman desk.

"Take a seat," Von Ribbentrop said, indicating the flimsy cantilevered Marcel Breuer chair in front of the desk.

Goering looked at it and frowned. He looked around for something less rickety but the only other seat in the room was a brutal Le Corbusier chaise that struck him as sure to be uncomfortable and possibly even dangerous. He settled on the Marcel Breuer.

Squashed awkwardly between the chair's metal struts, he looked around the room. The same marble floor ran seamlessly from the lounge into the office and the wallpaper was once again hand painted. On the wall behind Von Ribbentrop was a Picasso, the only painting in the room, Mercedes Olivier, if Goering was not mistaken, in a typical blue period composition.

"Take care, Joachim, if the Führer gets to hear of your private art collection, he will not take kindly to it."

"I take precautions. The Picasso is easily replaced with a portrait of our dear leader whenever I am visited by anyone whose artistic tastes are less well developed."

Goering smiled at the backhanded compliment. "Very wise."

Von Ribbentrop went on. "Before we got down to business, you must tell me what you think."

"It's very well done. I compliment you on your choice of craftsmen. There are one or two things I would have done differently For instance the furniture is not designed for a powerfully built gentleman such as myself," replied Goering, wobbling in his metal-framed chair. He continued, "But above all there's just too much foreign frippery for me, although I prefer it to the travesty Paepke prepared for me at Leipziger Platz, I'll never forgive Speer for selecting him as a consultant."

Ian Cassidy

"I didn't use Speer for these works, he was too busy with the Embassy. I'm surprised that you found Paepke wanting, surely he can be relied upon to come up with good solid German designs. You seemed very fond of the Biedermier next door."

"Not overly fond, no." Goering protested.

"Oh Hermann, do try to be a little less old fashioned."

"How dare you, my tastes are quite varied and modern."

"Really Hermann, perhaps then you are a closet fan of the designs of Herr Docktor Gropius. As a matter of fact I bumped into him at Southampton the other day, he was en route to New York. I believe he's doing very well over there," joked Von Ribbentrop.

"Best place for him," grunted Goering. "I shared the Führer's views about that subversive little outfit."

"There we must disagree again, I saw a lot of merit in the designs that emanated from Dessau but I suppose I am just more broad-minded than you and also a lot younger," Von Ribbentrop teased.

"Surely we are the same age," Goering spluttered.

"Oh I don't think so," Von Ribbentrop replied with supreme indifference. "Now, the Picasso?" He pointed to the painting.

"Impressive." said Goering. "But I'll say it again, anything by that smelly little Spaniard should be kept from the Führer's gaze."

"Of that I am only too aware," said Von Ribbentrop. "But he's unlikely ever to visit these apartments. When he makes his first visit to Britain, this place will not be part of his itinerary. The only destination for the Führer's Panzer will be Buckingham Palace."

"After calling at 10 Downing Street," laughed Goering.

Von Ribbentrop joined in.

Goering abruptly stopped laughing and asked, "Your decorators, where in Germany did they come from?"

"They were not German at all. I chose an English firm. After consulting with Goebbels, we decided it would be best. We did not want to be seen as depriving English workmen of their daily bread."

"Yes but was that wise, what about listening devices?"

"We took plenty of precautions. Canaris sent me some Abwehr boffins to poke around after the work was done and we didn't select an obvious firm, not a local firm or even one from London, so there was less chance of them being infiltrated by MI6. No, we chose a firm from the Midlands and one run by an Irishman. An employer of most excellent tradesmen but an out and out villain. We kept a very close eye on the silverware every time he visited his staff. I have his card here." Von Ribbentrop passed the business card to Goering who gave it a perfunctory glance and was about to hand it back.

"No Hermann, keep it, I have many more and you never know when you might need an English decorator. When the Führer is in Buckingham Palace, you will no doubt want a residence close by and believe me, some of these English grand houses leave a lot to be desired. You will need a decorator; these English aristocrats care more for their spaniels than for their homes."

"I've always had a yen for Balmoral," replied Goering. "Although the distance from London is somewhat prohibitive. I must ask Speer to look into the feasibility of moving it closer to London. Failing that I suppose I will have to settle for Kensington Palace."

"I believe Himmler already has his name on that one," smiled Von Ribbentrop.

"Damn that officious little pen pusher. Kenwood House then," suggested Goering.

"Hess's." Von Ribbentrop smiled maliciously.

Goering snorted. "Why wasn't I informed that London residences had been allocated?"

"There's been no sort of official allocation, old man, more of a first come first served selection. I've chosen Apsley House for myself."

"Oh have you, well as soon as I get to Berlin, I shall sort all this out, I'm not being fobbed off with some pokey little cottage in Chiswick."

"Of course not," said Von Ribbentrop, enjoying himself.

Goering had a brainwave: "Hampton Court," he ejaculated: "Who's got that?"

"I don't believe it's taken yet," said Von Ribbentrop: "Although I believe Rosenberg rather fancies it."

"Well, he won't get the chance, I shall claim it directly I reach Berlin" snorted Goering.

"I'm glad that's settled," mocked Von Ribbentrop. "Now shall we get down to business?"

As Goering struggled for the briefcase at his feet, Von Ribbentrop pressed a bell beneath the lip of his desk and soundlessly another footman appeared.

"Refill the Reich Marshal's glass and tell the chef we shall be through shortly," he barked at the footman, who bowed and left the room. Goering handed a bundle of papers to Von Ribbentrop and sat back waiting for his glass to be refilled.

Von Ribbentrop glanced over the papers before signing on the required dotted lines and handing them back. He stood up. "So, Hermann. Lunch."

12.23 pm. 66 Chasewater Road, Brownhills, Staffordshire.

James Coughlan settled into his armchair and unfolded the newspaper. He slurped his tea and turned to the crossword. His men were gainfully employed, decorating a local residence and earning him money whilst he sat at home. His healthy and engaging children were playing happily in the schoolyard and his attractive wife was arranging flowers in the local church.

Coughlan began with one across and made steady progress. As he swiftly completed clue after clue in his indecipherable spidery handwriting, his thoughts turned to his options for luncheon. He could wait for his wife to return from church duties or he could call in at the local pub – a drab cold meat sandwich and stilted conversation on subjects floral and ecclesiastical or a pint, a pie and pretty face behind the bar. He folded the newspaper, placed it under his arm and headed out of the door. All was right with the world in Staffordshire.

1.02 pm. Berlin, Office of Reich Marshal Hermann Goering.

With his employer engaged on important business in England, Luftwaffe Major Konrad Soellner left his desk and went in search of a long and lazy lunch. His in-tray was empty and he had nothing to do until Edvard's train arrived at Templehoff at 5.30. His 'friend' had been in Vienna since the Anschluss, ten days earlier where things had gone so swimmingly that he had been permitted an earlier than expected furlough. Konrad fully intended to enjoy every moment of this unexpected piece of good fortune. He took his usual table in the café opposite the Air Ministry and looked forward to an evening at the theatre and a convivial supper. All was right with the world in Berlin.

2.47pm. The German Ambassador's Residence, Frittenden, Kent.

After a substantial lunch of fois gras, brown Windsor soup, poached Scottish salmon and strudel, all prepared with a generous helping of English butter. Von Ribbentrop remembered Goering's quip about preferring to go without butter than guns. Goering excused himself and headed for the lavatory. He regretted having to leave his excellent cigar partially unsmoked but he had a little job to do that required both hands to be free. Von Ribbentrop called after him with a reminder to take note of the appointments and gadgetry in the room, which Goring waved aside.

Once safely inside, he ignored the space age gadgetry, the sunburst mirror with built-in lighting, the plug for an electric razor and once again the speakers for piped music. He could not resist playing with the chrome extending shaving mirror. Goering pulled it back and forth from the wall and looked at himself. *Ingenious*, he said to himself. He looked around the rest of the room which was typically art deco with an angular hand basin and WC, a profusion of swimming pool mosaic tiles and chromium plated rails wherever he looked. Despite the sharp blue and the glinting chrome, the room was strangely warm and snug. *Very comfortable,* he said to himself as he got down to the business at hand. He could not face the journey back to London in his present underwear. He had not brought an alternative with him but that was of no account, he was quite prepared to "go commando" rather than endure the constriction of his black satin panties on the return journey.

He sat on the lavatory and began to remove his boots, without the customary assistance of his batman; he found this something of a strain and was soon sweating profusely.

Ian Cassidy

With a heave and groan of relief he succeeded in getting the first boot off and started on the second. This proved just as difficult as the first and he was forced to stop several times to mop his sweating brow. One final heave sent the boot scuttling across the mosaic floor and Goering sat back on the lavatory panting heavily. He heaved his huge bulk to his feet and unbuttoned his breeches. He stepped out of them quite deftly for a big man and rapidly unhooked his suspender belt. He neatly folded his breeches and hung them over the chrome free-standing towel rail adjacent to the bath. After mopping his brow once again, he breathed a massive sigh of relief and began to pull off his panties.

Before rolling his stockings down his legs he cupped his gratefully unfettered penis and testicles in both hands, the song was not true, except perhaps in the case of Goebbels, and wafted them in the air.

He stood there wafting, feeling instantly cooler and more comfortable. He sat back on the lavatory and began to roll his stockings over his massive thighs. As he did so he looked around for his briefcase so he could stash the stretched lingerie safely out of sight. Damn, it was still in Von Ribbentrop's office. He hastily stuffed the underwear into his uniform pocket.

Naked from the waist down he looked at himself in the mirror. Damn! The bulge in his tunic pocket showed quite clearly. *It was not there when I came in*, he said to himself. *Von Ribbentrop will think I'm pilfering some of his toilet requisites*. He tried distributing the items more evenly throughout his pockets but to no avail, whatever combination he tried left a series of telltale bulges scattered all over his tightly fitting uniform jacket.

Exhausted and exasperated he sat down on the lavatory, now free of underwear; he recoiled from the cold plastic. The mod cons don't run to a heated seat. He grumbled. There's nothing else for it but to put them all back on. He groaned and reached into his pocket for the stocking. As he did so a loud knock came on the bathroom door. Goering almost fell off the lavatory seat. "Herr Reich Marshal, is everything alright?" asked the footman. "His Excellency is rather concerned."

Goering clutched his chest and choked back the "Fuck off" he was about to deliver. He struggled to keep his voice at an even level. "Fine, everything is fine, tell the Ambassador I will be with him shortly." Goering panted through the door.

I hope the dolt doesn't look through the keyhole. He thought to himself and commenced the laborious process of bending his massive torso, so that he could begin putting his stockings back on. He grunted as he rolled the fine silk over his toes and straining reached behind him to attach the tops to the suspender belt. Stretching the elastic suspender straps over his outsize thighs proved difficult and several times the straps pinged away from the silk stocking tops and hurtled dangerously close to his dangling penis. He swore and persevered.

As he did so one of the thin lacy satin strips that covered the clasps on his suspender belt came free and drifted through the air towards the floor. The strip of black satin with a red embroidered posy came to rest just behind the wash basin column. Goering did not notice; after all, the strip was designed to minimise the bulge in one's skirt caused by the clasp and the ruched silk. In loose fitting, cavalry breeches that is a problem one does not encounter.

After several minutes of hard labour he stood in front of the mirror, his lingerie restored to position, and commenced to put his breeches and boots back on. This proved easier than removing them and soon he stood at the bathroom door, composing himself. With the sweat dripping down his back and a visible film on his brow he re-presented himself to Von Ribbentrop.

"Is everything alright Old Man," asked the ambassador with mock concern. "You do look awfully warm. I hope the food has not disagreed with you."

"No, no everything is fine and in future I will thank you not to disturb me whilst I'm about my ablutions," barked Goering: "Now my case, if you please, I really must leave."

"Certainly Hermann, I'll call for your car." Von Ribbentrop called the footman and gave him instructions to call Goering's car. "Now Herman, let me show you out." Von Ribbentrop suppressed a smile as he led the Reich Marshal to the door.

The farewells were perfunctory to say the least and, with the help of the chauffeur, Goering was soon seated in the back of his Mercedes, moodily chewing on his now bitter tasting cigar.

Once outside the gates of the park, Goering tapped briskly on the divide. Before it was even halfway down, he barked. "Stop at the first tavern we come to, I need to buy some… matches."

"Has the cigar lighter in the rear malfunctioned, Herr Reich Marshal?" asked the chauffeur.

"I prefer to use a match, they give a more agreeable taste," Goering snarled.

The chauffeur reached into his tunic pocket. "Use mine, Herr Reich Marshal."

"No, no I don't wish to disturb you every time I need a light."

"Keep them, Herr Reich Marshal,"

Goering growled, "Just stop at the first tavern and don't question my orders again or you'll find yourself driving a garbage truck for our Embassy in East Africa."

"Very well, Herr Reich Marshal," said the bemused chauffeur, putting the screen back up.

The chauffeur slowed the car and pulled on to the forecourt of a half-timbered country pub: "Will this do, Herr Reich Marshal?" asked the Chauffeur.

"Yes, of course," said Goring.

With some difficulty, the chauffeur manoeuvred the large black automobile past the Land Rovers, dogcarts and the incongruous nifty little MG sportscar to the front door of the pub. He switched off the engine and opened the driver's door.

"I will be back with your matches directly Herr Reich Marshal," he said, getting out of the car.

Goering called him back. "No, no I'll get them myself," he said.

"As you wish, Herr Reich Marshal," said the chauffeur, hastening to open Goering's door.

Goering allowed himself to be helped from the car before announcing to the by now utterly confused driver: "You buy the matches, Hans.

I'll just take a look around the house, it looks to be an interesting old building."

"Very well. Herr Reich Marshal," stuttered the chauffeur. He made for the door of the pub and stood holding it open for Goering to enter.

Goering walked into the cold and draughty off sales and wrinkled his nose at the smell of stale tobacco, spilt ale and unwashed farm labourers. He looked at the two half glass doors, one announcing "Smoke Room", the other for the "Lounge". He tried to guess which one would offer the shortest passage to the lavatories. He opted for the lounge and directing the chauffeur to the off sales window, he took a deep breath and opened the door. Mercifully the room was free of local tosspots; they obviously preferred the smoke room. With the landlord occupied by his chauffeur, for a moment, Goering thought he might make it to the washroom unseen. He was making an uncharacteristic dash for the door at the far end of the room, when he noticed a couple sitting in the corner. A gentleman in the uniform of an RAF Flight Lieutenant, the owner of the MG, no doubt, and a woman in the uniform of the WRAF. On seeing Goering they hastily gulped down their drinks and stood up to salute him. He was after all wearing the uniform of a Lufftwaffe Field Marshall.

Goering returned their salute and looking away, moved towards the door as quickly as possible. He swore to himself. "This will get back, damn, damn. MI6 will amend my file to say I have a weak bladder, why else would I be stopping to use the lavatory not two miles from the Ambassador's residence."

He slammed the washroom door behind him and surveyed the cubicles. His first impression was that they looked frighteningly small. This was confirmed as he shoehorned his huge bulk through the door. Goering placed his case on top of the cistern and tried to work out how he could best achieve his underwear change. He looked about him at the cold white tiles rimmed with grimy, urine-yellowed grout and the flimsy plaster partitions also grimy and stained. He decided it would be best if he left the cubicle and reversed in, as he doubted if there was room for him to perform a pirouette.

Once he had reversed into the cubicle, he had to stand with a foot either side of the lavatory pan in order to close the door. He did not dare

Ian Cassidy

look down to see what he was standing in, just bemoaned the damage he was doing to his calfskin boots. He closed the cubicle door and swore. Bloody country. There was no seat on the lavatory, so he swore again and gingerly eased his ample buttocks onto the harsh white porcelain. Even through his cashmere breeches the bite of the cold ceramic was instantaneous. He winced and began to remove his boots. Because he had so recently removed and replaced them, but his boots came off with little or no effort and attempting to use them as stepping stones in the pool of agricultural effluent that covered the floor, he stood up and started to take down his breeches.

This too he achieved with little effort; he had overestimated the danger of falling into the flimsy partitions. In fact there was no danger at all, he was so snugly wedged in between them that he could only fall forwards or backwards. Once he had stashed his breeches on top of his briefcase, Goering almost tore at the clasp of his suspender belt. He snapped it open and wrenched down suspender belt, panties and stockings in one violent movement. He sat down on the lavatory to complete the task. ***Cretin!*** He swore at himself as the shark bite of the icy porcelain shocked through his thighs. Gritting his teeth he completed his task. After all he had endured far colder temperatures on the Western Front, although not often. Shivering on the cold pan, he removed his stockings from his ankles and performed the not inconsiderable feat of reaching behind himself to stuff the torn lingerie into his briefcase. He hauled himself to his feet and sighed. Balancing on his boots he pulled on his breeches and with less trepidation, as his warm milky buttocks had conducted a little warmth to it, he sat on the seat and pulled his boots back on.

Exhausted, he sat down on the lavatory. He took out his handkerchief and mopped his brow. Looking down he noticed the growing bulge in his trousers. ***Strange that such a god-awful place can have such an effect,*** he said to himself as he unbuttoned his fly. He took out his penis and fitfully masturbated. He was forced to perform a quite gruesome act of contortionism to ensure that his semen splashed onto the appalling floor and not his breeches and panting he sat back against the clammy porcelain. He buttoned his fly and stood up.

The **Unsinkable Herr Goering**

After straddling the lavatory again Goering opened the cubicle door and composing himself he headed for the outer door. He stopped; he could hear voices in the corridor. Some bloody yokels were heading his way; he turned back to the cubicle and shuddered. Telling himself, he was Hermann Goering, Reich Marshal of Germany and Commander-in-Chief of the Lufftwaffe, and not afraid of a bunch of carrot crunchers, he slung open the door and barged into the corridor.

The sight of Goering's massive bulk and crumpled formerly white uniform stopped the men in their tracks. Goering looked straight-ahead and hustled forward. He brushed past the farm labourers, cringing as the detritus on their overalls transferred to his tunic, and smashed into the lounge. The RAF couple made to stand again but Goering waved them back in their seats. He ignored the bemused glance from the landlord and showing a surprising turn of speed raced across the room towards the door.

He rushed through the Out door and stood under the porch of the inn, waiting as the chauffeur stubbed out his cigarette and opened the door for him.

"Hurry, dolt," he growled. "We must make London as soon as possible."

"Yes of course Herr Reich Marshal," panted the man. "And is everything alright… I mean… are you comfortable now for the return journey?"

"Yes, yes," barked Goering. "Now drive."

The chauffeur ran to his seat, started the engine and pulled away as fast as he could. As he accelerated towards the main road, he looked behind him and noticed that his distinguished passenger was sleeping soundly. He blew a silent raspberry into the mirror.

Some time later, the chauffeur pulled through the gates of the Embassy and drove into the underground car park. He stopped the car in front of the lift door.

Goering waited impatiently for his door to be opened and once outside the car he waited impatiently for the chauffeur to summon and open the lift.

When it arrived he shambled inside and after giving the chauffeur a perfunctory salute he pushed the button for the Embassy's lobby.

His staff awaited him in the lobby. He saluted and grunted in response to their enquiries about the success of his day.

The chief secretary made to take his case and Goering almost let him have it. Just in time he remembered that some of its contents were less than official and snatched it back. "There are some personal items in here which I must unpack first, come to my suite in five minutes and you may collect the papers," Goering snapped and headed off down the corridor.

4.52 pm.
Frittenden, Kent.

Back at the Ambassador's country residence, Frau Von Ribbentrop skipped up the back staircase and entered the private apartments. She wrinkled her nose at the piped muzak. "I could never stand 'Tales from the Vienna Woods.'" She said to herself as she violently tossed her riding hat at the Bugatti armchair.

She poked her head around the lounge door and waved at her husband who was contentedly sipping a post-prandial Armagnac in a chair by the bay window. Without stopping she headed for the bathroom. Once inside she pulled the hairnet from the bun at the back of her head and using both hands teased out her long blonde curls. Removing the knotted stock from her neck and unbuttoning her riding jacket, she looked at herself in the mirror. Pleased, she turned away.

Something behind the wash basin caught her eye. She bent down to pick it up. She examined the strip of black lacy silk. It was certainly not hers, far too tacky: "Joachim!" She screamed: "Who have you had in here?"

Annelies Von Ribbentrop stormed to the lounge bellowing "Joachim" as she went.

She met the now reanimated Ambassador to the Court of St James in the hallway.

"Yes my sweet." He said meekly.

"Who has been here while I was riding?"

"Just that oaf Goering. Why?"

"Then I suppose you're going to tell me this is his because it certainly isn't mine." She said brandishing the strip of black silk.

"Well one has heard rumours." Von Ribbentrop began to joke but quickly thought better of it: "It must belong to one of the maids." He said defensively.

"Don't be absurd even the cleaning wenches have better taste than that." She screeched, throwing the lace at him with unconcealed disgust: "You've had a call girl in here."

"Annelies, my sweet." Began Von Ribbentrop: "Don't be silly, where would I find a call girl out here in the wilds of Kent."

"Oh you'd manage it, you just can't help yourself, can you?"

"I haven't, truly I haven't," pleaded Von Ribbentrop. "And speaking of maids: 'Par Devant' as they say, come into the lounge."

"I don't care who hears," screamed his wife. "Let them all know what a filthy wretch you are," she said as she landed the first blow.

Von Ribbentrop ducked back into the lounge, where he took a hefty and regretful slug of his Armagnac. What a waste of such an excellent slow sipping cordial. He said to himself as he prepared for the onslaught that was sure to come.

7.18 pm.
66 Chasewater Road, Brownhills, Staffordshire.

James Coughlan made his second visit of the day to the pub and this time he was if anything happier than before as an unexpected windfall had recently come his way. Keith, one of Coughlan's more experienced operatives, who currently enjoyed exclusive responsibility for broom pushing, had called at Coughlan's home bearing a case of Scotch that had miraculously remained undamaged when it fell from the back of the lorry. Coughlan had taken it off Keith's hands for a fraction of its retail value and had then proceeded to relieve Keith of a substantial portion of the pittance he had just received by persuading him to try a few hands of three card brag. Keith didn't stand a chance and the proceeds of his piece of early evening larceny quickly dwindled as Coughlan won hand after hand. The rout was quickly completed and once they had adjourned to the pub, Coughlan even delivered a deft coup de grace by skilfully arranging that Keith picked up the tab for the first round of drinks. James Coughlan sipped his beer contentedly before launching into one of the hilarious, if oft repeated anecdotes that he was well known for. Once again all was right with the world in Staffordshire.

9.24 pm.
Kodeko Theatre, Nollendorfplatz, Berlin.

Luftwaffe Major Konrad Soellner and his "friend" outwardly enjoyed the show as Fraulein Trude Hesterberg and her troupe performed their usual Party-approved routines to great applause. Fraulein Hesterberg was a Nazi Party member and SS Support Group subscriber, so Konrad had not expected anything radical. He merely looked back wistfully to those heady nights in the Café Oh La La and the Stork's Nest before the Nazis came to power. He was careful to applaud in all the right places for the benefit of braying Brown Shirts who were dotted amongst the crowd.

In the darkness and amidst the occasionally forced hilarity, the other theatre-goers were blissfully ignorant of where Konrad's "friend" had his hand. Konrad was all too aware of it and contentedly tumescent. Once again all was right with the world in Berlin.

two
21st July, 1944

10.28am. Berlin, Office of Reich Marshal Hermann Goering. Goering tried to close his ears to the mayhem going on outside his office door. With a growing sense of irritation he looked at the teleprinter.

Amazing! he said to himself, *that funny little man, Von Stauffenberg, with his eye patch and crippled arm, who would have guessed he had it in him? Still waters run deep.* Rommel on the other hand and the others, those damned Junkers. He could understand them. They had never really taken to National Socialism, far too snobby, your average Prussian. He had really enjoyed crushing them underfoot when he was Governor of Prussia.

He let the tape fall from his hands and pressed the button on his intercom.

An aide appeared at the door.

"Konrad, can you step in here for a moment?" commanded Goering.

"Yes, of course, Herr Reich Marshal," said the man uneasily.

"I'm sorry to drag you away from your other duties, I realise things must be a little hectic today." Goering gave the aide an ingratiating smile. "Take a seat. I have a matter of the utmost importance to discuss with you."

"Yes. Herr Reich Marshal." Konrad clicked his heels together and made for a chair in front of his employer's desk.

Goering watched the tall young man's languidly fluid movements as he elegantly took his seat and found his mind wandering. He conjured up a picture of himself dressed in a French maid's uniform, all lace and frills with black fishnet stockings and a dinky little lacy bonnet, bending over as Konrad caned his back side with a riding crop. Each lash ringing deliciously through his tight black satin panties. He stayed with the thought for a few delightful seconds before announcing "So, Konrad, to business."

"Yes, Herr Reich Marshal?"

"This business yesterday has set me thinking. The current leadership of the Reich is secure."

"Heaven forbid it should be otherwise, Herr Reich Marshal," interrupted the aide, keen to show his loyalty to the party.

"Yes, yes, of course Konrad. It's just that we may soon discover that the current leadership is not best placed to secure ultimate victory or even to secure a reasonable, negotiated peace."

"I'm sorry, I don't follow you Herr Reich Marshal, surely it will be some time before we can negotiate the Allies' surrender."

"I admire your optimism Konrad. You must understand that the underlying cause of my anxiety, is that the Generals, arrogant, goose-stepping dastards that they are, may have been able to secure a negotiated peace that would have spared us from unnecessary and certainly painful war crimes trials. Once Müller and Kaltenbrunner's thugs have gone to work on the conspirators, no doubt taking blunt bread knives to their genitalia, no one else will dare to attempt to depose the Führer, so the possibility of peace with honour may perhaps have been extinguished forever."

"I'm sure your anxieties are misplaced, Herr Reich Marshal. The only war criminals to face trial will be Churchill, Montgomery and that murderer Harris."

"Please be realistic, Konrad," snapped Goering. "Look at the map. The Russians are on the Polish border, the Allies have secured Normandy and very little of Italy is left in German hands."

"An ideal situation for our counterattack," suggested the aide.

"Konrad, let us face facts. It is time to think about leaving," announced Goering.

"What… leave Berlin?" stammered the astonished aide: "Will it be possible to carry out your duties from your country estate?"

"I don't mean Berlin. I mean leave Germany. Once the Allies have taken over, I do not anticipate climate in Germany being to my taste. It is time to find a bolt-hole where conditions will be more conducive to my future well-being."

"I'm shocked, Herr Reich Marshal. The Führer is confident of our ultimate success."

"Please Konrad, drop the party line. This is not a test of your loyalty to the Führer ; that is not in question. This is a question of your loyalty to me."

"I hope that can never be in question, Herr Reich Marshal, I am your bondsman until death."

"Help me now, Konrad and it won't come to that. Wherever I choose as to make my new residence will of necessity be far away and very remote. I will need staff for the journey and to help me establish myself there. A very select few will accompany me. You are not married, Konrad?"

"No, Herr Reich Marshal," muttered the aide, reluctant to discuss his private life.

"That's what I wanted to hear, our little jaunt presents enough logistical problems as it is. We do not want to add them by dragging along an entourage of weeping wives and puking kids. Perhaps we can persuade one of those pretty typists in the outer office to come along with us. I will need secretarial assistance and you can avail yourself of any other services she may offer." Goering guffawed.

"Perhaps, Herr Reich Marshal," Konrad replied unenthusiastically. He was sure his choice from the typing pool would not meet with Goering's approval. Despite the rumours about Goering's sartorial perversions, and the curious pieces of direct evidence that he himself had seen, such as the size twelve diamante and satin dancing pumps in Goering's desk drawer, Konrad knew that Goering's kinks were purely auto-erotic. Goering would find Konrad's sex life degenerate and he was as enthusiastic about shipping homosexuals to Concentration Camps as the next Nazi. Konrad changed the subject. "Where are you… Where are we going?" asked Konrad, finally deciding to face facts.

"Now that is the question. I can't say I care for the Far East, although the remoteness of the jungle does appeal. It's just that I've never really cared for slant eyed nips. They're too inscrutable and also too small." Goering stroked his ample stomach. "I'd stand out too much."

"What about Australia?" suggested Konrad.

Goering was astounded. "Don't be absurd, Konrad, it's an Allied country and part of the British Empire."

"Yes, but it's very large, very remote and full of immigrants."

"That's true but as much as the delights of Wagga Wagga appeal to me, it is still an Allied country. I feel I need somewhere place where I can rely on a certain amount of co-operation from the local authorities. A certain sort of venality, somewhere place where I can purchase a blind eye or two."

"Very wise, Herr Reich Marshal," agreed Konrad. "Then on the same basis, we can dismiss Canada and South Africa."

"Yes, of course, especially South Africa after Seyss-Inquart's antics in Holland. Even the Boers would not be pleased to see me and they hate the British."

"What about elsewhere in Africa?" asked Konrad.

"I think not," answered Goering: "It's such a barbarous place, full of savages. I shudder even to contemplate the wild animals and the snakes. No, certainly not."

"That just leaves South America then."

"Yes, South America is my preferred choice. I'm glad you agree with me, Konrad."

"The south of the continent would be best, I think," Konrad said. "We may encounter a little too much British or French influence in the north. Argentina would be my choice."

"Yes, there or Paraguay or even Uruguay. But the final destination does not need to be settled just as yet," replied Goering.

"Shall I make some discreet enquiries with the embassies of those countries?" suggested the aide.

"No, no, Konrad We'll keep this on a need-to-know basis. I'm sure those damn places leak like sieves. If Müller or Himmler get to hear even the slightest whisper, then it's the blunt bread knife for us as well." Goering shifted uneasily in his armchair: "We'll just turn up, smuggle ourselves into the country and set ourselves up. We'll present the authorities there with a fait a compli and then hand out the bribes."

"Will Frau Goering and your daughter be accompanying you, Herr Reich Marshal?"

"Yes, berths must be found for Emmy and Edda, I could not possibly leave them to the mercy of the Americans. The British can be relied on to behave like gentlemen but the Americans with their gum chewing and barbaric music, a civilised woman could never be safe in their hands."

"What would you have me do, Herr Reich Marshal?" asked Konrad.

"We will need a ship and crew. Arrange it, but do it discreetly, very discreetly."

"Of course, Herr Reich Marshal."

"I think the safest place for our departure will be Spain. The ports of southern France are out of the question as it's only a matter of time before the Allies invade the Riviera and the Russians are so close that we cannot risk our own Baltic ports. You will have to go to Spain and purchase a suitable ship."

"I will have to go, Herr Reich Marshal?" gulped Konrad. "Won't that be risky?"

"I'm afraid we must all take a great many risks, Konrad. Leave immediately before the Allies take Southern France and use this." Goering reached beneath his desk. He heaved a large Gladstone bag from the floor: "It's bullion, with the Reich foundry marks removed so Franco's pen pushers should not suspect anything."

"Very well, Herr Reich Marshal," said the panicking aide.

"And Konrad, I understand that before the war you were posted to our Embassy in Lisbon."

"That is correct, Herr Reich Marshal. For three years."

"And how's your Portuguese?"

"A little rusty."

"Then polish up your Portuguese, as I suggest you pose as a Portuguese entrepreneur. We must try to eliminate any suggestion that the ship is required by a German buyer."

"Of course, Herr Reich Marshal," nodded Konrad. "Shall I hire a crew as well?"

"Yes, while you are in Spain you must do everything necessary to make our escape possible. The less we need to do from here the better. Himmler and Müller, remember."

"And Kaltenbrunner."

"Oh yes, him as well." Goering nodded.

"But that will mean a Spanish crew."

"That cannot be helped but you could look into the possibility of hiring a German captain."

"Very well, Herr Reich Marshal."

Goering opened the drawer of his desk and took out an envelope of papers. He passed them to Konrad. "There you have my full authority to cross every border, every checkpoint. Only the Führer himself can impede your progress. Now leave me and Godspeed. I must arrange for my personal items to be packed for the voyage."

Goering stood up and saluted. "Heil Hitler."

Konrad could manage only a half-hearted response. To Heil Hitler seemed just a little hypocritical. He left the office, struggling with the suitcase of bullion.

Before the door had closed behind the aide, Goering was working on the list of items necessary for the voyage and his new life in South America. The cellars at his residence on Leipziger Platz were already stocked with crates of bullion and US dollars, along with trunks full of jewels and precious stones recently borrowed from the Crowned heads of Europe. He smiled contentedly. Yes, he had enough cash, or items easily convertible into cash, for a few years at least. But he realised that life on the run would be rather costly.

When the cash and jewels ran out, he would sell the artworks he had accumulated. Most of these were at Karinhall, so moving them would be difficult but not impossible. Stripped of their frames, the paintings would be crammed many to a packing case. Much to his regret, he realised that the larger items would have to be left behind. There would simply be insufficient space on his private train for the Amber Room or the Sterzing Altar. He swore to himself and tried to think of a way around the problem of space. He could not leave the Amber Room behind but what could he sacrifice to make space, what other priceless treasures would have to be abandoned so that it could travel with him to

Ian Cassidy

South America? He threw down his fountain pen in frustration. This was a job for Konrad, the man was known for his efficiency and he could use it to see that all his Reich Marshal's possessions could be transported across the Atlantic.

Even with that problem solved, Goering was still swearing to himself. Damn Hitler's insistence that the French art collections remain inviolable. Goering recognised that in years to come the Impressionist and later collections in those galleries would be of most interest to collectors and investors. If he could have filled just one rail carriage with such works, then in years to come he would have enough money to bribe even the most untouchable war crimes investigator.

Was there a way of getting his hands on just a few of those paintings, he asked himself. After a moment's thought he decided against it. There was scarcely a railway carriage to be had in all of Western Europe, Eichmann had seen to that. To commandeer one in Paris would attract attention. It would risk exposing his escape plans. Besides, the cellars at Leipziger Platz contained a fine collection of Entarte Kunst, that little queer, Roehme's collection of works by Egon Schiele, plus works by Picasso, Braque, Leger, Kandinsky, Mondrian and Klee, "on loan" from Europe's art galleries.

He was satisfied that his monetary needs were well taken care of. After all, there were bound to be a few lucrative opportunities in his new country, especially for a man of his talents. Goering turned to the important business of things he would need to make life comfortable. He would take the fine Renaissance desk and chair from the hall at Leipziger Platz and the massive silver candlesticks that stood on it. The Ruebens "Diana at the Stage Hunt" also could go but at the last minute. To crate up such prominent pieces of his own personal collection would risk alerting visitors. The Vermeers, of course, Goering was proud of the deal he had struck with that corrupt little Dutch art dealer, what was his name? Van Meegeren. So quick to sell his national heritage and so cheaply too. Goering could not help but smile at his own brilliance.

Goering's thoughts turned to his stomach, He supposed he would just have to put up with Spanish cuisine on the journey - he might even get to like tortilla - but he could ensure he had something palatable to wash it down. The cellars at Leipziger Platz were the envy of the Reich and he was determined that at least some of his collection would accompany him. The Petrus would make the trip, every bottle he owned and the Margaux, although some of the lesser years could perhaps be left behind. After all he had to save room for his Dom Perignon and cognac and he really could not leave behind the case of Chassagne-Montrachet, from the cellars of Napoleon the Third.

Goering locked the papers in his desk and rang the bell. "Corporal, get my car," he barked before the man had gotten his head fully through the door. The journey to Berchtesgaden was long and arduous and he had already delayed enough. The quicker he was at the fireside of the Führer's mountain retreat the better.

three
2nd July, 1944

2.56am. **Berchtesgaden.** Goering turned over and woke with a start; the crossed wooden legs at the top of his inadequate camp bed had given way. With his feet several inches above his head, he flailed his arms and tried to struggle from the wreckage. He swung his massive thigh to his left and his great bulk surged wavelike to the floor. Supporting himself on the flimsy footlocker, he toiled to his feet. *Damn this place,* he swore repeatedly.

The bunker at Berchtesgaden was little short of hellish. The makeshift bed, the collapsible furniture and the blast proof curtains all seemed to be calling him Meyer. *Damn those Lancasters. Damn the RAF.*

He searched in his uniform for a cigarillo but found his leather cigar case to be empty. He drank reluctantly from the dusty water carafe on the campaign chest and brooded. Bomber Command and that bastard Harris meant such sleeping arrangements had to be endured in Germany but he was damned if he was going to be uncomfortable on his journey to freedom. He would not put up with cold, ironclad cabins and the reek of rotting fish. The very thought of a hammock made him shudder.

He would see that the ship that Konrad was en route to purchase was refitted. Nothing too fancy, just enough to make the long and arduous journey bearable.

Goering made a mental note to contact Konrad in Spain and instruct him to set the matter in hand. He stopped. No. No that would not do. Konrad would have to hire Spanish artisans to refit the ship and that could take forever. It was always mañana, mañana with them; the Russians would be in Berlin before the first coat of paint was dry. Goering was perplexed. His comfort was of the utmost importance but how was he to achieve his aims? To send a team of workers from Germany would be risky, Himmler or Müller might get to hear of it. Then there was the problem of finding workers skilled enough for the job. Everyone had been conscripted; he would be left with senile dodderers or invalids. He kicked his bed in frustration before commencing to limp across the room as he considered his predicament.

"Von Ribbentrop's Irishman." He said to himself excitedly. Yes he could do it, he certainly had the skilled workforce and if Von Ribbentrop's assessment of him was correct, then he could be relied on not to ask too many awkward questions so long as the money was right.

Yes, he could work out very well, Goering smiled to himself. There would be little trouble transporting three or four decorators from Dublin or Cork to Northern Spain and why should anyone get to hear about it in Germany.

Goering considered the proposition. The man had also worked on Von Ribbentrop's radio and music system, so he would presumably be able to install an up-to-date wireless receiver on the ship. That was very important to Goering. He did not wish to be completely cut off on the high seas with only the BBC World Service to rely on. He wanted access to as many wireless channels as possible so he could keep himself fully informed of any efforts to follow him. After all, he planned to slip unnoticed into his new country of residence and that would not be possible if the authorities on the ground were expecting him. Despite the minor difficulty of his nationality, Von Ribbentrop's Irishman seemed the best contractor available.

He was sure he still had the business card Von Ribbentrop had given to him at his country residence all those years ago. He would dig it out as soon as he got back to Berlin and see about making contact.

Goering propped the head of his damaged bed on the footlocker and gingerly tested it. Yes that would hold his weight. He hopped into bed and was soon sleeping soundly, dreaming of hand-painted wallpaper, cameo friezes peopled by classical maidens, Flemish tapestries and plush

Ian Cassidy

Persian carpets on polished parquet floors. His dreams did not remain untroubled for long. The hand-painted wallpaper began to peel from the walls, the classical maidens became malevolent classical warriors and the Satyrs depicted in the tapestries snarled cruelly at him as he writhed in his sleep. Finally he found himself sliding headlong over sparkling parquet floor before crashing into an ocean of Art Deco pastels where he came to rest trapped under a suite of Bugatti furniture. He woke with a start when an orange Bakelite telephone toppled from a hideously disfigured four-sided Bugatti tapering torchere decorated with bronze lozenges, each with a forbidding horsehair tassel flowing from it's centre, and clonked him on the head. Next came tumbling a truly ugly Clarice Cliff figurine of a seemingly disfigured dancing couple in evening dress and when that too bounced of his steamy pate Goering realised that he was still asleep. Finally and most worryingly a dog-eared copy of the London Times, folded to reveal the crossword half completed in faded, spidery script fluttered down and landed on his trembling belly. The dream Goering scratched his head as he watched its descent.

Goering spluttered into consciousness and found himself in a cold sweat and troubled by a painful erection. He groaned deeply but consoled himself that at least he could still get one at his age. He then climbed out of his rickety cot and kicked the footlocker across the room.

four
28th July, 1944

3.47pm. Office of Reich Marshal Hermann Goering, Berlin. Konrad dusted down his suit and knocked on the door of Goering's office. He was still in civilian clothing, having decided that his employer would wish to hear his news immediately. He had come directly from Tempelhof, having been lucky enough to secure a berth on an ageing Condor, making probably its last flight from Nice to Berlin. Konrad had spent what seemed an eternity crushed in the disused bomb bay with an assortment of injured SS infantrymen, supposed commercial travellers in those leather coats only Gestapo officers wore, and two foul-smelling U-Boat bombardiers.

Shaking off exhaustion and preferring not to notice the further damage wrought by the RAF in the six day nights he had been away, Konrad waited for Goering's response to his knock at the door.

"Enter!" bellowed the Reich Marshal.

Konrad popped his head around the door.

"Ah, Konrad," smiled Goering. "So soon and with good news I hope."

Konrad saluted. "I hopped on a flight from Nice, I was lucky and I had a little help." He tapped his suit pocket, indicating the letters of authorisation Goering had given him.

"Yes, it's good to know I still have some authority, in France at least. The way things are going at the moment, I will soon be powerless in Germany."

"Surely not, Herr Reich Marshal," said Konrad.

"No, that was just the ranting of a tired man. I am not without authority or influence although those bastards Himmler and Goebbels would have it otherwise." Sighed Goering: "Now, Konrad, our arrangements, how go they?"

"All is going very well, Herr Reich Marshal, I have completed the purchase of a medium sized tramp steamer, built in Bremerhaven in 1916 but now flying a Panama flag and called the "SS Atheling." She has no passenger accommodation, just berths for the master and crew, so no one will suspect you are on board. All in all I believe she is perfect for your needs, not large enough to draw any special attention but big enough for your requirements and to handle the Southern Ocean. She's a little rusty on the outside but totally seaworthy, well built and as tough as old boots."

"That sounds very promising, Konrad Well done." Goering sat back and crossed his legs contentedly.

"I have left instructions that she is not to be painted, a fresh coat of paint might make her conspicuous."

"Good thinking, Konrad. On the subject of painting, we must discuss the condition of the accommodation on board."

"Unfortunately it is basic at best, Herr Reich Marshal."

"As I expected; I have one or two plans for the interior of the ship, Before we get on to them, tell me about the crew."

"I have engaged the ship's current crew, and a pretty desperate bunch they are, too, cutthroats and desperadoes the lot of them. But they know the ship and they know the waters we intend to sail."

Goering slammed his fist down on the desk. "Really, Konrad, surely you did not reveal our prospective destination."

"No, no, Herr Reich Marshal," stammered the harassed aide. "I merely questioned certain crew members as to their experience in a very roundabout way, and managed to ascertain that a good many were familiar with the Southern Ocean."

"Good." Goering smiled. "And I am sorry that I underestimated you, Konrad. Now tell me about the captain."

"I took the liberty of dismissing the captain, he did not appear popular with the crew in any event and I feel we will all, passengers and crew, have a more comfortable journey under the guidance of a German captain."

"I couldn't agree more. Do you have anyone in mind?"

"There is a man who may be willing to take the job. His record as a seaman is second to none. He saw most of his service in command of a disguised surface raider and out of necessity had to be ruthless in his treatment of stricken Allied seamen, so he may be anxious to avoid the scrutiny of the Allies."

"Yes, I see," said Goering. "Those prigs the Americans are likely to try him for piracy."

"It's a possibility so I will speak to him at the earliest opportunity."

"Before you do that, I want you to arrange something else. I shall require proper quarters onboard our vessel, for myself, my family and my staff."

"Of course, Herr Reich Marshal, I will contact the boat dealer immediately. I'm sure he can arrange to have something knocked up."

"No, no, Konrad, that won't do at all. I don't want something just 'knocked up' as you call it; the journey will be long and tedious, so my requirements are a little more demanding than that. Also I've always been deeply suspicious of Spanish workmanship, good God, just look at the Segrada Familia. That is why I want you to contact this man." Goering handed the now tatty business card to his aide.

Konrad read it. "But he's English!" he said, astonished.

"Half-Irish as I understand it, but that need not be a problem. I think he will do it, in fact I'm led to believe if the money's right he will do anything. You will have to use one of our agents in England."

"Do we still have any agents in a position to help us?" asked Konrad.

"Yes of course. We still have agents of every description in England, from everyday economic moles to senior ones right in the heart of Whitehall."

"Shall I contact one of the senior ones?" asked Konrad.: "The Duke of Windsor, perhaps?"

"No, no, don't use him, Canaris would get to hear of it and in any case I could never stand him or his scrawny transatlantic trollop. What about those mad sisters, the writers, could they do it?"

"I don't think they would be suitable, Herr Reich Marshal, the younger one is no longer fit for active service. She shot herself, if you recall, when the Führer rejected her."

"The other one then, the one married to the 'English Fascist.'" Goering scoffed.

"I think she may have been interned for the duration. Even if she is at liberty, I don't think she would be a wise choice, Herr Reich Marshal. She is very well known and noticeable. I mean what would she be doing, meeting up with an Irish paperhanger from Birmingham."

"Well, do you have anyone in mind?" barked Goering.

"As a matter of fact I do, one of my contemporaries at Heidelberg joined the Abwehr and was posted to London before the war. We have had no contact for many years and I believe the agent in question is still there."

"Konrad, that's perfect, why didn't you mention it before. Contact him immediately."

"Contact her, Herr Reich Marshal," smiled Konrad.

"Good God! A woman?" spluttered Goering. "Can she be trusted?"

"She was very competent at Heidelberg and surely the very fact that she is still active in England speaks volumes for her continued proficiency."

"All right, Konrad, I will trust your judgement in this matter. Contact her immediately."

"Very well, Herr Reich Marshal. Anything else you require?" "Yes, Konrad I shall require some valuables and other personal items for my new life abroad. As our final destination is uncertain I cannot transfer the funds direct from Switzerland and besides that would risk creating a paper trail."

Konrad nodded and Goering continued, "I think it best that a consignment or two of bullion and other easily convertible assets make the journey with us. Here is a list of the items I will require shipped to Spain," he said, handing Konrad several sheets of paper.

The aide poured over the handwritten notes. He looked anxiously at his employer. "There is rather a lot here, Herr Reich Marshal. Won't moving all this arouse suspicion?"

"We will need considerable funds to establish ourselves in a new home so it is a risk we must take. In any event I do not think the risk is overly great." Goering paused and looked about him conspiratorially. "Of course you know not to repeat what I am about to tell you but they're all at it. I have it on the highest authority that Bormann recently took a second vault at his Geneva bankers to house all his loot. And Goebbels' clod-crunching relatives dare not dig anywhere in their Westphalian smallholding for fear of damaging the Tsarist Faberge enamels he has buried there."

"Very well, Herr Reich Marshal, I will make the necessary arrangements."

"Do that, Konrad, open a file marked Top Secret for your and my eyes only."

"Of course, Herr Reich Marshal."

"And Konrad, do not mention anywhere the nature of the final shipment."

"Yes Herr Reich Marshal and what shall I call the file?"

"I'm sure you can come up with something.,." Goering said lazily.

"Er … how about Operation Red Sea?"

"Why ever would we call it that?" snapped Goering.

"Well, the parting of that sea did facilitate a rather miraculous escape," replied the aide.

"Oh, I follow your reasoning Konrad but I think not, I do not like the Semitic overtones. Can you not think of any other famous escapers?"

What about Operation Airey Neave? Konrad thought but kept it to himself. "Robert the Bruce," he suggested.

"No, no, Konrad, I don't like that either, although he did defeat the British. What about that Greek fellow, Icarus?"

"He didn't actually make it though, Herr Reich Marshal."

"The other one then, the one who did get away," snapped Goering, losing his patience.

"Daedalus?" said Konrad hesitatingly.

"That's it!" bellowed Goering in triumph. "The removal of myself and my chattels will be called "Operation Daedalus."

"As you wish, Herr Reich Marshal." Konrad bowed.

"That will be all, thank you, Konrad." snapped Goering. The aide left the office.

five
27th July, 1944

9.56am. **West Coast Main Line. Near Rugby.** Katherine Baatjer, or Anne Cole as she was known in the Great Marlborough Street publishers where she had worked since arriving in London in 1937, shifted awkwardly in her seat as an NCO in RAF uniform entered the third class carriage.

To the unconcerned observer she was a quiet, mousy technical editor's secretary, aged 36, owner of a large tabby cat and her employer's mistress. Every Wednesday she had a half-holiday and entertained the senior editor at the rented flat she shared with Susan, an art gallery assistant from Norfolk, who was underemployed but just busy enough to be out every Wednesday. Sharing a flat made communicating with Germany a problem but it provided excellent cover. Not that there had been a lot of communication with Germany in recent months. She had come to London with such high hopes. After reading languages at Heidelberg, she had joined the Ministry for Tourism before being specially selected for the Abwehr. She had finished top of her class of apprentice agents. Canaris had sent her on assignment personally, with instructions to work her way into the heart of Fleet Street and gain access to the many snippets of priceless information floating around its smoky corridors. How she had got side-tracked into working for a publisher of technical manuscripts she would never know. For the last few months, she had finally begun to accept that her employers in Berlin had no important jobs for her. There were no glorious schemes for her to mastermind. She was not going to get the chance to further Germany's interests. In short, Canaris had forgotten her.

She pushed her feet as far under the carriage seat as they would go. She was wearing her best suit and her last pair of silk stockings and she did not want to ruin them. Her work did not bring her into contact with any American servicemen, with their penchant for making gifts of hosiery, and there was very little prospect of buying another pair. Money was not a problem. She did, after all, have a stash of ready cash and a pile of gold sovereigns provided by the Abwehr, with absolute discretion about how she spent it, but there was simply nothing like that to be had in the London shops.

She regretted not coming into contact with the American forces and not just because of the improvements that would mean to her wardrobe. She was sure she could still do important work for the Fatherland, especially with all the Americans in London. They were so loud, so confident and so cocksure that she was certain she would hear information of importance to German Intelligence.

And what was she doing, travelling half way across the country at the behest of a Lufftwaffe SturmbanFührer … no, the Lufftwaffe did not use those ranks, Konrad was just plain "Major" at the behest of a Lufftwaffe Major she barely remembered, to send a Brummie paper hanger to Spain.

Anne Cole sighed and tried to think of her time with Konrad Soellner at Heidelberg. Her memory was hazy but she remembered a tall and elegant youth, studious and efficient and painstakingly well dressed. That was something you did not often encounter in penniless Weimar Germany, so much so that she and her friend Maggi were convinced that Konrad preferred the company of other men to a degree that was decidedly dangerous in National Socialist Germany. Still she was pleased that he had risen so high in the service of the Fatherland, although she could not understand why he needed an English house painter.

Still worrying for the safety of her stockings, Anne Cole sat back in her seat and took out the Times. She started the crossword and eighteen minutes later she contentedly put it down, completed. She had been a little a slow today but still English was not her first language and she looked on completing it at all as a mark that she was truly bilingual. She tried to sleep for the remainder of the journey.

Ian Cassidy

Anne was dozing fitfully as the train struggled into Birmingham. The signs for New Street shook her to life. She hurriedly collected her belongings and strained to reach her valise on the rack above. The NCO from the RAF did not offer to help. She bumped the case down and lugged it behind her. She had only brought it as part of her cover story and to provide a hiding place for the large amount of cash her assignment required her to carry. She did not intend to be in Birmingham long enough to use any of its contents but if questioned she would say she was visiting relatives. She frowned at the NCO and left the compartment unnoticed.

On the platform she joined the throng of transient servicemen and returning Midlanders, her case banging against her right leg. She tried holding away from her body but the strain on her shoulder was too much. Thinking to hell with it, she let the case go were it might, if it laddered her stockings, then so be it. She would soon learn to draw straight lines with an eyebrow pencil on the backs of her calves.

The office where she worked possessed a disused cobwebbed library and its fusty shelves contained an out-dated Bradshaws, so Anne knew she had to catch the connecting train to Lichfield. Wartime restrictions on signage made it difficult to find the correct platform. She cornered a red-faced porter and quickly ascertained that a train stopping at Lichfield was leaving Platform 4 very shortly.

Anne shuddered at the prospect of climbing the precipitous footbridge but pressed on. Once again the youthful servicemen ignored her struggles with her luggage. That was one of the perils of being almost forty and artificially dowdy. Sweating, she made it to the other side and waited with the other travellers.

As she stood there, Anne noticed that the vast majority of passengers bound for Lichfield were servicemen, infantry to be exact.

She remembered that there was a barracks in Lichfield, the Headquarters of the Staffordshire Regiment, to be precise. She wondered if she would have time to check it out. It might be important; there were certainly a lot of troops on the move and all this activity might mean that the Parachute Regiment, of which the Staffordshire Regiment was part, had a major operation planned.

She decided to concentrate on her own mission and not add to it with jaunts of her own. After all, it was only to be expected that at some point the Paras would join their comrades in France. She would just be reporting something that was already known in Berlin and something that Berlin was powerless to stop.

With a cloud of smoke and screeching brakes, the Lichfield train pulled into the enclosed platform, blotting out the sun and waking Anne from her reverie. She picked up her case and joined the mass of uniformed humanity heading for the train. Anne was swept along to the nearest door, buffeted by kit bags and bruised by rifle butts.

If the platform had been uncomfortable then the inside of the train was a nightmare. All the seats were taken and their occupants huddled behind crumpled firsts of the Evening Mail, so as not to catch the eye of any distressed female.

Stoically, Anne stood in the corridor and told herself this leg of her journey would not take long and soon she would be able to take her shoes off in the comfort of her hotel room. She purposely forgot that she had not booked a room in Lichfield. In fact, she had no idea what the standard of accommodation was like in the City, so she preferred not to think of the pokey little attic above some smoky taproom she would have to rent.

As the train chugged out of the station, the corridor was filled with acrid black smoke; Anne hastily turned to the window and tried close it. It would not budge. A burly Red Beret came to her assistance but still the window would not move. With no prospect of relocating further down the carriage, Anne pulled her hat as low as it would go and prayed that the wind would change. She smiled her thanks to the soldier and then scowled for the rest of the journey.

After a similar if slightly less hectic experience on the platform at Lichfield, Anne presented her ticket to the stationmaster and walked through the booking hall to the street. She had no idea where she would find suitable accommodation but she decided not to ask any of the station staff. She was officially visiting relatives, so what need would have of a hotel room? She mentally tossed a coin and turned left out of the station grounds. She saw the cathedral's three famous spires poking through the trees in the distance, took the first right and headed towards them.

She walked past the elegant buildings of Bird Street. ***No bomb damage here***, she said to herself and pressed on into the city. The road opened out as she walked past the school and Anne came upon the imposing edifice of the George Hotel. She walked past; the George was a little too grand for her, on this assignment at least. With her stash of white fivers and gold sovereigns, it was not beyond her means but she required something less conspicuous.

Fortunately there was an inn opposite. She took a quick look and decided that the King's Head would be more than adequate for her purposes. Heaving her suitcase, she entered the passageway at the side and headed for the entrance. She stopped and read the plaque at the side of the door.

> *"Colonel Luke Lullington raised a regiment of foot at the King's Head on 25th March 1705. This regiment became the 38th Foot in 1750 and was given the title of the 1st Staffordshire Regiment in 1782. In 1881 the 38th Foot became the 1st BN The South Staffordshire Regiment."*

Anne wondered if it was an omen. Should she spend some time investigating the proposed deployments of the Staffordshire Regiment? She decided to check in and think about it later.

Anne pushed through the sparsely populated bar and asked for the landlord. After a few minutes a large man with a wide slug of a black moustache who, judging from the memorabilia that littered the bar, was a former sergeant with the Coldstream Guards and who, judging from his waistline, was now secretly glad not to be in Normandy with his former Regiment, snapped: "What do you want?"

Anne asked politely if he had any rooms free as she noticed that his shirtsleeves were held back with elastic bands not those funny expandable metal bands that were specifically designed for the purpose.

"How many nights?" barked the landlord.

"Just a couple," replied Anne, finding it hard to smile.

The **Unsinkable Herr Goering**

After examining Anne's papers and asking the other required questions, the Landlord withdrew to a back room. He reappeared two minutes later carrying a single key. "This way," he said, not offering to carry Anne's luggage.

On the way to the room, he asked Anne what she was doing in Lichfield and she conscientiously stuck to her story, she was visiting relatives in the area. To make her cover story complete, she even informed him that she would not be requiring an evening meal, as those relatives would feed her, although she had absolutely no idea what arrangements she would make for feeding herself that night.

Anne asked about the times of buses running to Brownhills, the neighbouring town where she expected to find her paperhanger. After noting down the times and directions to the bus station, Anne closed the door on the landlord and surveyed the room.

It was dusty and unaired; the smell reminded Anne of an old board game that had been left in the bottom of a wardrobe. Otherwise the room seemed quite comfortable. Business had obviously been slack since 1939 and the furniture had not suffered from a procession of commercial travellers and illicit love-making couples. Anne tested the small sink in the corner of the room and after a few seconds of throaty clanks the tepid water ran clear. She hastily washed her face and smiling approvingly at the firmness of the bed, sat down and removed her shoes.

She rubbed her aching stocking feet and smiled ruefully, she was a little disappointed that the room was not a pigsty. She had a slightly masochistic streak and a more than slightly masochistic approach to this assignment. She would dearly have liked to be able to report that she had put up with the most awful conditions, squalid room, flea ridden bed, MI6 agents and predatory bar flies to get her job done.

She got off the bed and opened her suitcase. Anne reached underneath the hastily packed lingerie that she hoped she would not need and pulled out two brown envelopes. One contained a bundle of white fivers, the other a basic set of plans that she had picked up from her contact at the Portuguese Embassy, a man she hardly recognised; it had been so long since she had had any contact him.

She had studied them along with the rest of her instructions and was singularly unimpressed. The blueprints contained the specifications for constructing a series of wooden framed rooms, decorating the same, and appointing them with plumbing, lighting and cooking facilities. To her untrained eye, it all seemed very basic. Surely there were artisans in Spain capable of doing such work? Why did she have to travel half way across the country to find this Irishman? Why did she have to risk blowing her cover before she had had a chance to achieve something? To discover something important, the Allied plans for the invasion of Greece perhaps? Anne shook herself from her reverie; half-heartedly she told herself that every little cog was important, even the smallest task was important to the Führer's great plan.

She was off again. Did she really believe in the Führer's great scheme any longer? Was it just because she had been exposed to six years of John Bull propaganda or was she genuinely disillusioned with National Socialism? If the vague stories that were slowly filtering through about the horrific goings on in Eastern Europe were true, then she would feel justified in abandoning Katherine Baatjer forever; that was not what she had joined the Party for. Anne looked at the bundle of money. If she spent it on this assignment, she would have nothing left for emergencies; hopefully her contact at the Portuguese Embassy would replace it, but even that was uncertain now. If it was replaced, at least she would have a little something she could use to make herself invisible to the Allies. Feeling more contented and determining not to become side-tracked again, she picked up the envelopes and stuffed them into her handbag.

Next she ferreted around in the case for her second best shoes. Stuffed in each toe was a leather drawstring bag containing gold sovereigns. After rattling them in her hands, she jammed them into her handbag and threw her second best shoes onto the floor. She was ashamed of them anyway, they were crushed out of shape and the soles were filled with holes. They had only made the journey as a result of her increasingly spinsterly thinking, she could not risk travelling with just one pair of shoes, what would she do if she got her best pair wet. She put her good shoes back on and, after going back to hide the worn out pair under the bed so that the chamber maid, if the hotel boasted such an extravagance, would not see them, she headed off in search of the bus station.

The rattling single-decker let her off in the dreary town of Brownhills, opposite a half-timbered but definitely not Tudor public house. She looked it over and considered relocating. Perhaps this one would have a more genial host. It was certainly very convenient for her paperhanger, whose offices were in this very road.

She decided not to move, better that no-one knew where she was staying, Checking the house numbers, she set off in search of Number 99.

She walked along the road pleased not to be burdened by her suitcase and soon found herself outside a newly constructed bungalow, with a large double gate at the side. On the gate was a badly painted brass and enamel plaque announcing:

"James Coughlan & Sons.
Painters, Decorators & Industrial Cleaners.
Registered Office."

Whatever could Konrad's office want with this man? Anne asked herself. She lifted the latch on the gate and walked into the yard.

The driveway was lined with ramshackle sheds and huts, many without roofs. One was a huge but thankfully disused dog kennel, big enough to house a whole pack of rottweilers, but now full of rusting paint cans.

She walked down the driveway and looked at the garden at the rear of the bungalow, the flowerbeds now filled with vegetables, a run for chickens and a smaller one for ducks.

At the end of the driveway she was confronted by a huge shed with a Belfast roof constructed from Anderson Shelter sheeting, no doubt diverted from their proper purpose. Next to the shed was a once delightful sunken garden. Its mellow brick walls were sadly no longer clad with delicate climbing plants, as it had become a depository for rickety ladders and forgotten scaffolding.

Beside the sunken garden was the car park, in which was parked a battered van of indeterminate manufacture and age. It was old and square and had covered over rear wheels. The van was not sign-written and

Ian Cassidy

Anne guessed why. When you're making off with a load of purloined scrap iron or fly tipping asbestos, you do not want to be identified.

Anne was shocked to see an ageing Rolls Royce next to the van. A 1926 20 Hp James Young saloon, recklessly maltreated, with a homemade roof rack full of peeling wooden ladders.

Finally, in front of the office was a sleek Armstrong Siddley saloon, black and shiny, obviously the proprietor's vehicle.

Anne turned to the office, a converted stable, and knocked. She entered the office and smiled at the dumpy secretary sitting behind the desk.

Anne looked around the office. Despite its former agricultural use, it was decorated in the style of a traditional front room or parlour, although the roof sloped dramatically away from the doorway to a rear wall of Lilliputian proportions. A small and inadequate fireplace of awful light brown treacle glazed tiles dominated the rear wall. The room was decorated with dingy brown wallpaper, its faded flower pattern, here and there interrupted by a framed certificate of public liability insurance or a sepia photograph of ant-like workers daubing paint around the interior of some echoing steel plant. Finally Anne's eyes came to rest on a certificate of Royal Appointment. Obviously a forgery.

She smiled at the large, dark woman behind the desk, "My employer has a commission for Mr Coughlan."

The woman behind the desk smiled back. "Industrial or domestic?"

"Domestic" said Anne, not wanting to give too much away.

"Oh that will be nice" smiled the secretary: "The men always prefer them, so much cleaner and warmer."

"I wouldn't have thought the cold was a problem." Anne smiled. "We've had such a lovely summer." **Stick to the weather**, she told herself, ***always a safe subject with the English.*** "Is Mr Coughlan available?" she asked.

"I'll see," said the secretary. "Do take a seat." She stopped hammering the ancient typewriter and pushed aside the nicotine-stained white Bakelite telephone before pushing a button on an intercom-like contraption that took up half of the desk.

After a pause she began, "James, there's a client here to see you."

Anne heard only static, but the secretary seemed to understand everything clearly. "He'll be with you as soon as he finished his call to LMS. We're repairing their train sheds, although I've probably said enough." The secretary winked at Anne.

"Oh yes, loose lips and all that," Anne beamed back.

"I'm Mary by the way, Mary Hilton."

"Anne, Anne Cole."

"Can I get you some tea?" asked Mary: "It won't be very strong, I'm afraid, I must have used the same wretched leaves about half a dozen times."

Anne looked at the rusting gas ring and chipped tea wares and declined.

Mary smiled again. "I'm glad you said that. I'm trying not to walk around too much today. I'm stretching these shoes for James's… Mr Coughlan's wife. They're off to a do on Saturday, the local Lodge, although James… Mr Coughlan is not a member and Diana, Mr Coughlan's wife, has bought these new shoes, which are a little tight for her. So as we're the same size but I'm a wider fitting, I'm trying to stretch them a little for her." Mary pushed her leg from behind the desk: "Beautiful aren't they?"

Anne looked down at the waving foot and admired the petrol blue grosgrain sling back, with a tapering square heel and just the hint of a platform. Mary's workaday wool stockings spoiled the effect somewhat but Anne gushed enviously: "Yes very, but how do you get hold of a pair of those nowadays?"

"Oh if you've got the money and the contacts it's not difficult."

Sighed Mary: "They're starting to pinch so I'm trying not to walk on them. I've been up and down all morning making tea for those two reprobates, which hasn't helped." Mary half shouted in the direction of two men haphazardly working behind Anne. The men shouted back, "Oh, but you love us really," and carried on cleaning paintbrushes. Anne turned around. She had not noticed that the second half of the office was a quasi-workshop, filled with benches and brushes, paint mixing cans and primitive spray equipment. Two men in grubby painters' overalls were cleaning brushes and rollers. One of them, a tall decorator, with a cheeky grin and pointed nose, caught Anne's eye and openly leered at her. She hastily turned away.

"We're not very busy at the moment," explained Mary. "Although Mr Coughlan probably won't thank me for saying so."

Anne looked at Mary. They were roughly the same age and Anne guessed that their situations were probably very similar. They were both sleeping with the boss. Anne would work on this, who knows what information she could find out? Something important about the Ministry of Defence contracts that Coughlan & Sons were carrying out. Something important to remind Canaris that she still existed. She was sure a rapport was building up between them. She would use all her training to turn this already budding friendship to her advantage. Anne whispered: "Who's he?" indicating the long-nosed lecher in the back room.

Mary whispered back, "Oh that's Jack, he's a legend in his own lifetime. Before he joined us he was a deliveryman for the local bakery. Let's say that a lot of housewives got more than just a sliced white." Mary laughed quietly.

"Oh I see," Anne joined in. "I'll have to keep an eye out for him."

Mary was about to reply when the door of the office opened. James Coughlan stood in the doorway. Coughlan was forty, average height, balding and red faced with heavy stubble although he had shaved that morning. His eyes glinted and went to Anne's legs. Silk stockings, he smiled lasciviously.

"James," Mary began, "This is Anne Cole, she has a job for you."

"I don't exactly, but my employer does," said Anne, getting up and straightening her skirt.

Coughlan came over to her, his eyes darting from her face to her silk stockinged legs. They shook hands. "Shall we go into my office?" said Coughlan. "Has Mary offered you a cup of tea? Or maybe you'd prefer a real drink?"

Anne smiled: "No, thank you." She noticed that there was no trace of an Irish accent, the man spoke pure Black Country and was obviously the second generation of an Irish immigrant family. She hoped that would not be a problem.

Coughlan held out his arm, indicating that Anne should go on ahead.

As she walked in front of him, Anne felt his eyes burning through her barathea skirt. *Well it's for the Fatherland*, she said to herself and tried to wiggle her hips. *God I'm out of practice*, she thought as she tried to master the unfamiliar manoeuvre. *Not that I was ever very good at it,* she sighed silently as she sat down.

Coughlan's office mirrored that of his secretary's, the roof sloped away markedly and with his desk positioned at the rear he had to shoehorn himself behind it, with his head almost touching the ceiling.

Anne looked at the slightly obese, red-faced man, with his chubby boyish cheeks and self-centred sexual confidence. *Pull my skirt up a little and this will be a piece of cake*, she said to herself.

She began, "I'm here at the behest of my employer, who at present wishes to remain anonymous. He has some alterations that he wishes you to carry out."

"We're very busy at the moment." Coughlan gave the standard reply without even realising he had said it. It was a reflex. He always had an eye for the main chance, even if his entire workforce was sunning themselves behind the sheds or perfunctorily doing a few odd jobs for his wife. Odd jobs that were never finished since as soon as he had set a couple of the lads to working at his home, a big job would come in and he would have to drag them away, leaving the hallway half papered or the bathroom half plumbed. Even if he had every man available, he would always tell the client that he had pulled them off another job and try to charge a little more.

Anne smiled to herself. "I expect the two men kicking their heels outside would jump at the chance to do something more interesting than washing brushes," she laughed.

"They're doing very important preparation work for an important job we're starting next week," Coughlan lied effortlessly.

"Well, if you can't help, I shall have to look elsewhere." Anne hitched up her skirt.

"I didn't say we couldn't do it," Coughlan backtracked.

"That's better," said Anne: "Now, my employer has a job that will require six of your best men for around a fortnight. To begin immediately."

Ian Cassidy

"The best thing is for me to come and look at it and give your employer a quote," suggested Coughlan.

"That won't be necessary or in fact possible at the present time, but I have a set of plans from which you may prepare an estimate. You are to provide labour only, all materials will be sourced by my employer's agent on the spot." She took the blueprints from her handbag and passed it to Coughlan.

Coughlan looked at them briefly and said: "They're a bit rough, I don't think I can produce a final quotation from these alone. For a start, whoever drew them up has left out the windows."

This man is no fool. Anne said to herself. She shifted in her chair. "I understand the plans to be complete, the designer has not included windows because they will not be required. The suite of rooms is to be constructed in the hold of a cargo ship."

"What! A ship, I'm afraid Miss Cole that's not really our thing. You need a shipyard for a refit like this."

Anne had expected this. "Come, come, the job looks simple enough. You are to construct a series of partition walls, roofs and floors and then decorate and fit them out. And upgrade the ships' communications room. It seems hardly much different from converting these stables. You just have to forget that the whole thing floats."

"If you put it like that, I suppose we can do it but I must ask. Why?"

Anne had planned her cover story: "My employer has many business interests throughout the world and he travels extensively to keep an eye on them. Given the present world climate he requires a vessel that will allow him to do this unnoticed."

"You mean he's a smuggler," Coughlan said looking pleased as he sensed a big pay-day.

"Shall we just say that he prefers to keep a low profile and to conduct his business affairs out of the glare of officialdom." Anne smiled. "Is that a problem for you?"

Coughlan grinned. "No, no, he sounds a man after my own heart. I don't like petty bureaucrats poking their noses into my business either. As a matter of fact, I've just been prosecuted for storing inflammable materials without proper authorisation. We're painters for god's sake; we have to store paint and turpentine. Admittedly I had got a few gallons in the pantry at home but it was all a fuss over nothing." Coughlan pointed to a framed newspaper cutting on the wall. "It made the local press because I told the magistrate it was all a load of piffle. It didn't go down too well and I got fined an extra couple of guineas for my trouble."

"So I can take it that you are willing to do it?"

"Let me have a proper look at the plans, cost it all out and work out a price. Come back tomorrow afternoon and we can sort things out." Coughlan got up from his chair. "I'm sure that I'm free all afternoon but make an appointment with Mary on your way out." He held out his hand.

"Thank you, Mr Coughlan," said Anne, shaking his hand. Coughlan held on just a little longer than propriety allowed and Anne could have sworn he winked at her. She left the office and Coughlan's eyes never left her legs.

In the outer office Mary Hilton looked up from her work. "Everything all right?" she asked.

"Yes, fine, I'm coming back to see Mr Coughlan tomorrow afternoon." Anne smiled, "I've got to arrange a time with you."

"Right, let me see." Mary consulted the desk diary. "Three o'clock suit you?"

"That's fine," agreed Anne, although she had no idea how she would fill in the time between now and then. She began, "Now, I've been on the go all morning. I really must eat, is there anywhere local that you recommend?"

"I'm just off to the local pub for my lunch, why don't you join me?" Mary enthused.

"Why not?" said Anne.

"It's nothing much but they can usually manage a sandwich or something. I'll just finish up here and we'll be on our way."

Anne waited as Mary pulled three sheets of paper interleaved with worn out carbon from the typewriter. Mary put them in a rusty out-tray and picked up her handbag.

"Hadn't you better change those shoes?" Anne suggested. "I don't suppose they're suitable for lunch in a village pub, even if we go into the lounge bar."

"They're not suitable for walking to it, that's for certain, even though it's only round the corner," said Mary, going back to her desk and rummaging underneath it for own shoes.

Mary slipped on her down-at-heel work shoes and the two women set off. They went back up the driveway, chatting as they went, Anne thought it was a wise move to get to know Coughlan's secretary. If nothing else, she would get some background information that might come in handy for tomorrow's meeting.

They went through the gate and Mary waved at the scruffy old man standing at the gate of the terraced house opposite. She ushered Anne along, nodding towards the man at the gate: "We don't want to get captured," she whispered.

I certainly don't, Anne said to herself "Bit of a talker is he?" she asked.

"I'll say," agreed Mary: "Once he's got you, you just can't get away."

The two women rushed up the street, passing a ramshackle motor repair shop, and presently came to a double fronted tavern, constructed around the turn of the century and not decorated since. Anne looked at the untended half-barrel flowerbeds and the rickety cricket tables.

"That's a shame," she said. "If these tables were nicer, we could sit outside. It's such a lovely day."

"Not a good idea," Mary confided. "There's always all sorts of strange smells and noises coming from the garage we just passed. Inside's a much safer bet."

Mary led the way into the pub and the two women were soon seated with a glass each of unspeakable sherry whilst the landlord's wife knocked them up something for lunch.

"What made your employer choose Coughlan's?" Mary asked.

"I understand he was a guest at a house you renovated before the war," Anne answered.

"Oh really, which one?"

"I'm not sure, somewhere down south." Anne thought it best not to say it was the German Ambassador's country retreat.

"Yes, we did quite a few back then, some very grand commissions. Of course that's all stopped at the moment. Nowadays all we seem to do is repair bomb damage."

"Yes, awful isn't it? London's becoming unbearable, especially now the doodlebugs are coming over."

"Is your employer a Londoner?" asked Mary.

Anne hesitated. "He moves around a lot but originally he's from the south, yes." Anne omitted to say the south of Germany.

"Well, it's nice to have some domestic work for a change. I know the lads will be pleased, they like to do something a bit more interesting than lime washing, it keeps their hands in."

Anne changed the subject. "Tell me about Mr Coughlan, how long have you worked for him?"

"Oh, for nearly twenty years," Mary said enthusiastically. Anne noticed that at the mention of Coughlan's name Mary's eyes lit up and she became more animated and talkative. She pressed on: "He pays well then?"

"Not too bad."

"Is he married? I didn't notice a ring."

"Yes, I was wearing Mrs. Coughlan's shoes if you remember."

"Yes, of course," said Anne. "Silly of me to forget."

"He doesn't wear a ring, he doesn't wear any kind of jewellery. I do so hate this modern fashion for men to wear rings, don't you?"

"I agree with you. Children?"

"Yes he's got two lovely little boys."

"The '& Sons'." suggested Anne.

"Eventually," smiled Mary. "At the moment they're still at school but I expect they'll join the family business. Mind you, that doesn't stop James."

"Doesn't stop him what?" asked Anne.

"You know, with the ladies, always one for the ladies is Mr C."

"Are you speaking from experience?"

"Is it that obvious?"

"Well, you see, I'm speaking from experience also," Anne confided. "My boss and I have an arrangement every Wednesday afternoon."

"Oh, I see. And yes, you're right. James and I, shall we say, see each other on a more than professional basis. Have been for years. Not that I'm the only one. I know we shouldn't but…"

Ian Cassidy

"Yes, I know the feeling."

"I can still remember the first time, he used every hackneyed old line the book, he even said he'd still respect me afterwards. Can you believe it?"

Anne just smiled. Mary reached inside her blouse and pulled out a thin silver chain, on the end of which was a polished stone. Anne looked at it and although she was no mineralogist, she was convinced it was nothing more than a piece of gravel. She waited for Mary to elucidate.

"It's little memento of that first time. We were at a conference in Scarborough and made love on the beach. This little stone got stuck somewhere intimate…"

Anne interrupted: "You mean… " She said looking down at her lap.

Mary Smiled: "They say sand gets everywhere when you're on the beach, well I can tell you that the same is true of pebbles. After I'd extracted it, I had it polished and drilled and wear it as a keepsake."

The two women laughed but their enjoyment was cut short by the arrival of their lunch. Anne looked at the grey bread and indifferent yellow-edged salad leaves and suddenly didn't feel like laughing. She sat back and took a sip of her sherry. At least she had gained some very useful information. She would inform Konrad of Coughlan's propensity for womanising and for large women in particular if Mary was anything to go by. Perhaps they could arrange for him to be caught in some compromising situation in Spain. They could then use him as an agent or at the very least blackmail him into accepting a lower price for his work and save the Reich some money.

She was moving her indescribable salad around the plate when the two workmen she had seen in Coughlan's office entered the bar. The smaller of the two went up to the bar. Jack, of bread round fame, came straight over. He was skilled at being backward in coming forward, especially when it was his round.

"Mary, introduce us to your new, pretty friend." He was off instantly.

Before Mary could reply, the squat painter at the bar called over, offering to buy Mary a drink.

Mary refused. "Nothing for me Keith, I must be getting back."

"What about your friend then."

"Oh no, nothing for me, thank you," Anne gulped. "I must be going as well."

"Don't be silly," said Mary. "Stay, it may not be the Café Royale but it's better than moping around at your B&B."

"We don't bite," Jack leered.

Anne hesitated. What would her mother say if she could see her now, in the bar of a grotty English pub with two strange men in grubby overalls. *It's for the Fatherland*, she thought, *Besides, I might learn something useful from a brief conversation with these two men.*

She looked them over. Leering Jack was interested in only one thing and the bulldog-like man at the bar was certainly not the sharpest knife in the box. With her education and training, getting information out of them would be a pushover.

"Yes, why not?" She smiled. "A small sherry please."

Mary left and Jack introduced himself. Bulldog-like Keith came over with the drinks and sat down, smiling inanely.

"And what do you do for Mr Coughlan?" Anne asked.

Jack began: "Whatever he tells us at the moment but when we're doing proper work, I do the metalwork, welding and blacksmithing."

"Oh, right and what about you?" Anne looked at Keith.

He stuttered, "Oh… I'm a jack of all trades, woodwork, painting, you name it. And I drive the van," he said proudly.

"Have you worked for him a long time?"

"Longer than we care to remember," Jack laughed.

Anne joined in, "You must have lots of stories?"

"Not many for your ears Miss."

"Oh come, I'm more broad-minded than you think."

"You wouldn't want to hear us talk about painting factories, Miss."

"Oh, but I would, my employer wants as much information as possible before he selects a contractor."

"Well." The two men looked at each other.

With uncharacteristic hesitation Jack began: "Well, he throws Keith into his swimming pool every Christmas Eve, doesn't he, Keith?"

"Oh yes," gulped Keith: "Without fail, he gives me my Christmas bonus and a bottle of whisky, then throws me in the pool."

Ian Cassidy

"So he's a generous man, Mr Coughlan?" Anne asked.

"Oh yes, he always has the all the lads for a drink at Christmas in his snooker room. This year we had fish and chips and posh wine, Chateau du pop or something that he'd got cheap on account of it having fallen of the back of a lorry."

"Very generous," Anne agreed.

"Oh we had a high old time, we always do, he knows how to entertain."

"Tell me about the jobs you've done." Anne asked.

"You name it we've done it, Miss. From lime washing factories in Tipton to hanging hand-made wallpaper in Newtonards.

"Newtonards?" said Anne. "So you do work in Ireland as well?"

"Yes we do a lot of travelling, he's got a lot of contacts in the old country."

Anne finished her sherry. "Well thank you, gentlemen, you've been most helpful."

It was Jack's round so he did not offer to buy her another drink. The two men said goodbye and Anne left quite satisfied with the information she had picked up. Coughlan obviously enjoyed a lavish lifestyle, with swimming pools, snooker tables and Chateauneuf du Pape. He would naturally be on the lookout for lucrative work to sustain it and he regularly worked in Ireland, so it would not be too problematic to get his men out of the country. Konrad had chosen well.

Feeling slightly light-headed from the sherry and the smoky atmosphere, Anne headed for the bus stop. *What the hell am I going to do for the rest of the afternoon?* she asked herself. She could not go back to the King's Head, as the landlord would think it strange that her reunion with her "relatives" had been so brief. She got onto the bus and tried to think of something to do.

She looked at her watch as the bus set her down once again in Lichfield. A quarter past two, that left her with about six hours to kill. She walked through the city, lingering outside the birthplace of Dr Johnson and walking aimlessly around the statue of Boswell that stood opposite. She headed in the direction of the cathedral close.

She walked around the close looking at the buttressed walls and then walked all the way round again, swinging her handbag and gazing skyward at the three spires.

She completed a third circuit before she looked at her watch again. The gold Rolex, a gift from her boss in the publishers, said two fifty five. She swore under her breath. She decided that a fourth circumnavigation might arouse suspicion. After studying the massive carved front of the cathedral she went inside, trying hard to picture how the statues of the saints would have looked when they were originally put in place, all sharp and brightly painted.

Once inside, she walked along the left side, studying the tombs and other inscriptions. She did the same on the right side and finally settled in the Lady Chapel. She took a seat and resisted the temptation to consult her watch again. She sat there as long as she could but finally she began to suspect that she was attracting the attention of a beer bellied canon and, not wishing to become engaged in a discussion about her spiritual well being, she got up and left.

At the doorway she was confronted by a less than harmonic crocodile of yellow capped schoolboys, choristers from the Cathedral school on the way to pre-evensong practice. The boys politely stood aside and Anne smiled as she pushed her way out.

She left the close and headed back towards the city centre. The road she walked down was flanked by two parks. She chose the one on her right. She was met by a series of uninteresting, badly tended flower beds, muddy lawns and two tennis courts, now churned up and put to the cultivation of vegetables. A stone statue of Queen Victoria, covered in pigeon droppings, guarded the entrance to the park but it was the bespattered bronze statue of a sea captain that caught Anne's eye. She walked up to it and read the inscription.

"Commander Edward John Smith RD RNR
Born January 27 1850, Died April 15 1912
Bequeathing to his Countrymen
The Memory & Example of a Great Heart
A Brave life & a Heroic Death
Be British."

Ian Cassidy

"Be British!" Anne scoffed. Only the British could see something heroic in steaming straight into an iceberg and sending hundreds of people to their deaths.

At least he went down with his ship, Anne thought. She had read about this while she was researching this area of south Staffordshire. Smith was born in Stoke-on-Trent but following his misadventure on the Titanic, the people of his hometown had been keen to disassociate themselves with him. When it was proposed that a statue be erected of their famous but accident-prone son, they had objected, so the statue was erected thirty miles away in Lichfield. She read the inscription once more before selecting a bench and sitting down.

She sat back and enjoyed the late afternoon sunshine. She slipped off her shoes and dozed. At five twenty Anne roused herself and commenced a slow walk back to city. She realised that she was hungry. She had missed breakfast in order to get to Euston in time and since then she had had nothing but an unspeakable sandwich that masqueraded as lunch. She began to look for a suitable inn or café for an early evening meal. The first pub she came to had not yet opened and the elegant half-timbered Tudor café had closed; apparently it only opened for lunches and afternoon teas. She pressed on, once again coming to Dr. Johnson's birthplace.

At the other side of the marketplace, beyond Boswell's statue and nestling in the shade of a dinky little church, that seemed to Anne to be unnecessarily close to its big sister the cathedral, Anne saw a pub with its doors open. Its large grimy windows were frosted and dark. *Beggars can't be choosers*, she said to herself and walked across the square.

She went into the lounge bar and without looking at the surroundings - *I'll save that delight for later*, she thought - she ordered a lemonade before enquiring about the possibilities of obtaining a repast in the establishment.

Anne and the barmaid discussed the possibilities of obtaining something hot from the limited menu of cold chicken of unspecified vintage, meat pie with no further information available and mouse dropping sandwiches. Anne settled on a hot platter centred on something porky and, scarcely looking forward to the anticipated confection of gristle and offal, she retired from the bar.

She took her lemonade to a nearby table and sat uneasily. She surveyed her surroundings, the unprepossessing exterior had prepared her for the most awful spit and sawdust establishment, so she was pleasantly surprised as she noted the cosy interior of polished wood, log fires and mercifully few topers at the bar. Her experience of pubs was limited, especially on her own, but she thanked providence that she had chanced upon an establishment that was just suitable for the single female traveller. She sipped her lemonade and waited for her meal.

Presently the barmaid appeared with a diabolical concoction of off-white pork belly, lurking greens and watery potatoes. Anne was less than eager to dig in so she was not displeased when the woman began to chat.

"You're not from these parts?" she asked.

"No, I'm up from London for a few days."

"Are you a commercial traveller?"

Struggling with a rubbery mouthful, Anne could only shake her head.

"Or maybe a lawyer in town for the Assizes?"

"Nothing so grand," Anne replied after she finally performed the awkward task of swallowing: "Just visiting relatives."

"Really, anyone I know?"

Anne paused. "Oh, I shouldn't think so," she said noncommittally.

"Try me, I've worked at a lot of pubs, if they like a drink, I bet I'll have run into them."

Anne frowned briefly. **Nothing else for it**, she said to herself. "James Coughlan, do you know him?"

"I know the name, from Brownhills right?"

"Yes that's right." said Anne, cringing inside.

"I'm sure our potman used to work for him, he's in the cellar now; I'll ask him when I get the chance."

Anne forced a smile and the barmaid left. Anne pushed the surprisingly palatable food around the plate and cursed. She was not looking forward to the prospect of discussing a man she had met for less than ten minutes but now claimed as a relative with one of his old acquaintances. Despite her hunger, she could not enjoy her meal at the thought of such an awkward, not to say dangerous, encounter. She decided to try and bolt it down and make her exit before the potman finished doing whatever potmen do in the cellar.

She was unsuccessful. She had worked her way through her meal to a point where she calculated that she could leave it without arousing comment, when a portly aproned man appeared at her table. He did not smile: "I hear you're a relative of Jim Coughlan's." His voice dropped as he mentioned Coughlan's name.

"Yes, but quite distant," Anne said, trying to convey a confidence she did not possess. "I wanted to get away from London for a few days and as my finances won't run to a hotel I had to look up second cousin James for the first time in years."

The fat man with sweaty grey hair appeared to lighten up: "I'm glad to hear you say you're a distant cousin, Miss. May I sit down?" he asked conspiratorially.

Anne nodded.

"A word of advice Miss, I've known Jim for a lot of years, his father as well, and as you've not seen him for many years I probably know him a lot better than you."

"I'm sure you do." agreed Anne, wondering what the man's point was.

"Well, Miss, it's not a wise move to go bandying Jim's name about in the local pubs. He's made a lot of enemies and you never know when one might be sitting at the bar."

Anne was intrigued and although her better judgement told that there was little to be gained and a lot to be lost in prolonging this conversation she asked: "Really? Tell me more?"

"I don't really think it's my place to do that," the potman said, although Anne sensed he was bursting to dish the dirt.

"Oh, please do," said Anne. "As I said it's been many years since we ran into one another and I'd like to hear what's been going on in James' life."

"I wouldn't want to spoil your holiday, Miss."

"Forewarned is forearmed," smiled Anne.

"Well." The potman shifted eagerly in his seat. "It's a case of where do I start, Miss. His old man is a rogue, more than a rogue, an out-and-out crook. He was a bookie before the war, still is if the truth be told, despite the government making it illegal."

"That sounds fairly harmless to me," said Anne: "Men will always gamble and in times like this I'm sure they need a bit of innocent excitement."

"It's not quite so innocent Miss, in times like these men can't afford to lose their cash to the bookies and they can't afford to lose their ration books."

"He can't take those surely?" Anne asked.

"He takes payment in any form he can. He was a wrongun before the war and nothing's changed. He worked the tracks, Newmarket, Aintree, you know."

Anne nodded.

"The things he got up to, he used to give out tickets with a different name on them."

"I'm sorry?" asked Anne: "I'm not familiar with the racetrack."

"You see, Miss, he'd put up his board and his sign, saying "Steve Coughlan, Turf Accountant" and start taking bets; he'd take the punters' money and give them a ticket with a totally different name on it. People rarely look at their ticket until after the race and when the lucky winners did, they would go looking for a bookie standing under a board with the same name as on their ticket. They wouldn't find him and all they'd know was that they had the bet with a man in a hat and an overcoat."

Anne smiled to herself, with lineage like that Coughlan appeared perfect for Konrad's scheme: "Do go on," she said.

"There's worse than that, Miss. Do you remember the Pontefract Tote disaster of 1929?"

Anne had no idea what he was talking about. She had been at Heidelberg in 1929, studying languages, including English, but her battle with English grammar had been fought across a field of dusty textbooks, not imported English newspapers, so she had been blissfully ignorant of English affairs. Her passion for the Times crossword had developed in later years.

She coughed. "Vaguely, as I said the turf has never really been an interest of mine."

"The race course was so full, Miss, that all the grandstands were full and many racegoers climbed onto the roof of the Tote building…"

Anne interrupted. "Tote building?" she asked.

"It's a betting office inside the track, Miss."

"Oh I see, forgive me, do go on."

"With the weight of all the people, the roof of the building gave way crushing the racegoers and the betting office workers below. Many were killed and a lot more badly injured. Old Steve was right outside when it happened and joined in with the rescue efforts, that is until he got to the tills, he filled his pockets with as much unattended cash as he could and was out of there like a rat from a drainpipe."

"Dreadful," said Anne. "But tell me about James?"

"In his own way he's worse, Miss, but his vice is different. He's still as interested as his father in looking for ways to make a dishonest buck. Plenty of poor sods will tell you that but Jim's always on the lookout for something else. Not to put too fine a point on it, he can't keep his trousers on."

Anne smiled inwardly. "He was the same all those years ago," she gambled.

The potman warmed to his task: "He's got children littered all over the country, the poor little bastards! Beg your pardon, Miss. He leads his wife a dog's life. The stories that people have to tell about him, well it's beyond me."

"Oh no," said Anne, shocked. "Oh, I'm sure they're just malicious rumours." Seeing a means of escape she went on, "Thank you so much, it's been very illuminating but I really must be getting back." She got up and was making for the bar to settle her bill as the potman whispered again, "Just be careful where you mention Jim's name, Miss, that's all."

"Oh, I will and thank you again," Anne muttered back and quickly made for the bar. She paid her bill and left.

As she walked back to her hotel, she pondered on what she had learnt. Nothing of consequence, she decided, it was always likely that anyone prepared to accept her commission, no questions asked, would be a little dubious, if not outright crooked. She was sure Konrad would have no problems with them in Spain, after all, Konrad would probably be accompanied by a platoon of Panzer grenadiers and what would these petty Staffordshire crooks have? A paintbrush and a stepladder.

She hurried across the city and made it to her hotel, a little earlier than she had planned but she explained her premature return to the landlord by saying that she had had such a long day travelling that she was simply unable to enjoy the fun at her relatives for a moment longer. He was not particularly interested in any event and when Anne bought a large brandy from him, sorely needed to wash away the lingering taste of pork belly, he was completely appeased.

Anne shut herself away in her room for the rest of the evening. She began to mentally compose her report to Major Soellner but after such a tiring day it was far from complete when she fell asleep.

six
28th August, 1944

8.24am. **King's Head, Lichfield, Staffordshire.** Anne rose early the next morning and after briefly popping out to pick up a morning paper she presented herself for breakfast. After all, she had paid for it.

The landlord's wife, whose existence Anne had seriously doubted, served to her a bowl of burnt, lumpy porridge and a cup of undrinkable coffee. Despite the constant outpourings of Churchill's propaganda machine, Anne scarcely believed that the acorn coffee they were reportedly drinking in Berlin could be worse than this. She ate what she could and returned to her room. She passed the landlord on the stairs and explained to him that her relatives had to work that morning so she would not be visiting them. Once again he showed scant interest and Anne decided that her constant explanations to him might become counterproductive. She was over-thinking her mission; the days when publicans looked out for counteragents and Quislings amongst their guests were long gone. No one would take any notice of a prim secretary in her late thirties but they might take notice of a prim secretary in her late thirties who was always giving unnecessary explanations.

She got back to her room and locked the door. She took her suitcase from under the bed, opened it and took out her camera, unfortunately not the sleek, state of the art Leica she had owned at Heidelberg, but a creaky Houghton folding Klito she had purchased at a stall on the Portobello Road. She considered her plan of paying a visit to the

Staffordshire Regiment's barracks at Whittington but one look at the camera told her it was out of the question. The cumbersome piece of equipment would be noticed by even the most apathetic sentry and besides she was hardly equipped to pose as a rambler. She had brought only her city clothes and she was sure the sight of a woman trudging through the countryside in a business suit, silk stockings and high heels would alarm even the previously mentioned apathetic sentry. She took solace in the Times crossword and watched the hours pass slowly before her meeting with Coughlan.

Anne presented herself at Coughlan's office five minutes before the appointed time and after exchanging pleasantries with the ever cheerful Mary she was shown into the tinpot director's low roofed office.

She endured the expected scrutiny of her legs without complaint and sat down.

Coughlan began, "I've got a few figures based on the plans you gave me, I was thinking in the region of…"

Anne stopped him. "Before you go on, Mr Coughlan, there's one extra detail you need to know. The work is to be carried out in Spain. In the port of Sitges, to be exact."

Coughlan sat bolt upright, almost banging his head. "What!" he exclaimed. "Where?" He puffed and went slightly redder in the face. "It may have escaped your notice that this is north Birmingham not north Barcelona. It's not very convenient to travel to Spain every morning plus the little matter of the war going on. And where the hell is Sitges?"

"Funny that you should mention Barcelona because it's very near there, just to the south, on the Mediterranean as it happens." Anne said calmly. "We are not at war with Spain, so travel between the two countries is possible."

Coughlan whistled. "Theoretically, yes, but there's a lot of paperwork involved. I think we would need permission to travel, and I'm certain we wouldn't get it quickly enough to complete the job in the time scale you mentioned."

"My employer is most anxious that the existence of this contract is known to just ourselves. He would be forced to withdraw if the authorities were to be informed."

Ian Cassidy

"So what do you want me to do?" asked Coughlan reluctantly.

"I understand from your secretary that you regularly work in both Ulster and the Republic of Ireland."

"Yes, what of it?"

"So both you and your men have travel papers."

"Papers to cross the border from Ulster, yes, they may not be enough to get us into Spain."

"My employer will take care of things in Spain," Anne lied. She had no idea how those amongst Coughlan's party without passports would enter Spain. She would include it in her report. It was just one more detail for Konrad to take care of.

She continued, "So it would be possible to send a party of workers to Ulster, let them slip over the border into the Republic and then they could travel without restrictions between two non-combatant countries."

"Possible, yes." agreed Coughlan sweatily. "Possible but very expensive." He said brightening up.

"My employer will compensate you more than adequately."

"Just how adequately?" Coughlan asked sharply.

Anne hesitated, she had been given carte blanche in these negotiations with no upper limit but she felt like making Coughlan work for his money.

"My employer is a very generous man but he did not reach his position of wealth by being overgenerous. He will require a certain amount of value for money. What figure did you have in mind?"

"You're asking me to scrap these figures and start from scratch," Coughlan barked.

"No, I'm asking you to produce an estimate for the work already discussed and for the incidental travel and accommodation costs."

"Let me see," said Coughlan whose mental arithmetic was excellent as befits a bookmaker's son. "Six men plus myself to travel to Liverpool, the ferry to Belfast, accommodation in Belfast, diesel for driving to Dublin. It will be much easier and safer to cross the border in our own transport than getting the train to Dublin. We'll need accommodation in Dublin because we may have to wait for a ship going to Bilbao. From Bilbao we'll have to get a train to Barcelona, from where we'll travel to Sitges and start the job. We do fourteen days' work and then do everything in reverse. We will be away for at least five weeks. I'll have to pay my men for that, I can't just pay them for the two weeks that they are on the job."

"My employer understands that," said Anne.

"Well, let's call it twenty thousand pounds." Coughlan's voice was perfectly calm. He could give the most outrageous estimates without the slightest embarrassment.

Anne, on the other hand, was less calm. She gulped, she knew he was a villain but he was asking for more money than she would ever see and being completely blasé about it. And how was she going to tell Konrad that she had just spent twenty thousand pounds of his Department's money? Although she had a suspicion that such a vast amount would never be paid, a platoon of Panzer grenadiers can put off even the most determined of creditors.

Coughlan filled the silence. "In advance." He even smiled.

Anne started to protest but she knew she had no choice. She began unsteadily, "The total amount is fine but we are unable to make over such a sum in advance. My employer has authorised me to let you a substantial sum now, but not the full amount."

"How much?"

Anne opened her handbag and placed one thousand pounds in white fivers and fifty gold sovereigns enticingly on the front of Coughlan. She noticed the avaricious look on Coughlan's face and said, "There's one thousand pounds in cash and fifty gold sovereigns there, so shall we call it fifteen hundred pounds in total."

Anne watched as Coughlan did a quick calculation. "I don't think so," he said, sharply indicating the sovereigns. "They're worth about eight pounds each, so we'll call it fourteen hundred."

Anne shook her head. "I checked in the Times this morning, an ounce of gold is worth almost nine pounds."

Coughlan smiled his "don't try to kid a kidder" smile. "Now I know you're trying to have me over, gold prices aren't quoted anymore. The London gold market closed in 1939."

Anne had to concede that Coughlan was quicker than he looked. "Shall we split the difference?" She suggested, smiling and crossing her legs as she did so. "Let's call it four hundred and fifty for the sovereigns."

Coughlan smiled and looked at her legs. He nodded. "So that's fourteen hundred and fifty on account, leaving a balance of eighteen thousand five hundred and fifty to be paid. When?" Coughlan asked.

"When what?"

"Will it be paid?"

"On completion," Anne suggested.

"No, that won't do, won't do at all. I'll have used up a lot of this just getting to Spain, I'd like some money paid when we arrive in Sitges, for digs and that sort of thing."

Anne was not altogether sure what "digs" meant, her fluency in English did not extend to Midlands vernacular but she nodded anyway. "I'm sure that will be acceptable. I'll suggest to my employer that you receive three thousand five hundred and fifty pounds on arrival in Spain and the final fifteen thousand on completion."

"That sounds fine," said Coughlan. He pointed at the pile of cash in front of him on the desk. "You don't mind if I count this?"

Anne nodded. Coughlan began to count slowly, examining every note.

"I can assure you they're genuine," said Anne.

"All the same, I think I'll check. The Jerries are supposed to have flooded the country with dodgy notes."

"Surely that was earlier on in the war. And besides, where would I get hold of forged Nazi fivers?" Anne smiled disingenuously. Also she knew that the money was one hundred per cent genuine, Canaris would never risk one of his agents being captured because of an infringement of currency regulations.

Coughlan stopped counting. "Actually I've just had a thought, I'd like the balance to be paid in Swiss francs. That way I can arrange to have it paid directly into my Swiss bank account. I don't really fancy trying to smuggle that amount of cash back into Blighty. It won't be a problem will it?"

"I don't think so, I will inform my employer as soon as I get back to London."

Coughlan nodded in agreement and greedily pocketed the cash and sovereigns. "I'll contact you in the next day or so and tell you when we propose to leave."

Anne reached into her handbag for a card. "Call me on this number any evening, you'll find me in. And you'd better call me when you're ready to sail from Dublin, so I can arrange for you to be met in Spain."

"Yes, of course, we don't want to get turned away at the border." Although Anne suspected that would suit him very nicely, that way he would pocket the best part of fifteen hundred pounds for doing nothing and Konrad could not send the bailiffs in to retrieve his money, could he?

Coughlan stood up and held out his hand. Anne stood and they shook hands.

Once again Coughlan left his hand in hers a little longer than propriety required. He smiled his winning smile and suggested: "Why don't I drive you back to your hotel, so much better than the bus."

This was something Anne was hoping to avoid so she hastily changed the subject: "I will need a receipt for the money you've just been paid."

Coughlan looked askance and muttered something unintelligible.

"Shall I ask your secretary?" Anne suggested.

"No, no!" Coughlan blurted and hastily scrabbled in his desk drawer for a suitable piece of stationery. He scribbled a panicky note on the firm's dowdy headed notepaper and handed it to Anne. He stood and quickly regained his composure: "Now what about that lift?" The winning smile had returned.

Anne was about to refuse but the thought of another bone shaking journey over South Staffordshire's potholed highways was too much to contemplate. She returned Coughlan's smile and agreed.

Coughlan roared away in the Armstrong Siddely and Anne sat back as the stately boat-like machine rolled along. *More comfortable than the bus*, she said to herself, *but rather like being part of a funeral cortege*.

Coughlan changed gear and his hand slipped effortlessly onto Anne's stockinged knee. She demurely moved it away. Coughlan did not appear to notice.

"Tell me about yourself, Anne," he began.

"There's nothing much to tell," Anne replied robotically.

"Oh I'm sure there is," Coughlan pressed.

"Well." Anne began reluctantly, she was confident in her cover story but the less times it was wheeled out the less chance of there was of her being exposed. "I work for a publisher in central London. I live just south of the river, I'm unmarried. My parents are no longer with us and I have one sister who married a South African and moved to Cape Town. All in all, a very ordered and very boring existence."

Anne noted that Coughlan listened very well. He nodded in all the right places, made agreeable noises and smiled where necessary. She also noted that he had not the slightest interest in what she was saying. He was just doing what was necessary to get into her cami-knickers.

"Why would a publisher need a ship refitted?"

Anne was taken aback. "I'm sorry?"

"You said and I quote: 'the job is for your employer.'"

"So I did." Anne stalled. "My employer as I referred to him is in fact a client of my real employer."

"Oh I see," said Coughlan, "He's a writer is he? Would I have heard of him?"

"That I cannot say, Mr Coughlan and I am sorry but I am not authorised to reveal his identity."

"Please yourself." Coughlan grunted. "Why does a writer need concealed apartments on a cargo ship."

"I did not say he is a writer. I said he has many business interests, business interests that led to him having dealings with my firm. Shall we leave it at that."

"Fine," said Coughlan, not entirely convinced. "Now what do you do for enjoyment?" he asked.

"Oh I read a lot," Anne replied.

"But working for a publisher as you do that's almost work, there must be something else."

"Crosswords," said Anne. "I'm a Times crossword addict."

"I'm a Manchester Guardian man myself," said Coughlan.

Anne looked surprised.

"It is possible, you know, to be a capitalist and a supporter of Mr Attlee. My father-in-law's a coal miner, you see. So despite what he's doing now, the family can never really be fans of Churchill. It will be a long time before the colliers forget what went on in Wales in 1923."

Anne nodded knowledgeably but she was inwardly panicking. At least she had a vague inkling about the events to which Coughlan referred but she wished she had spent a little more time studying recent British history.

"Yes, it was an awful thing to do," she said noncommittally.

"Anyway, enough of this serious talk," Coughlan said breezily. "Tell me about the man in your life. There must be someone in London waiting for an attractive woman like you." His hand was back on her knee.

"No, no, there's no-one." Anne found herself blushing despite her best efforts not to. She tried to brush his hand from her knee.

"That is a shame, what a…"

Anne interrupted. "Here we are!" she blurted as the King's Head came into view. *Saved by the bell*. Anne said to herself but Coughlan was not easily put off.

"Why don't I buy you dinner?" he suggested.

"Isn't it a bit early for dinner?" Anne said evasively. "There'll be nothing doing in the way of food here for at least an hour."

"Well what about afternoon tea then." Coughlan had the bit between his teeth."And not here, we'll go across the road, it's so much nicer." He said nodding towards the George Hotel.

Coughlan spun the car around before Anne could reply. He accelerated past the grand front portico of the George, took the first left, then a left again, through the archway that had been the hotel's entrance in its former days as a coaching inn and brought the car to a halt at the rear entrance.

He's done this before, Anne said to herself. She attempted to speak to Coughlan but he was already out of the car and heading for her door.

With a flourish he opened the passenger door. Anne made her excuses before she moved. "Really Mr Coughlan, it's very kind of you but I really must settle up at the King's Head and get the next train to London."

"Nonsense," said Coughlan. "You can catch a later one, all work and no play."

"Really, Mr Coughlan, my employer will want a progress report."

"There's nothing to tell him that can't wait until tomorrow morning and it's Jim, none of this Mr Coughlan business."

Anne realised further resistance was futile. "Perhaps a cup of tea then." She said, getting out of the car.

Coughlan showed her into the hotel. Judging by the plush interior, Anne guessed that wartime privations meant little here. Just a hint of the fine Aberdeen Angus roast lunch hung in the freesia-scented air. Anne smiled inwardly. *Why not,* she said herself, *I deserve a treat after a night in that unspeakable room and the nightmare train journey before it. Just so long as it's not too costly,* she reminded herself.

Her feet sank into the thick carpet as Coughlan showed her to a table in the lounge. She sat down worrying that her obviously twice-worn blouse would not escape the notice of the over-attentive staff.

While Coughlan ordered tea, she excused herself and made for the ladies where she retouched her makeup, tried to tug the creases from her suit and straightened the seams of her stockings.

Feeling slightly more comfortable, she returned to the hotel lounge. Coughlan was chatting easily with the maitre d'. She realised he was very well known here. Obviously not the first time he had made use of the George for an assignation. She sat down and they chatted while waiting for their afternoon tea.

Coughlan continued in similar vein to the conversation in the car. He listened well without listening and was quick with the anecdotes and quicker with the compliments. He brushed her knee whenever possible, stroked her cheek and her arm, although he seemed more taken with her watch than her shapely wrist: "Beautiful timepiece." He observed.

"Yes, it was a gift from a friend."

"A very generous friend."

"Yes, he is."

"He is." Said Coughlan: "I thought you said there was no-one in your life."

"There isn't," said Anne hastily. "It was a very long time ago but I expect he's still as generous now, only with someone else."

"I'm sorry it didn't work out," said Coughlan, trying and failing to sound empathetic. All Anne noticed was his relief that his planned seduction was still on track.

"These things happen." She said quite sharply.

A vast afternoon tea of cream cakes, freshly baked brown bread with no crusts and real butter arrived on a sliver tray. Anne was disappointed that the teapot was silver plated but that aside she had few complaints and despite her efforts to peck demurely, she feared she ate an unladylike share. The previous twenty-four hours had not been kind to her digestion.

Coughlan chatted easily and watched her eat. Anne squeezed the last drop of tea from the pot and Coughlan excused himself. Anne was happily gazing out of the window, watching the first of the town's office workers making their way home, with her shoes kicked off under the coffee table, when Coughlan returned. He looked pleased with himself.

"I've just checked with the concierge." He announced: "There's a train bound for Euston leaving here at eight thirty, so why don't we adjourn to the bar for a cocktail while we're waiting." Anne was sure he had a room key in his hand.

"No really Mr Coughlan… Jim, you've been too kind, I really couldn't impose on you anymore."

"Don't be silly. It would be my pleasure and a couple of stiff gins will make the train journey that much more bearable."

Anne had to agree with him, she was not looking forward to the return journey and after a drink or two, she would perhaps be lucky enough to sleep for some of the trip home. She said yes.

Coughlan led her through to the bar where the barman perked up when he saw Coughlan and hastily ceased his glass polishing. He was poised for action as Coughlan helped Anne up to a barstool.

"Mr Coughlan, how nice to see you again. Your usual, Sir?"

"Thank you, Lewis." said Coughlan slipping the barman a ten bob note. "And for the lady I think the Jupiter."

"Nothing too strong please," said Anne, feeling outnumbered.

"Try it, you'll love it," Coughlan laughed. "Lew here is a genius. He gets his cocktail recipes from the Savoy Cocktail Book." He went on in a whisper: "He pretends he worked there before the war but really he was pulling pints at a spit and sawdust joint in Wolverhampton."

Anne was lost but before she could ask for an explanation Coughlan went on. "The Jupiter is one of his specialities; it's gin, vermouth, orange juice and Parfait Amour. Which is very hard to get hold of nowadays but Lew keeps a bottle hidden especially for me," Coughlan said, winking at the bartender.

"I would think orange juice is just as hard to get hold of," observed Anne.

"You're right, it's probably powdered but after the first two or three you won't notice the difference."

"It's been that long since I even saw an orange that I can't remember what they taste like anyway." Anne began and then hastily changed the subject; she did not feel like a discussion about shortages and rationing. Not that Coughlan would have joined in anyway, his mind was on other things and his hand was on her knee.

Anne crossed her legs and brushed it off. She took a sip of her cocktail and stifled a cough. *No doubt as to Coughlan's intentions and no doubt as to the barman's complicity*, she said to herself. If Lewis wanted to keep the ten bob notes coming his way he had to be heavy-handed with the gin.

Coughlan prattled away with another series of meaningless compliments and another round of drinks appeared. Anne felt Coughlan's hand on her knee again but this time underneath her skirt. He ran his hand up her silken thigh and looking into her eyes said: "Why don't we go somewhere quieter? Away from all the noise." Coughlan looked around at the bar which was slowly filling up.

"Let's have another drink first," suggested Anne, feeling slightly light-headed.

Lew was there instantly with two more drinks. Coughlan did not waste any time with his scotch and before she knew it Anne was being ushered up the hotel stairs with Coughlan's hand pressed limpet-like to her backside.

He came to a stop outside room number nine and fumbled for the key.

"A room," said Anne blearily. "I thought we were going to a quieter bar."

"No, you didn't," leered Coughlan, squeezing her backside.

"No, I didn't." Anne giggled. Coughlan swung the door open. He was kissing Anne before they crossed the threshold. He kicked the door closed behind them and pressed Anne against the wall. She returned his kisses and, fearing for the buttons on the only presentable silk blouse she owned, she brushed his fumbling hands away. "Let me do it," she gasped before his mouth closed on hers again. The two of them tumbled towards the bed.

It's my duty to the Fatherland, she said to herself as he pushed up her skirt.

Anne awoke with a start. She shuddered as tried to focus on the unfamiliar surroundings, the hairy arm between her legs brought it all back to her. She sighed and slumped back into the pillow, listening to the violent snores of the man beside her. Regrets bubbled up inside her but she never completed her *What have I done?* lament. "My train!" she blurted, looking for her watch. Coughlan grunted but showed no other signs of stirring. Anne groped around on the bedside table, fearing that Coughlan may have snaffled it. She had noted his interest in it and after the events of the last few hours she did not doubt that he was capable of stealing it.

She was relieved when her hand closed on it. She turned on the bedside lamp and looked at the dial. A quarter to eight. She shook herself to life and gently elbowed the stirring Coughlan, "Jim, if I'm going to get that train I really must be making tracks."

Coughlan grunted. She elbowed his hairy back once more. "Jim!" she yelled and poked at one of the reddening scratches that she had put there less than an hour earlier.

Coughlan spluttered into life.

"Jim, I really ought to think about leaving, unless you were planning to make a night of it." She ran her hand down his back.

Coughlan flipped over and sat bolt upright: "What, er… yes… er… no. I've got to get back, got to get home. I'm late as it is."

Ian Cassidy

"Oh," said Anne, pouting although she had expected nothing more. Coughlan was already pulling his socks on. Anne turned away and reached for her stockings.

Anne crept back from the shared bathroom to find Coughlan waiting for her in the doorway of their room. He was awkwardly passing her handbag from hand to hand; he smiled sheepishly and handed it to her. They went down the stairs in silence.

Before reaching the reception desk, Coughlan took her to one side. "Why don't you nip across the road and settle up there, while I do the same thing here, then I'll run you to the station."

Anne nodded and turned on her heel. She walked across the unlit street, checking that the buttons on her blouse were all safely done up and, ignoring the desultory tosspots in the bar, headed for her room.

Once inside, Anne hastily checked that she had left nothing behind and picked up her case. She presented herself to the landlord and asked for her bill and a receipt. The landlord grumbled and looked askance. Did she really want a written receipt? Anne would have preferred to have no evidence of her trip to Lichfield but she insisted on a written receipt anyway just to annoy the landlord.

Several minutes later he passed her a sheet of lined paper torn from a duplicate book. Anne read it and was shocked at the amount. She paid without complaint and with a sigh of relief said goodbye to the King's Head.

Coughlan was revving the Armstrong Siddely in the street outside and Anne stumbled around to the boot with just the dim light from its shaded headlights to guide her. She fumbled with the lock, scowling at the now less than chivalrous Coughlan. She banged her case inside and got into passenger seat.

"Everything all right?" Coughlan asked breezily.

"A little pricey but I suppose it's to be expected."

"Well, next time stay at the George, I can get you a very special rate," Coughlan grinned knowingly.

"I don't expect I shall be visiting the area again for a very long time."

"Oh, you must come again," Coughlan said mechanically, barely concealing his indifference.

Anne said nothing. They had already covered the short distance to the station and she could feel the heavy car slowing down.

This time Coughlan got out of the car and pulled her suitcase from the boot. He presented it to Anne at the station entrance and gave her a perfunctory and clumsy kiss on the cheek.

"I'll call you as soon as we're ready to leave," he piped and was gone.

Anne lugged her case, which suddenly seemed even heavier, up to the ticket counter and bought a single to Euston. She ambled to the platform, trying not to think of Coughlan. She could not help herself; she had to say it.

"Men." She blurted a little loudly but fortunately there was no one on the station to overhear. They were all the same, Maupassant had rutted himself into a syphilitic grave at forty, Henry VIII at fifty and now this man Fleming had perfected his drug to cure it. He'd spent eleven years getting it right so that men could put it about with impunity and just pop a few pills if they were unlucky. She testily kicked at a loose stone and put it from her mind. She was composing her report to Konrad as the train pulled in.

James Coughlan pulled into his driveway and brought the car to a halt. He skipped up the steps and breezed through the front door. With confident unconcern he looked into the lounge where his wife was listening to Alvar Liddel on the radio. In the unlikely event of her asking him about his movements he would have a plausible answer or even an implausible one. If the worst came to the worst he would just deny everything and keep on denying it. If said with enough conviction, you could make a trusting spouse disbelieve the evidence of their own eyes. He knew from experience; even if caught in flagrante, deny everything. Coughlan was well aware that it isn't hard to fool someone who loves you but then he took it a step further and it became, it's hard not to fool someone who loves you. He just couldn't help himself.

Diana smiled as he cruised through the drawing room door: "Good meeting?" she asked.

"Not bad" he replied noncommittally. "Could be quite lucrative." Diana Coughlan may have been the company secretary and a major shareholder in the business but that did not mean she had to be informed of the questionable contracts her husband engaged in.

"That's good." Diana smiled and returned to her needlework.

"Kids in bed?" Coughlan asked.

"Yes, of course, hours ago." His wife yawned.

"I'll just pop up and say goodnight."

"Don't, you'll only disturb them. Sit down and I'll warm your dinner up."

"What is it?" Coughlan asked, doing as he was told.

"Brawn I'm afraid, my coupons are running low."

Coughlan winced: "Put the kettle on as well." He was teetotal at home, confining his drinking to the pubs and cocktail bars he frequented so regularly.

Diana Coughlan got up and went into the kitchen. Coughlan watched his wife leave and tried to listen to the radio. He aimlessly fiddled with the dial but could find nothing that interested him. He had other things on his mind. In fact the more he thought about it, the more he regretted turning down Anne Cole's suggestion of making a night of it. He definitely had an urge.

Coughlan fidgeted and soon followed his wife into the kitchen. He looked her up and down as she stood at the front of the clunking gas oven. He leered at her shapely ankles; her dainty suede high heel shoes and fine silk stockings. Unlike Anne Cole, Diana Coughlan did not have to worry about the supply of such items running dry. Coughlan's eyes went up her elegant calves. One of the things that had attracted her to him was her long and beautiful legs. He looked at her pert behind poking through her impeccably tailored suit and up to her small breasts that still excited him even after two children. He slavered towards her long and stately neck but looked away from her finely sculpted face and perfectly coiffed hair.

Coughlan smiled lasciviously, a second tumble with Anne would have been nice. Still, there was always the wife.

Diana Coughlan stood beside him as she put his meal in front of him. He took the opportunity to run his hand up her stockinged leg, right up her skirt. He squeezed her left buttock. Diana pulled away: "Not tonight Jim, it's that time again." She smiled apologetically.

"I don't mind."

"Well I do." She pulled away from his creeping fingers.

Coughlan bridled at the rare refusal. He grunted and perused the uninspiring plate of brawn. He did not push the matter; Diana was usually very accommodating on that score. They had once made love in a closet at a cocktail party with all their friends chattering away unwittingly on the other side of the door.

He started to eat, very quickly. As the product of a large Irish Catholic family, it was a habit he could not break. With twelve or more seated at his father's table, a tardy eater was likely to have his choicest cuts pinched by a mischievous elder sibling. He finished his meal in record time and ill naturedly slurped the remains of his tea. He made no effort to make conversation with his wife, banged the empty cup down and left her to the washing up. He crashed around the lounge for several minutes, complained again about the lack of "anything worth listening to" on the wireless before stomping up to bed without a word to his wife.

seven
29th july, 1944

4.30pm. **Coughlan's Yard, Brownhills, Staffordshire.** James Coughlan heard one of his work's vans rumble down the driveway and poked his head out of the office window. He watched a bulldog-like driver/painter/broom-pusher climb from the driver's seat and attempt to liberate the lowest of the teetering pile of ladders strapped on the roof rack.

Coughlan stepped in before the bulldog-like driver/painter/broom-pusher was buried in an avalanche of antique wooden access products. He shouted: "Keith, leave that and get in here and tell that dumb bastard to come with you."

"Who do mean?" asked Keith. "Don or Bert?"

"Both of 'em but make sure you leave that dozy bastard where he is," he said, indicating the thin man in painters' overalls sitting under one of the trees that shaded the yard, alternating between strumming a clapped out banjo and blowing puffily on a scruffy clarinet. This was Gordon Lyle, graduate of Emmanuel College, Oxford and sadly unsuited for life away from the dreaming spires. He wanted to be a musician but not one of your BBC types in a dandruff stained evening suit, playing middle of the road concertos for conservative listeners in Tunbridge Wells. Gordon was breaking the mould with his earthy compositions based on the stark realities of life in the back-to-backs of Birmingham.

It was unfortunate that at that present moment Gordon was the only person to appreciate his mould-breaking talents. Talents that were also engaged in composing a witty and challenging collection of songs based on the saying and phrases used by his employer and colleagues as they went about their day-to-day business.

He had the titles but little else. "There's a bon load at the Vic." "Hallo Sir." "Don't talk like a berk." "Pop goes the diesel." "I'll be alright for Wednesday." "Paid to do as you're told." "Walking about like a poacher's dog." "I don't know how to mop." "Any tea in?" and finally "I'll ring him tonight."

Sitting alone outside Coughlan's shabby armour-plated office, Gordon put aside his clarinet and took up the battered banjo. Borrowing unashamedly from Lewis Carroll but almost drowned by an unusual, avant garde blues refrain of his own invention, Gordon began to sing.

"There's a bon load at the Vic. The foreman cried as he stirred his tea with care. There's a job of work to do, answered the crew."

He stopped and gave verse two a try.

"He would answer to Bri or any loud cry, such a fisher or thingamajig."

Gordon stopped again and crossed out thingamajig. *Must find a better word,* he said to himself. He frowned for a minute or two, frustrated that inspiration would not strike. Finally, to console himself, he struck up one of his finished works. One that he was really proud of.

"Met a girl from Baton Rouge,
my god her tits were awful huge.
When I saw her huge behind,
it almost blew my mind.
And her thighs just tantalised my brain."

He performed, or more correctly, attempted an ambitious riff on the banjo before commencing the chorus.

"And sodomy's another word for coming in behind,
Me and Emily do it naturally."

Keith lingered a while and listened to the caterwauling, he rather liked it although he was not too keen on one of his work mates forever dodging the column to get in some extra music practice. This was a complaint Keith would repeat almost constantly twenty years in the future when, towards the end of his working life, he would be saddled with a teenage apprentice who was a most unwilling window cleaner but who would go on to become one of the Seventies' foremost glam-rockers and the writer of England's most enduring Christmas song.

Coughlan shook his head at the noise and as he closed the window he shouted to Keith.

"And fucking hurry up, everybody else is already here."

Keith rounded up the other two and together they mooched towards Coughlan's office.

Coughlan was waiting for them in the outer office, his own room being too small for a full gathering of his workforce.

Coughlan looked over his men, or more precisely the six men he had chosen to make the trip to Spain. He would be leaving his foreman Bernard Fisher in charge while he was away, along with Gordon and two men who had fought in the Spanish Civil War, on the losing side, who were probably not welcome in Spain. Also they were a little weird. They wore their hair long, below the collar, always wore working denims and sports shoes and smoked strange plants they cultivated themselves. All in all, Coughlan preferred for them to remain in England.

The majority of the six men chosen to make the trip, all raggeddy trousered and decidedly un-philanthropic, were too old for military service but still young enough to do a lot of work for a little pay. Sitting right in front of him, helping himself to free tea and the office biscuit jar, was Don the carpenter. Six feet six of wiry muscle with lank flyaway hair and serial killers' eyes. Next to Don sat Keith, the bulldog, never without a cigarette and with a shining bald pate but hair everywhere else, his chest hairs poked above his scruffy shirt and tie. Then there was Bert, with variegated teeth and infamous pipe; he billowed smoke from his filthy briar constantly. He was jack of all trades, carpenter, bricklayer, you name it but his responsibility on this trip would be the electrical work. In everything, even pipe smoking, he was slow and methodical but highly skilled. His real name was Archibald Horace but he hated both Christian names and so he insisted on being called Bert, a truncation of his surname, Bertram. Of course Coughlan, much to Bert's annoyance, rarely respected this wish and could be relied upon to bellow 'Archibald' or 'Horace' at the top of his voice whenever he needed Bert's services. Then came Jack, the would-be lothario of the bunch, whose much-vaunted prowess with ladies had been hard-earned as a delivery boy for the local baker. Once at work, he was picky and pernickety with neatly pressed, spotless overalls. He kept his work's van just the same.

And finally the brothers, Maurice and Ivor, the monkey men and also Welsh. The fastest painters in the west, or the West Midlands at least. Maurice was small and Gollum-like, with unruly hair, numerous tattoos and forearms like thighs. Renowned for his cheek but usually charming enough to get away with it, Maurice had once sent his employer's wife on an errand to buy him some "sky hooks," a gallon of tartan paint and a long weight. Amazingly he kept his job. Ivor was equally squat and potentially violent but strangely his skin was free of artwork. As usual, he wore Wellington boots. Unlike their work mates, these two were young enough to be called up but ineligible for other reasons, most notably their string of previous convictions for theft, assault, housebreaking, you name it. Ivor even had a conviction for theft, assault and criminal damage all related to one incident. He and a friend had stolen twelve dozen eggs and stood on a footbridge above the platform of the local railway station and bombarded the alighting commuters. Ivor had received his first period of Borstal Training for that little escapade. All in all the authorities had decided against calling them up. Probably a grave mistake. Just think of the havoc the brothers could have wreaked amongst the Wehrmarkte. Ivor had a posthumous Military Medal written all over him but Maurice was the true loss to the Armed Forces. His cunning and his conniving, his sixth, seventh and eighth senses would have made him an ideal company sergeant major. Every Tommy would have wanted to go over the top with him because CSM Perry was invulnerable. His intrepid actions in the trenches would have got him a 'Mention in Dispatches', and then another gong or two, perhaps even a battlefield commission and finally Captain Perry, MM, DSM and Bar would have settled into an interesting retirement. If only the recruiters had not been so short-sighted.

Coughlan called them to order. Bert lit his pipe Don moved his chair away. "Like sitting next to a tramp steamer," he complained.

"Right, we've got a rush job on. Five weeks in Ireland, starting Monday."

The men hooted their disapproval.

"Alright, alright, there's a big bonus for everyone on completion." Coughlan knew that this would be enough to satisfy his men, especially Don and Jack who were both notoriously careful with money. "And there's some up front. See Mary afterwards." That would be enough to satisfy the others. All four were unable to make their wages last the week. It was not unknown for them to be penniless the morning after they picked up their money.

"What we doing, boss?" asked Ivor.

"Building a few partition walls and painting them, it's a piece of piss." The men slurped their tea indifferently.

Coughlan went on, "Right, be back here at half five tomorrow morning." He left them to their grumbles.

Bernard Fisher followed him into his office: "Anything important to do while you're away?" he asked.

"There's only Gordon and the fucking weirdoes to find work for." He passed Fisher his desk diary: "It's all in there, plenty to keep them busy and you."

"What makes you think Gordon isn't a fucking weirdo as well?" Fisher asked as he studied the book.

"He's alright, just keep them busy. And Bernie," Coughlan said warningly, "go easy on the petty cash."

Fisher smiled naughtily. "Would I?"

31st July 1944. 5.26am.
Coughlan's Yard, Brownhills, Staffordshire.

Keith the bulldog-like driver/painter/broom-pusher parked the van outside Coughlan's office. He was the first to arrive, so he jumped over the low privet hedge that separated Coughlan's yard from his home and went up to his employer's back door.

He knocked. "Come on, Jim, the birds are singing."

Coughlan came to the door with a cup of tea in his hand. Keith looked at it expectantly. Coughlan noticed. "Make some tea for the lads, I'll get my things together." He left Keith pottering around in the kitchen. As he was getting the milk from the larder, Keith noticed a bottle of brown ale, he didn't hesitate and he was guiltily guzzling it down as the other five travellers came to the door.

Jack greeted him. "At this time in the morning? You're getting worse."

"Just a livener," Keith smiled sheepishly.

"Well, I've got news for you, you drunken bleeder, you threw up while you were driving home from the boozer."

"How do you know?"

"Cos there's puke all up the side of the van."

"Ah," said Keith even more sheepishly: "Better go and clean it off before God sees it."

He had just finished hosing it off when Coughlan led the rest of his Spain-bound work force out to the van. They loaded up their bags and squabbled over the seating arrangements. Coughlan claimed the front seat and Jack, who had smelt Keith's brown ale breath, volunteered to take the first shift behind the wheel. The other five grumbled into the back where they bedded down as best they could. Much to everyone's disgust Bert began stuffing his infamous pipe with the horse manure and bus ticket flavoured tobacco of which he was so fond. As he put a match to this obnoxious heap, the others loudly voiced their opposition but Bert smoked on obliviously, almost vanishing beneath a billowing blue cloud.

The journey to Spain had begun. Coughlan lit a cigarette and pondered on when would be the right moment to reveal the true destination.

8.51am.
The Same Place.

Bernard Fisher pushed at the office door and breathed a sigh of relief. Still locked, so Mary had not arrived yet. He unlocked the door and went straight to the strong box containing the petty cash. He pocketed most of what was inside and looked hungrily at the office safe.

Later, he said to himself as he put the kettle on.

3.35pm.
Office of Reich Marshal Hermann Goering, Berlin.

Konrad knocked the Reich Marshal's door and entered.

"Ah, Konrad, sit down, sit down." Goering said energetically. He was in an expansive mood that morning. His officials at the Air Ministry had just informed him that the first of his V2 rockets would be operational by the end of the month. More importantly, he had attended a meeting the previous evening where Hitler had vehemently backed Speer in his ongoing dispute with Goebbels over diverting manpower from the front into armaments production. A short-lived victory, no doubt, as Hitler's mood was currently so volatile that by next week he was likely to be siding with Goebbels again. Still, Goering had greatly enjoyed seeing the odious little man publicly humiliated.

"What news?" he asked.

"I have our agent's report. Herr Reich Marshal," replied Konrad, handing it to Goering, who gave it a cursory glance and placed it to one side.

"Our man is en route," Konrad continued.

"Excellent!" said Goering, sitting back in his chair.

"There is however one small problem. It appears that not all of his contingent have the necessary papers to satisfy the Spanish immigration authorities."

"We can arrange something?" Goering asked.

"Yes, I have made discreet enquiries with my contact at our embassy in Madrid. He is willing to meet them at their port of entry and issue them with diplomatic papers."

Goering was concerned: "Is that safe, Konrad? Won't it be noticed in Berlin?"

"I don't believe so. Spain is a very low priority at the moment. My contact tells me that they are feeling very isolated in Madrid, so I do not believe that the movements of a junior embassy clerk will be noticed by the authorities here."

"I hope you are correct, Konrad, there's a lot riding on this. Nevertheless, give him the go ahead to meet our man and do the necessary."

"He will require some funds, Herr Reich Marshall."

"See to it Konrad," Goering snapped.

"With Ministry funds?" asked the aide.

Goering paused, as much as he hated spending his own money, he appeared to have little choice: "Perhaps you're right. I will have to arrange it with my Swiss bankers that the man receives enough for our purposes."

"And perhaps a little for his own purposes," Konrad suggested.

"Yes, we must guarantee his silence." agreed Goering. He passed Konrad a pad and pencil: "Write his details on that so I can arrange things. Now, our departure, how are the preparations progressing?"

"Very well, Herr Reich Marshal, your possessions are almost all dispatched. There's one, perhaps two shipments left to go."

"Excellent work, Konrad. I hope everything is being stored securely in Spain."

"Yes, of course, Herr Reich Marshal. The crates go direct to the ship and straight to a strong room in the hold."

"Is this so called strong room secure, Soellner? If the ship is as rusty as you say, my priceless collection will be at the mercy of anyone with a sturdy can opener."

"It is sufficiently robust for our needs and besides the crew are indifferent to the contents of the packing cases. A packing case is a packing case to them and nothing more. Furthermore they have been hired to transport cargo and passengers to South America, their wages depend upon said cargo and passengers reaching their destination intact. Once they have been paid, then that may be a different matter."

"Yes, we will have to be very watchful at the other end." Goering clapped his hands in satisfaction: "Very good work, Konrad, I will accompany the final shipment." He announced.

Konrad stuttered. "I had not anticipated your departing so precipitously, Herr Reich Marshal."

"It's time Konrad, our intelligence suggests that an allied expeditionary force is poised off the Riviera as we speak. When does the last shipment leave?"

"It is ready now, Herr Reich Marshal. I have just to give the go-ahead." Konrad hesitated. "It's just that I do not think it would be wise for you to leave immediately."

"Really, why not?" Goering snapped.

"Our man has only just left England. If he is progressing as planned, then he has yet to reach Dublin. It could take another ten to fourteen days for him to reach his final destination. Added to that, the time it will take for him to complete the conversion will mean almost a month will elapse between your departure from Berlin and us taking to the relative safety of the high seas."

"I see what you mean, Konrad. That would give too much time for any potential pursuers to trace us. I will delay my departure." Goering paused. "But not for too long, I cannot risk my escape route being cut off by the Allied advance and also I'd like to be in Spain to supervise the work."

Konrad plucked up the courage to disagree with the Reich Marshall once again. "I don't think that would be wise either, Herr Reich Marshal," he said timorously.

"Why ever not?" Goering demanded.

Konrad shifted uneasily in his seat: "Firstly, the fewer people who see you once you have decamped the better; we don't want news of your whereabouts reaching the Gestapo and also our man may not give a hoot about his employer's identity so long as he is being paid."

"And extremely well paid!" Goering interrupted. Konrad looked shocked. "Yes Konrad, I read a little more of that report of yours than you thought, he's being paid an extortionate amount."

"As you say Herr Reich Marshal, our man is being paid handsomely, so I think we can rely on his cooperation regardless. Even if he discovers the true identity of his paymasters, it will be of no consequence to one so corrupt. He will do anything to get his hands on twenty thousand pounds. The same will not be true of his employees. They will not wish to work for the Reich; therefore we would have to keep you hidden from them and from anyone else in the area who may disclose your presence to them. You would find that extremely uncomfortable and inconvenient."

"Very well, Konrad, make arrangements for my family and me to travel as soon as soon as you believe it to be safe."

"As you wish, Herr Reich Marshal." Konrad always found it expedient to let his employer believe that he had reached these decisions by himself.

The **Unsinkable Herr Goering**

"To be on the safe side, Konrad, it might be prudent to rent a bolt-hole for us, somewhere convenient for the ship, just in case we have to leave earlier than planned."

"That will be difficult from here in Berlin, Herr Reich Marshal."

"That problem is very easily solved, Konrad. You will go on ahead of us and make all the necessary arrangements. Also you can meet up with this Irishman; I want someone trustworthy to supervise the work. I don't want his gang of navvies just papering over the cracks and producing a hovel."

"Very well, Herr Reich Marshal. I will leave as soon as I can," Konrad said reluctantly.

"Sooner than that, Konrad. Go now, this minute."

"As you wish, Herr Reich Marshal." Konrad gulped, saluted and turned to leave the office.

Goering called him back: "Before you go, Konrad. Do we have a captain?"

"Oh, yes, Herr Reich Marshal, I was able to secure the services of the man I mentioned to you."

"You had better tell me a little more about him. I am after all entrusting him with the safety of my family."

"As a seaman his record is second to none. Many years exemplary service with our merchant fleet. As you are no doubt aware Herr Reich Marshal, at that time opportunities to see service on warships were very scarce."

"I'll say," Goering interrupted: "Versailles left us with barely a couple of yachts on the boating lake."

"Once we broke the shackles of Versailles, he transferred to one of our capital ships as number two…"

"Really!" exclaimed Goering: "Which one?"

"The Gneisenau," answered Konrad.

Goering nodded and Konrad continued. "After that he was given his own command on a surface raider."

"And it was while in command of this surface raider that he had his little trouble?" Goering asked.

"That is correct Herr Reich Marshal, after four years of valiant service and an almost unparalleled tonnage of Allied shipping sent to the seabed, he made a rash decision. Unable to accommodate any more survivors aboard his vessel, he ordered the machine guns to be turned on the stricken crew of a doomed tanker."

"I don't call that a rash decision, Konrad, and neither will the allies, they will call it murder."

"That, Herr Reich Marshal, is why he is so keen to accompany us. He does, however, look on his decision to open fire as an act of kindness. The crew of the tanker were stranded in burning diesel-strewn water with no hope of rescue."

"I'm sure that would make an interesting defence," Goering scoffed: "I understand why he is not keen to air it before a war crimes tribunal. That aside, I have your assurance that he is capable of delivering us all safely to our destination."

"Yes, Herr Reich Marshal, there can be no doubts on that front."

"Where is he now?"

"I have him secreted in a small village to the north of Sitges. He is comfortable enough there and the Spanish are very accommodating; several of the hoteliers of Sitges are supplying him with the bratwurst and Reisling that he seems to consume by the tonne. He can be with the ship in less than a day, this I know because even though he has been in Spain for but a short time he has made several trips to a brothel in Sitges."

"The man sounds like a barbarian," Goering barked.

"He is a sailor," Konrad finished abruptly as if this was sufficient explanation.

"Well I don't like it, Soellner; boozing and whoring, what will my wife think."

"He is also a German officer, so I am sure that when the time comes he will behave impeccably."

"I hope you're right, Soellner."

"I am sure of it, Herr Reich Marshal, but I will endeavour to persuade him to desist from visiting the port in future, he has very little English so it will not be to our advantage for the contractors or the crew to see too much of him."

"For the reasons set out above," smiled Goering. "Very good, Konrad. That will be all."

Konrad stood. He looked expectantly at Goering.

"I'll see that you have sufficient funds before you leave," Goering barked as he dismissed his aide.

Konrad saluted. "Herr Reich Marshal." He clicked his heels.

"Konrad, it may be wise if you stopped calling me Herr Reich Marshal From now on it may be better if I am just a plain Mister."

"A plain Mister Meyer perhaps," Konrad said quietly.

"What was that, Major?" Goering snapped.

"Mr Miller perhaps."

"Why the devil should I call myself Miller?"

"It's an unobtrusive sort of name."

"No, no Konrad, I don't like Miller but we will keep it simple. From now on I will be Herr Weiss or rather Mister White." Goering could speak excellent English when required. "Now convey that information to our agent in London and then on to the contractor He will need to have a name to ask for, once he reaches Spain. That will be all."

"Very well, Herr Reic…Weiss."

Konrad closed the Reich Marshal's door behind him and took a deep breath. He crossed to his desk where he stood behind his chair, unable to decide what to do next. *So that's that*, he said to himself, *I must leave the Fatherland.* He reached for his briefcase but hesitated. *No*, he said to himself once again. *To cover my tracks I'll finish my duties here as normal and then begin my journey, leave Germany, perhaps forever.* He gulped for air and reached for the telephone One call to Himmler's office and this ridiculous escapade would be terminated. He put down the receiver without dialling the number. He could not betray Goering; it was more than his life was worth. Goering's vindictive tentacles had a long reach and he would have ways of exacting revenge even from the interior of a Gestapo torture chamber. And besides he had no wish to become one of Himmler's informers. It was such a grubby occupation and he was well aware that their life expectancy was notoriously short.

Konrad picked up the telephone again and dialled his father's number in Nuremberg. His mother answered but Konrad said nothing, merely listened to the sound of her voice. His parents did not approve of his lifestyle. They had ended all contact with him when they began to suspect that his friendship with Edvard was a little more than just friendship. He hung up and sighed. ***Edvard, I must speak to him before I leave but what can I say to him.***

He tried Edvard's number at the Ministry of Armaments but it was engaged. Vowing to try again later, Konrad picked up the photograph of Edvard that stood on his desk. He had told his colleagues and his secretarial staff that the photograph was of his brother. He was not sure whether they believed him and he was sure the secretaries sniggered behind their hands when he passed. In fact he was sure that they were doing it now. He scowled ineffectually in the general direction of the typing pool and then quietly took the picture of the tall blonde man in immaculate uniform from its frame and put it in his wallet. With a sigh he remembered to conceal the empty frame in his desk drawer.

He was too preoccupied to convincingly carry out normal duties as if nothing untoward was planned. He called out to the pretty dark-haired secretary who sat closest to him.

"Maria, I have an appointment at the Ministry of Labour."

"An appointment Herr Major? There is nothing written in the dairy."

"Not everything is documented in that diary, Girl." He tapped his nose conspiratorially. "I shall leave now and I will not return again today." Konrad stood up and reached for his briefcase before adding unconvincingly, "See you in the morning."

Maria wished him good evening. He was sure she turned and made some sort of mocking sign to her colleagues. He scowled again. Before he left, Konrad studied the map of Europe on the wall behind his desk. He ignored the rapidly shrinking red line that indicated the skies controlled by the Lufftwaffe. Instead he studied the route to Spain. It seemed so very simple that his eyes shifted to the map of Britain, to the centre of the country, to Birmingham. He speculated that if everything was going as planned, then the contractors would be well into their journey. He followed their likely route on the map. Birmingham to Liverpool, a ferry to Belfast, then Belfast to Dublin. Yes they would be in Dublin by now. Then they would travel overnight to Bilbao and finally journey by train across Spain to Barcelona. They could be with the ship in less than four days. He had no time to lose.

Maria watched as Konrad stood dreaming in front of the map. She stifled a sigh, oh Major Soellner, so handsome, such a waste. She winked at the other girls in the office. Their lips began to twitch as one by one they reached for their make-up or handkerchiefs.

Konrad left the office. He was convinced that yet again the secretaries were laughing at him behind their powder compacts.

3.46pm.
Whitehall.

A dingy little man with ink stained fingers and a prominent squint meandered slowly up and down the dingy and stained underground corridor. He had been kicking his heels for over an hour waiting for the Section Commander to return from lunch at Rules. He thought of the insipid cheese salad he had eaten in the MI5 canteen and meandered a little slower.

Finally the Commander's secretary raised her eyes and motioned that he could go in. Knocking first, he pushed open the chipped door and entered the plush world of the upper ranks.

"Well, Harrison, what have you got for me?" asked the Section Commander, not inviting him to sit down.

"It may be nothing, Sir." Harrison hesitated.

"Don't prevaricate, man." snapped the Section Commander. Lunch with the Director had been trying and the pheasant had been tough.

"It may be that a suspected German sleeper has been activated."

"May be?" The Section Commander snapped again.

"Well…" Harrison stuttered, "These events may be unrelated but three days ago the boffins at Station X picked up a transmitter signal. We had presumed that the receiver was dormant or destroyed as there had been no activity for thirty months."

"And?" the Section Commander interrupted.

"Then two days ago one of our old suspects made an uncharacteristic journey."

"So you are assuming that he was acting on instructions contained in the signal that Station X picked up."

"We cannot say for certain, Sir, but it is possible."

"I see, Did Station X manage to decipher the signal?"

"No Sir, they are unable to shed any light on the contents of the message she received."

"She! A female spy."

"Yes, Sir."

"Weren't you watching her?" demanded the section Commander.

"No Sir, it had been thought unnecessary. As I said, there had been no activity for almost three years and no other evidence. In fact we were beginning to think our suspicions were unfounded."

"You are watching her now, I hope?"

"Yes Sir, of course. She has recently returned from her journey. She went to Lichfield…"

"Lichfield? I don't like the sound of that. That's where the Parachute Regiment is based isn't it?"

"Yes Sir, I believe at least one battalion is there."

"Well you better hope the Nazis haven't got wind of our plans for the Paras."

"What plans for the Paras, Sir?"

"The little matter of Arnhem, you dolt."

"Oh, those plans."

"Yes, those plans and if we cock it up the Yanks will go berserk. What did the suspect do in Lichfield, did she go snooping around the barracks?"

"Not as far as we know Sir, she went to a couple of meetings with a painter and decorator."

"A what?"

"A painter and decorator."

"Why?"

"We don't know, Sir, but one thing's for sure it was not on family business, our suspect is not related to this painter."

"Well, just to be on the safe side you'd better try and find out It's a little odd, don't you think, to travel all the way from London to speak to a paper hanger."

"Yes, Sir." Harrison agreed.

"Well, open a file and keep me informed." With that the Section Commander dismissed Harrison. Before giving any thought to the matter just raised, he called his secretary over the intercom and asked for a large helping of Alka Seltzer. *Bloody Rules*, he said to himself, *why the Director always insisted on lunching there he could not understand, they did you so much better at Boodles.*

5.27am.
Templehoff Station, Berlin.

Konrad lowered his still sleepy body into the first class seat and waited as the train got up steam. He was pleased that the compartment was empty as he planned to sulk for the entire journey. He had been unable to meet with Edvard and had to console himself by sending a hastily scribbled billet-doux promising to explain everything to his lover as soon as he could. Konrad was composing this heartfelt letter as the shiny iron wheels began to turn. At the same time two Normandy bound Panzer officers barged into the carriage. Konrad was distraught and barely managed to return his fellow officer's pleasantries. Fortunately the combat weary soldiers were soon asleep and Konrad was able to sulk uninterrupted.

eight
11th August, 1944

9.02am. **Sitges, Northern Spain.** Coughlan tiredly threw his suitcase onto the platform and jumped out after it. He stretched his aching limbs and inhaled deeply, filling his lungs with the fresh Spanish morning air, so welcome after blue grey fug of cheap tobacco, unwashed socks and stale breath that had pervaded the compartment. His dishevelled, down-at-heel, drunken, party of tatty tradesmen shambled from the train after him.

It had been one hell of a journey and things had not gone entirely according to plan. The trip had started uneventfully enough, they had reached Liverpool in time to catch the ferry and Belfast had been great fun. Old friends had been looked up, the Guinness had flowed and old beds had been shared.

Dublin had been even better, more Guinness and more bed hopping but amidst all this debauchery a snag had arisen. There were no ships bound for Spain leaving Dun Loaghaire that week. Four days they had to kill in Dublin, four days that the bar owners of Grafton Street were very grateful for. An unusual incident occurred on the third day of this binge when Coughlan and his men had been snoozing off the lunchtimes' excesses in the leafy surroundings of St Stephen's Green. Don had returned from relieving himself in the thicker undergrowth in something of a panic. As he'd stood there, dick in hand, he had been spoken to by another man ostensibly in the bushes for the same reason.

"What did he say to you?" Coughlan asked barely suppressing a smile.

"No idea, I got the hell out of there PDQ I can tell you. They're all over the place." Don grumbled.

The other men tittered and went back to sleep.

Later that same afternoon as the men were leaving the park, Don suddenly froze.

"He's here, what's he fucking want?"

"Who's here?" Coughlan asked rubbing his eyes.

"The bloke who spoke to me in the woods. What's he after?"

"He's not after anything, he's on his way home, same as we are. Now come on, let's get back to the digs, we haven't got time for all this crap."

Don grumbled but followed along with the rest.

Maurice, who was bringing up the rear anyway, slowed to light a cigarette when he felt a tap on the shoulder.

He turned to find himself face to face with Don's 'friend.'

"We know what you're up to," the man whispered.

"That's more than we do, mate," Maurice replied chirpily and carried on walking.

The man drew alongside Maurice and from the side of his mouth breathed: "You could find yourselves in a lot of bother." With that he was gone.

"I'm always up to my neck in bother," said Maurice to no one in particular, before hurrying after his employer. He told Coughlan what had just happened and asked, "Has this got anything to do with bloke who's paying for us for this job?"

"Maybe, I really don't know."

"Well, just who are we working for?"

"You met the woman. We're just doing a little conversion job for her boss, Mister White. A lick of paint for his place and his boat, that's all, somewhere called Weissgarten." I can't see anyone having a problem with it."

"It sounds a bit iffy to me, Jim; it also sounds a bit German."

"Don't be silly. Weiss is a Jewish name, so it can't be anything to do with the Germans can it?"

"I don't know." Maurice hesitated.

Ian Cassidy

"I'll tell you what, there's an extra fifty quid for you if you keep your mouth shut."

Maurice readily agreed and so Coughlan kept his suspicions that their little jaunt had attracted the attention of the Security Services to himself, although he was sure that the man was bluffing and they did not know what was going on. Blissfully ignorant, the rest of the men set upon the alehouses of Dublin's fair city with the usual gusto.

Finally, hung-over and behind schedule, Coughlan and his men sailed out into the Irish Sea en route for Spain. Coughlan told them where they were really going as the ship passed under the towering edifice of the lighthouse at Blackrock. The journey was slow and sooty but uneventful. Bilbao was anything but.

After a surprisingly smooth ride through Customs, which Coughlan suspected was the work of a tall blonde shadowy man who chivvied the Spain officials mercilessly and met every query on their part with a wad of cash.

"Who was that at the port? The bloke who helped us out," Jack asked as he and the others left the docks in search of the railway station.

"Who do you mean?" asked Coughlan, feigning ignorance: "I didn't see anyone."

"You must have, the bloke in the long leather coat, who was talking to the Customs men, he persuaded them to just wave us through."

"You're imagining things. He was just travelling through the same as we were."

"There's more to it than that. Why would he help us?"

"I don't know, just a good Samaritan I suppose." suggested Coughlan before adding under his breath, "Or maybe a good Bavarian."

"Perhaps he's got something to do with the bloke we're working for."

"Maybe, I don't know, you're reading too much into it, he was just being helpful."

"Who are we working for?" Jack asked, standing his ground.

"We're working for that woman, the one you fancied."

"The one you screwed."

"Yeah, well, that's one of the benefits of being the boss." Coughlan smiled his most self-satisfied smile: "Now let's get a move on, we'll miss our train."

Before Jack could continue the interrogation, Coughlan breezed off to buy seven rail tickets and so the men went to the nearest bar to buy seven beers, to begin with.

"This place looks a little rough." Jack pondered as they entered the dockside bar. They crowded around the bar and waited for the barman.

"Bloody hell," said Don, peering beadily through the tobacco fumes. "Just look at this place…and the customers? I've never seen anything like it."

"Has he got horns?" asked Bert, indicating the rough looking merchant seaman to his left.

"That's nothing, that one over there has got tusks."

"You're joking."

"I'm not and he's the good looking one of the bunch. That one's got a hammer head."

"And I've never seen anyone as hairy as that. Look."

"The Sasquatch lives and sails out of Bilbao."

"And him, he looks like he's got four eyes?"

"No."

"He has, I'm telling you."

"And what's that noise!" Don wailed, cupping his hands over his ears as protection against the weird Basque ballroom tunes that were permeating the smoky saloon. "It's so bad it makes me nostalgic for Gordon's caterwauling."

"You're right, they make Gordon sound good."

"And look good, just take a look at them, that must be about the evilest looking bunch of musicians in Western Europe."

This amazed perusal of the patrons was interrupted by a commotion. The barman was busily ejecting two sailors of possible African origin, it was hard to tell because they were caked in soot and grime: "We don't serve your kind in here," he announced before returning to his place behind the counter. He ignored the six thirsty house painters.

Maurice leaned over the bar and tugged at the back of his shirt. Maurice was trying to place an order when a piggy faced salt with grey skin and red eyes confronted him.

"I don't like you," the piggy faced man growled.

"I don't like you either," Maurice replied and turned to face the barman.

Piggy-Face was drawing back his fist when Ivor came to his brother's aid. "This little one isn't worth the effort, now let me get you something."

Piggy-Face swept Ivor's hand away and went for Maurice. He never got near, Ivor's right fist crashed into his rib cage, simultaneously his knee made brutal contact with the man's groin and as the man doubled up, Ivor kicked him neatly and efficiently under the chin. At the same time Maurice dragged the barman over the counter and dropped him with a couple of deft blows to the head. The other customers backed off from this scene of supremely efficient mayhem.

Jack surveyed the grumbling drinkers before making a decision. "Come on, lads, let's make ourselves scarce before one of those beauties decides he fancies his chances."

"And before the Law shows an interest in Ivor's handiwork," Bert added pointing to the piggy-faced man who was bleeding heavily from the mouth and nose.

"Yeah, let's find Coughlan and get the hell out of here."

"Not too fast though, lads, don't let them know were scared."

They walked swiftly to the door. Once outside they broke into a run.

"Which way's the station?"

"No idea, just keep running."

"There was at least thirty cut-throats in that bar. If they catch up with us, they'll eat us alive."

Coughlan stood at the corner and watched as the cream of his workforce careered over the slimy harbour-side cobblestones towards him. As they passed he hefted his suitcase onto his shoulder and joined in the stampede: "Who's Ivor chinned this time?" he asked casually as they jogged along.

"Just some sailor and it was him who started it."

"Of course he did. The station's down here. Follow me."

The seven men spent an anxious hour waiting for their train but were not troubled by a visit from either angry matelots out for revenge or inquisitive Spanish police officers.

The Unsinkable Herr Goering

The journey across Spain was slow and dusty. The train stopped frequently and without apparent reason. "Adlestrop." Coughlan opined at one point but only Bert understood the literary reference.

"I was there you know," Bert said chugging away on his pipe.

"You were where, you silly old bugger?" Coughlan asked.

"Arras in 1917, when he got it."

"When who got what?"

"Edward Thomas, the poet. He was killed at Arras."

"Come off it, you were in the Pay Corps."

"I saw action, more than I care to remember. Ypres, Passchendaele, I went right through. The things I saw," Bert mused, his eyes misting over.

"I know," said Coughlan in an uncharacteristic tone of empathy.

"I lost a lot of friends, good friends. I've got no time for the Germans, never have had."

"Well it's a good job we're going to Spain then. Now get some sleep, you grumpy old sod."

"Wouldn't cross the road to help a German," Bert grumbled before knocking his pipe out and closing his eyes.

Finally they reached Barcelona and then made the short hop to Sitges.

In Sitges the six men stood bleary-eyed on the platform as Coughlan called them to order.

"Give your bags to Keith or Bert." He shouted above the noise of the solitary departing train. "They're coming with me to find some digs. The rest of you can go to the docks and find this boat, the Atheling."

"The what?" asked the confused Jack. Coughlan's pronunciation had left a lot to be desired.

"The Atheling." repeated Coughlan.

"Funny name, sounds German to me."

"Don't be silly, it's a Scandinavian name, great sailors the Scandos, Vikings and all that."

"Alright," said Jack reluctantly. "Where is it?"

"It's in the port, a place called Aigualdoc."

"Where? I can't even fucking say that," said Jack.

"According to the map, it's about a mile out of town in that direction," said Coughlan, pointing.

Jack and his three charges hesitated.

"Look you won't have any trouble finding it but take this with you." Coughlan wrote the name down on a scrap of card torn from his cigarette packet and gave it Jack. "Just show that to one of the locals and they'll tell you the way."

"Okay, boss," said Jack, taking the paper.

Of course you won't understand a word they say to you. Coughlan said to himself before turning to his men. "And when you get there, make a start."

"Do what?" they complained in unison. The unfortunate four selected to commence work immediately turned angrily towards their employer. They couldn't start work, they didn't know what to do, they not had breakfast, they needed to take a crap. Coughlan shut them up. "Jack, you're in charge, just go and show your face, piss about in front of the dagos, look busy. I'll meet you there as soon as I can and buy you breakfast. Now clear off. I'll see you there in half an hour," he commanded good-naturedly.

Jack led his ramshackle team off in the direction of the harbour. Coughlan waited for them to leave and got in to the first taxi. He motioned to Keith and Bert to follow him with the bags and in broken and heavily accented, Black Country spiced Spanish he attempted to get the taxi driver to take them to somewhere offering reasonably priced lodgings.

9.14am. Sitges,
Northern Spain.

With no information beyond a brief communiqué from his contact at the embassy in Madrid, informing him that the men had passed through immigration at Bilbao, Konrad had to assume that the men could, subject to the vagaries of the Spanish rail network, arrive at any time. He had no choice but to present himself on the quayside every morning and await their arrival. The Atheling was berthed at the extreme end of the overlapping breakwaters that made up the fishing port of Sitges, third in importance on the Catalan coast to Barcelona and Tarragona.

He sat precariously in the shadow of the Atheling, on a canvas covered pallet of he knew not what. He did not recognise the consignment as being part of the authorised ship's manifest and suspected the crew of engaging in a little private enterprise. Konrad decided he would attend to the crew later and went back to his struggles with the Spanish newspaper. He was slowly getting to grips with a review of the latest production at the local theatre when he was surprised by the unmistakable sound of English voices coming from the other side of the port.

Jack and his party were standing on the townward side of the port, scanning the smooth harbour waters for a likely ship. As usual they were not doing it quietly. They squabbled as they looked out over the two substantial concrete and shale breakwaters that jutted out into the sea like the malevolent jaws of a giant grab crane. The breakwaters overlapped at the seaward side like a pronounced and uncorrected overbite. Sheltered within these great concrete groynes were rows of jetties with fishing smacks and the occasional pleasure boat moored to them. As it was too large to pass within the narrow confines of the jetties, the great rusting hulk of the Atheling was tied to the inner breakwater at its far end, near the mouth of the port.

"That must be our boat," announced Jack. "The big fucker at the end." So saying he commenced the long trek over the dusty, sun-baked quay.

Konrad looked over the harbour walls to where the voices came from and watched in amazement as four dishevelled figures came more sharply into view. His unease grew as he studied them more closely. The group was led by a wavy haired giant with spider-like limbs and the blackest staring eyes. Next came what he could only describe as a pair of Neanderthals, heavy set bundles of tattooed hairy muscle. Working for the Air Ministry, Konrad had been spared any involvement in Germany's unsavoury experiments in social engineering. It was a subject he found highly questionable – that is, until he looked at these two. Now he was not so sure. Finally came a tall man, almost respectable, squinting at a piece of tatty paper. Konrad singled him out as the most approachable and reluctantly moved toward the band of desperadoes.

"Mr Coughlan?" he squeaked quietly and uneasily.

"He's following a bit later, we're the advance party," Jack joked.

"The canaries." added Maurice.

"Canaries?"

"Yeah, we go in first and field all the crap before the real people go in."

"Oh." said Konrad, still confused and slightly affronted that Coughlan had not taken the trouble to accompany his workers. "I must speak to Mr Coughlan," He said haughtily.

Jack said nothing. He was himself a little uneasy about being accosted by a flamboyantly dressed stranger with an impenetrable accent.

As part of his cover as a Portuguese entrepreneur, Konrad had adopted a more Latin style of dress. He was wearing a cream linen suit, brightly coloured striped shirt with no tie and white shoes. He had enjoyed the relaxed atmosphere during his short sojourn in Spain and not just the freedom to dress in manner more expressive of his sexuality. He thought of Edvard back in Berlin and felt guilty. **How easily one is tempted.** He thought to himself.

He was also struggling to speak English with a Portuguese accent, which was no mean feat for a German. He pressed on. "Where is Mr Coughlan?"

This time Maurice the monkey man piped up: "He'll be here in a two ticks. Where do we start guv?"

Konrad was stumped and looked around helplessly.

"What's the matter with the dago puff?" Maurice asked his brother.

Jack was sure that Konrad did not understand but just in case he stepped in between the belligerent brothers and the nonplussed Nazi. He smiled at Konrad and began, "We're expecting Mr Coughlan to be here in about half an hour, what do you want us to do in the mean time?"

"I prefer to give my instructions to Mr Coughlan," Konrad said rudely.

"Please yourself but what are we going to do?"

"That is not my problem, why don't you have a look over the ship?" Konrad said. "Now I have an appointment in the town, I will return and meet with your employer after lunch." Konrad turned on his heel and left.

The men were not overly bothered as they now had the perfect excuse for an impromptu tea break. They stood on the quay and watched

Konrad leave, unable to resist wolf-whistling the rather effete Nazi as he walked away. They were just commencing a slow trundle back along the breakwater with a view to making an unauthorised excursion into the town when they met Coughlan coming the other way. "Where are you wankers going?" He announced by way of greeting.

The men explained and Coughlan decided that now was as good a time as any to buy them the promised breakfast. He selected the nearest café and ushered them in. "Get in here and behave." He said, looking mainly at Keith, Ivor and Maurice.

The men hesitated, it was nothing like the cafés back home. There was no smell of burnt grease and harsh English tobacco, inside all was dark and threateningly exotic with a lingering aroma of spilled wine, garlic and cloying Spanish high tar. Coughlan led the way and selected a table. His men warily joined him. With a judicious use of hand signals, Coughlan succeeded in ordering six teas and a coffee. Cunningly he avoided tea himself, reasoning that in a Spanish café tea would be a beverage of rare antiquity likely to consist of little more than dust and mouse droppings, certainly displaying no evidence of ever having been near the temperate slopes of Ceylon.

The drinks arrived and the fun began. Don spat his tea across the table, announcing loudly that it tasted "like piss." The others agreed.

Coughlan pretended not to hear the uproar. "What's it be then. Seven full breakfasts?" he asked.

The men nodded, all except Don. "Not for me, no more fucking grease. I'll just have some dry toast," he complained.

"I'm paying," said Coughlan.

"Right then, I'll have two eggs, bacon, sausages, tomatoes, fried slice, tea and toast," Don said, his appetite rapidly returning.

Coughlan had expected that reaction so he called the waiter over and did his best to place the order. He began by slowly and deliberately placing an order for bacon and eggs and all the trimmings seven times. Despite the fact that this was done in a voice many, many decibels higher than was necessary, unaccountably the waiter didn't understand. Coughlan tried again but this time he spoke even slower and even louder.

That would surely be enough to make the man understand. But no; the waiter still did not understand.

"They just don't try with other languages do they?" Maurice opined.

Finally Coughlan had to resort to hand signals, he mimed a sleeping man awakening, rising from his bed before cooking and eating his first meal of the day.

The waiter nodded and rushed away from the table, he took the order to the kitchen and left the chef to do his best.

Seven plates of streaky bacon with fried eggs, cheese and croissants duly arrived. Naturally the men complained, the bread was sweet, what was the cheese doing on the plate and oh god the bacon. Coughlan tucked in with a greedy lack of concern for the predicament of the unadventurous 'gastronomes' surrounding him. Also he was somewhat amazed that they could complain. He was certain that not one of them had eaten bacon for a long time, certainly not since Ivor and Maurice had stolen a pig in the spring. Starved of meat by wartime rationing, the men's complaints were short lived. They were happy to eat proper food for a change but reluctant to show it.

After another round of unspeakable teas, Coughlan announced that it was time to start work.

"We can't, boss." Jack informed him. "The Spanish puff in charge won't be back until the afternoon."

"What we gonna do then? asked Coughlan.

"We could have a beer," suggested Keith.

"No we fucking couldn't," snapped Coughlan. "We've got work to do and I know I'm the only one here with any fucking money."

"What we gonna do then?" Keith whinged.

"We'll have a slow walk back to the harbour and you can have a kip in the sun. You're fucking good at sleeping on the job, you've had enough practice."

Coughlan took charge and keeping the gently lapping waters of the Mediterranean on his left he strolled off in the direction of the Aigualdoc.

The men followed kicking up dust on the promenade.

"Water looks nice," Ivor announced, eyeing the ochre expanse of San Sebastian Beach.

"Yeah, let's go for a swim. What do you say Jim?" Keith suggested.

"But we haven't got any bathing costumes."

"So what," said Ivor pulling off his Wellington boots.

"We can't swim in the nude. Not here, we'd all get nicked."

"Keep your pants on then. That's what I'm gonna do," said Ivor running bow-legged over the sand.

The others watched him go and then began to undress, all except Bert. He stood on the beach, deaf to the entreaties of his work mates. He had a deep mistrust of water at all times, more so if it came accompanied by a bar of soap but seawater was bad enough. He preferred to smoke his noxious churchwarden and he chugged away behind a rapidly growing smokescreen as the others made their way over the warm sand to the sea.

Don's ancient string undergarments would not stand up to scrutiny so he plunged straight into the benevolent surf and spared himself the inevitable comments about skid-marks. Coughlan and Jack folded their clothes neatly before making a more dignified dual entry into the Med. Ivor, Maurice and Keith entered the balmy waters in a bizarre tableau of hairy arses, cell-block tattoos and profanities. Soon the six men were enjoying the unexpected treat of swimming in water free of choking fish, drowned cats, pig iron and dud munitions illegally brought home from the front, such as they encountered in the canals around Britain's industrial heartland.

They pelted each other with seaweed, splashed and swore in a perverse, orgiastic scene far too comically grisly for even the sauciest seaside postcard.

After a quarter of an hour Coughlan returned to the beach and stood on the sand waiting for the sizzling midday sun to dry his already singeing skin. His spluttering employees joined him one by one. Don and Ivor dressed quickly but the other four hesitated.

"I'm not putting my trousers on top of these wet underpants." Coughlan grumbled. Jack agreed: "Nothing worse than wet trousers," he said and flung his thick woollen trousers over his shoulder. His employer did the same and swords swaying in their now transparent Y-fronts, they set off up the beach to the promenade. Keith weighed up his options and decided to join the trouserless faction of Coughlan's weapon-waving warriors on their bandy-legged incursion into Spain. Maurice also chose to join the frightening phalanx of bare-legged sword-swingers

So began a priapic swashbuckle along the esplanade, as the salt-streaked gang of labourers with four men without trousers at its head marched on the town. They drew astonished looks from the locals as they swaggered through the slumbering streets, their swinging rapiers barely concealed by the wet gossamer fabric clothing their lower bodies.

Mothers pulled their frightened children indoors as Coughlan and his braves made their cutlass march towards the port. Mangy dogs, so common in Spain, turned tail in the face of these scimitar-wielding cavaliers. Even the hardened stevedores who frequented the docks hunched their shoulders and scurried along the opposite side of the street as Coughlan and his men continued their sabre-dancing advance towards the harbour.

2.09pm.
Sitges Harbour.

Konrad paced the quayside impatiently. Where was this damned Irishman. He swore to himself and walked the length of the ship once more. He was starting another turn when he heard it. A potent, terrifying mix of laughter and profanities recognisable in any language with an underlying ear-splitting dash of pure white noise, like a swarm of locusts or a Zulu impi banging their shields. *They're back*, Konrad said to himself. *It can only be them*. Konrad tensed but despite his growing terror, he stood his ground.

The malodorous bunch of drunken Midland mercenaries, some of them seemingly naked from the waist down, turned the corner and struck out along the breakwater towards him. Never having seen active service, Konrad had little experience of fighting men but he could not believe that even a division of the Waffen SS, battle hardened on the Soviet steppes, could be as frightening as the men who confronted him now. Konrad forced himself to stand still. He regretted dressing in civilian clothes. His uniform would have given him the authority to deal with these men. He'd always found that jackboots give you power.

Swallowing hard, he stepped forward: "Mr Coughlan, I presume." He quailed.

A red faced man with an alehouse glow and bare hairy legs stepped forward. "That's me," Coughlan said, hand outstretched and Claymore still prominent beneath his slowly drying underwear. He noticed Konrad's astonished countenance and announced, "We've been swimming.". Konrad smiled uncomfortably and Coughlan continued, "And you are Mr White?"

Konrad was wrong footed. "Mr White? Who? No I'm not Mr White … I am er … his agent."

"And your name is?" Coughlan asked, holding out his hand once more.

Konrad took the proffered hand and panicked. He could not remember the name on his false Portuguese passport. It had not been needed at the border as he had used German diplomatic papers, the hotel in town had asked to see it but he handed it over without giving it a second glance. "MMManuel." He stuttered. "Manuel Cervantes." He could think of nothing else. *Please don't notice*, he quaked to himself.

"Like the writer," Smiled Coughlan: "Never managed to finish it myself."

"What?" said Konrad, confused. He recovered himself: "Oh Don Quixote, it has been many years since I read it also." He said, calming down. The red faced amiable man with his beery confidence seemed pleasant; it was just his men who were scary. He smiled at Coughlan. "Shall we go aboard?"

Coughlan nodded and roused his men to action. Konrad studied the contractor as they waited for the men to assemble what little equipment and tools that remained in their possession. He normally did not have a thing for older men, but there was something about James Coughlan. The balding, virulent face with chubby, high cheekbones was strangely compelling although the mono-brow worried him slightly. What was the old saying, "Beware the man whose eyebrows meet for in his heart there lies deceit." For a man of forty, Coughlan was in very good shape, although Konrad realised that this was the effect of rationing and conscription compelling Coughlan to engage in a bit of unaccustomed manual labour. Konrad watched the lithe and swarthy contractor assemble his men and smiled.

Jack and Don were the first to cross the Atheling's rickety threshold. They trod warily around the rusting ship while Maurice and Ivor, who came next, were totally unconcerned about being aboard such a death trap. They were happy to spit voluminously over the ship's rail. Finally Bert and Keith wobbled up the gangplank; they shared Jack and Don's reservations.

The men watched as Konrad took Coughlan to one side. He produced a set of blueprints from his briefcase and handed them to Coughlan. "I will leave you to study those at your leisure," he said: "If there is anything else you need, come and see me at my hotel." He said passing Coughlan a card with the name and number of his hotel written on it.

Coughlan jumped at the chance: "I need something, some money."

"Yes of course," said Konrad. "Come to my hotel for cocktails at seven-thirty and we will arrange things." Konrad looked towards to mingling partially dressed painters, in particular the spitting, monkey-like ones and added: "Come alone."

"But of course," replied Coughlan: "Give us chance to get properly acquainted."

"And you will dress a little more er…appropriately?" Konrad laughed indicating Coughlan's continuing state of spear-swishing dishabille.

"But of course," Coughlan joined in the laughter.

Bert and Keith, who were standing closest to their employer, heard every word. They could not wait to share this valuable information with their mates. As he reached the forecastle Keith began excitedly: "He's at it again."

"Who?" asked Jack.

"Fucking JC that's who, chatting up the dago site agent, I tell you he'd fuck a dead hedgehog."

"He'd fuck a scrubbing brush," laughed Jack.

"Yes, but he wouldn't do a bloke would he?" asked Keith.

"He'd fuck a frog if he could stop it jumping," laughed Jack seriously.

By this time Coughlan had taken his leave of Konrad and came to join his men. He overheard some of Keith's comments about his sexual appetite and he was not altogether displeased by the back-handed compliment. Suppressing a smile, he told them all to shut the fuck up and put their fucking trousers back on.

Coughlan called Don and Jack to him and the three men set about studying the plans. The remainder of the firm of James Coughlan & Sons began to make an inventory of the tools and materials provided for them. Bert set light to the filthy smelling shag in infamous pipe; he found it an invaluable aid to mental arithmetic as the possibility of selling any surplus materials was not far from anyone's mind. Next, Bert compared his quickly computed inventory with the genuine article provided by Konrad, and came to the conclusion that there would be very little surplus. Sulkily everyone condemned the efficiency of the man who had purchased the materials. It was that famed German efficiency but they didn't know it.

Next they turned their attention to the tools that had also been provided. Those that weren't irreparably damaged by the time the job was completed could be stolen and sold. The tools in first consignment were Spanish made and not to the men's taste. They told Coughlan who was unconcerned, he knew that he could rely on them to improvise and besides there was a pallet full of much better looking tools right there.

"What's the matter with these?" he asked, pointing. "They're much better."

The men had to agree, the second consignment of tools and paint was of an infinitely higher quality.

"Look! That's a 'GKN' logo on most of them, they're made in Brum, good old British workmanship," said Keith delighted at the prospect of working with such precision instruments.

Coughlan had a look. He found the 'N' a little hard to make out mainly because it wasn't there and the logo simply consisted of 'GK'. *Probably George Krupps*, he said to himself and winced, but not long enough for the men to notice.

"Right! Leave all that lot for now and follow me," Coughlan barked at his men and they silently followed him towards the hold. Coughlan stood to one side and instructed Keith to open the hatch. After a brief struggle he managed to prise it open. He jumped back as if he had been stung by a particularly large and nasty wasp. He swore. "Fuck me, Jim, what have they had in there?"

Coughlan crept to the edge and peered over. He took a deep breath of the noxious fumes coming from the hold and expertly concealed his reaction: "It's just a bit of stagnant water; we'll give a mop out in the morning." He said with typical understatement.

"Stagnant water my arse," said Jack as he joined them at the hatch "They've been transporting animals down there."

"It's nothing," said Coughlan. "We've all been in much worse and besides Maurice and Ivor love getting black."

Maurice and Ivor smiled resignedly, they did indeed get all the dirty jobs.

Taking a deep breath Coughlan breezed down the ladder into the hold. He suppressed a very strong desire to wretch and called up to the deck: "Once you're down here you hardly notice it." He lied automatically.

The men reluctantly followed, each swearing loudly as he crossed the threshold, each coughed and wretched as he descended the greasy ladder. As he got to the floor of the hold, Bert took the precaution of lighting his pipe and for the first and last time. His colleagues were glad of the masking effect of the smoke screen that emanated from his filthy briar.

On the floor of the hold, surrounded by spluttering labourers, Coughlan looked about him. The removable roof of the hold would have to come off to give them sufficient light and ventilation and then he foresaw no problems. He was rubbing his hands at the indecent profit he was going to make.

With Jack and Don to help, Coughlan made rudimentary marking on the walls and floor and before long they had a good idea of how the project would pan out. They may have been scruffy, dirty and tired but they were surprisingly good at their jobs.

Coughlan called his men to order: "Right, first thing in the morning we'll clean this place out. It shouldn't take us long."

He silenced the hoots of derision: "Bollocks, it's a piece of cake. We'll get it cleaned out tomorrow and start work proper the next day. Now let's get back to the digs and get some dinner."

Coughlan led his gang of workmen out of the hold. He was grateful for the fresh air but would not show it. They left the ship and headed into the town.

After stopping once or twice for a quick beer, Coughlan lead the men onto the main thoroughfare. He walked them swiftly past the plush hotel recommended by the taxi driver to the run down guesthouse that stood in its shadow.

Coughlan pushed open the peeling front door and, ignoring the men's complaints about the strange garlicky smell, he collected three sets of keys from the stunned duenna at reception. He pointed the men towards the luggage that he had deposited with the porter, or more correctly the porter, gardener, handyman and duenna's husband, that morning.

Coughlan bundled the men up the stairs and allocated their rooms. He had reserved just three rooms, a single with an en suite for himself – the only one in the place – and two trebles for the men. Maurice, Ivor and Keith took the first room, Jack, Don and Bert the second. Both were sparsely appointed with three narrow beds, a doorless wardrobe, a slanting chest of drawers and a clanking sink unit in the corner. All six men threw their bags onto their beds and dashed for the bathroom. Maurice got there first.

The remaining five disappointed tradesmen settled on their bunks, crossed their legs and grumbled.

Forty minutes later, the six men assembled on the steps of their boarding house awaiting their employer. They were arrayed in all their finery, anticipating a night on the town. Maurice and Ivor sported flyaway open-necked shirts beneath their carefully patched sports jackets. Bert as usual wore a suit and tie, although he was already regretting it and his choice of suit was causing him some concern. His heavy wool suit, his only suit was, to say the least, unsuitable for a July evening on the Mediterranean. Jack had also gone for the open-necked looked and carried his jacket over his arm. With his thick, dark hair and already tanning swarthy skin, he was comfortable in the heat and he was ready to go on the prowl.

Don and Keith wore identical Prince of Wales check sports jackets. Back in England they had agreed that they would not wear them at the same time but the arrangement had been forgotten in the rush to get ready. Their thirsty work mates had refused to let either of them go back and change, so now the two men stood at either end of the group, Don scowling angrily and Keith giggling at the joke.

They turned as Coughlan blustered out of the hotel, brushing aside the landlady's broken English request for a down payment on the rooms. She had appraised her new guests and decided that it would be in her interests to get hold of a deposit against breakages.

Coughlan handed Jack a bundle of pesetas. "That's all I've got left," he lied: "Get yourselves a drink over the road, while I go and see Manuel." He left to hoots and wolf whistles from the assembled painters.

Coughlan quickly concluded his business with Konrad, they shared a couple of drinks and Coughlan relieved the Nazi of a large amount of cash. He also noted with envy the expensive camera that was slung around Konrad's neck, a Leica if he was not mistaken. Coughlan was hatching a plan to 'borrow' the camera as, pockets bulging with pesetas and Swiss francs, he pushed though the smoky tapas bar to the table where he had left his men less than an hour previously. Having very little Spanish, he greeted the local drinkers with a tried and tested greeting of his own invention. He simply said "Javon" to everyone as he pressed past and remarkably everyone returned the pleasantry. Coughlan joined his men at the far end of the bar.

He brushed aside their snide remarks about his assignation with Manuel/Konrad and joined them in a beer before leading them onto the street in search of an evening meal.

Coughlan herded his men into the first restaurant that looked likely to serve large amounts of food in return for small amounts of money. He soon pushed his men out again, not because he had been wrong in assessment but because he wished to avoid yet another violent incident involving Ivor. As the men took their seats the waiter had bustled over enthusiastically. He heard their harsh northern European tones and assuming that they were German he recommended that they try the excellent bratwurst that just been delivered. He'd got it special from the Austrian butcher in Barcelona because there had been a lot of demand for it recently.

"Must be a German ship in the port," Bert speculated.

"Do you think the crew will be in here tonight?" Maurice asked with an evil grin. He nudged his brother.

"Oh I hope so," said Ivor. "I wouldn't mind doing a bit for the war effort and cracking a few Kraut skulls."

At this Coughlan suggested, nay insisted, that they leave.

He bundled them into a neighbouring bar which, to his annoyance, looked a good deal pricier and also a good deal more exotic, which was sure to cause problems with his gang of culinary Luddites. However, his worries about any adverse reactions to the intricacies of Spanish cuisine proved unfounded. Don and Jack, as ever, ate and drank anything and everything so long as someone else was picking up the bill. Maurice and Ivor, with long residences at Her Majesty's pleasure behind them, were happy to eat anything that was not accompanied by grey vegetables boiled in the contents of the cell piss pot. Bert and Keith were initially reluctant but soon tucked in with gusto, years of rationing having cured them of their aversion for anything other than meat and two veg.

Coughlan ordered brandies all round and discussed the coming fortnight with his men. He winced at the harsh kick from his balloon of Fundador, a far cry from the cocktail bar of the George in Lichfield or that of his favoured holiday destination, the Palace Hotel in Torquay. Steeling himself, he poured it down in one. "Right, I'll get the bill. I fancy an early night so I'll see you back at the hotel." He had not got out of his seat before six disappointed painters accosted him.

"Any chance of a sub?" Maurice pleaded. The rest of them joined in.

Coughlan gave each man an advance on that weeks' wages and left them with the imprecation to behave themselves. He needed to get back to his hotel room and secrete the piles of funny foreign money that was currently bulging from his jacket pockets.

Coughlan dodged past the landlady and made it to his room without parting with the overdue down payment. Once safely inside, he counted the brightly coloured notes and, smiling contentedly, he looked around his room for a hiding place. The floor was covered in terrazzo tiling so that was no good as a hiding place and the carved oak armoire was too heavy to lift. Coughlan scowled and tried his en suite bathroom. He emptied his toilet requisites from his travelling wash bag and stuffed the notes inside. Coughlan climbed onto the toilet seat and lifted the lid of the wall-mounted cistern. He placed the bag inside and wedged it just above the waterline. Satisfied that the landlady or her jack-of-all-trades husband would not notice it, Coughlan switched out the bathroom light and returned to the bedroom. He stretched out on the bed and began to read one of the many library books he had brought with him.

When not engaged in other horizontal activities, Coughlan was an avid reader and an insomniac, although it was not his conscience that robbed him of sleep. He was dozing with the book open on his chest when all hell broke loose. Six slightly befuddled painters were making their bad-tempered way up the stairs and along the badly lit corridor. Coughlan climbed off the bed and stood in his doorway as they filed past.

"Didn't expect to see you back so soon," he began.

"Nothing doing in the town. I've found more action on a wet Wednesday in Great Wyrley," grumbled Maurice as he grizzled along the corridor.

Ivor backed him up. "What a piss corner," as he disappeared into his room.

Jack and Keith came next, giving Coughlan disappointed shrugs as they passed. "Even the port's dead as a doornail." Only Don and Bert, the older members of the party, looked relieved to be having an early night.

"Early start in the morning," Coughlan announced: "So an early night won't hurt you. Keith, call me at half five," he said as he closed the door.

nine
12th August, 1944

3.47am. **Sitges.** Ivor awoke and rubbed his eyes. He listened to the throaty snores of his brother in the adjoining bed and remembered where he was. He grunted and decided that he needed to urinate. He got to his feet but did not even bother looking in the direction of the door. He headed straight for the sink unit in the corner.

Keith felt a fine mist hit his cheek and dreamt he was back in England on a rainy day. The first of a series of more substantial droplets struck his face and he awoke with a start.

"Always a bad move to pick the bed next to the sink," Ivor laughed maliciously as he carried on relieving himself.

Barely awake, Keith repositioned himself with his feet at the danger end and went straight back to sleep with "dirty bastarrrr" dying on his lips.

6.03am.
Sitges Harbour.
After complaining about having to work on a Saturday and grumbling their way through an indecently large amount of unfamiliar breakfast material, the men engaged in a violent dash to the toilet before assembling outside their lodgings to wait for Coughlan. He was making leisurely use of his own private water closet and as was his habit he lingered in the lavatory. He sat there complaining about the laxative effect of Spanish beer and sulked. Before providing the men with breakfast the

landlady had insisted upon her down payment and Coughlan had had no choice but to dip into his stash in the cistern.

Coughlan joined his men and led them down to the harbour. Once aboard ship they set reluctantly to work. The cover of the hold was removed and, once ventilated, the dingy cargo bay took on an altogether less unwholesome aspect.

Also as the light flooded into all four corners of the hold, it revealed a heavily padlocked door partly concealed in the stern bulkhead, obviously the entrance to a strong room. The men were intrigued and Coughlan had to call them away with instructions to keep their thieving hands to themselves. Maurice and Ivor looked longingly at the bolted door before taking up mops and buckets. Dreaming of riches and aided by Keith, they commenced cleaning the walls and floor of the hold. The other three who regarded themselves as skilled workers refused to contemplate such menial work so they set about modifying and adapting the tools Konrad had provided.

To show willing, Coughlan joined Keith, Maurice and Ivor with the cleaning, much to their annoyance. As usual he set to work at breakneck speed urging them to keep up with him. They did nothing of the kind. Keith, Maurice and Ivor plodded away at their own pace and true to form Coughlan soon decided that this kind of work was not for him. He also noticed that cleaning the hold was a major job and detailed the whole contingent to join in the work. When all six men were busily swishing mops or shovelling the muddy detritus from the hold floor into buckets ready to be hauled up to the deck and deposited over the side, Coughlan quietly took his leave and went in search of a mid-morning coffee.

He returned an hour later with a billycan of lukewarm brown liquid masquerading as tea for the men. He need not have bothered, Maurice and Ivor had already located the ships galley and with a mixture of pidgin English, hand signals and Seaman's Polari charmed the Serbian cook into providing hot and cold drinks for the workers in the hold at regular intervals.

The afternoon passed without incident, Coughlan sunned himself on the deck, pretending to study the plans while keeping an eye out for officials from the Spanish Ministry of Labour. It went without saying that no work permits had been obtained.

Occasionally he gave the man hauling the buckets of waste oil and animal faeces up to the deck the opportunity to take a breather and did the job himself. Each of these stints was punctuated by the bucket accidentally on purpose becoming snagged on its way up. Coughlan would skilfully and with a wicked smile violently tug the bucket free, ensuring that its malodorous contents were upended onto one of the unfortunate men below.

Coughlan was dozing on the deck when, at shortly before five-thirty, six effluent-caked tradesmen dragged themselves wearily from the hold. They surrounded him as he lay in the warm Mediterranean sun, making sure some of the muck that covered their overalls dripped onto him.

He shook off their basically good natured complaints and had a quick look at the now shining hold. He announced: "We'll spray it out tomorrow and start building on Monday." He looked at the state of his men. "I'd buy you a pint but I don't think they'll let you in anywhere."

"We'll sit outside." The six men said in unison.

"Alright we'll give it a try but try not to frighten the locals."

After more than one quick drink, with the men crushed out of harms way but nonetheless distressing the locals with the malodorous miasma they broadcast over the corner terrace of a portside bar, Coughlan led his team back to their hotel.

Once there, he luxuriated in his own bathroom while the men jockeyed for position in the queue for the inadequate shower.

A familiar evening ritual followed, the men complained about the food but ate everything that was put in front of them. They complained about the beer but drank gallons. Don and Jack, as befitted their status as charge hands, even unsuccessfully tried the vino tinto. They turned down the waiter's offer of a glass of Reisling, deeming it unpatriotic but yet again didn't think to ask why the town's restaurants and bars appeared so abundantly stocked with Teutonic comestibles.

Once the restaurant bill had been settled, the men headed off in search of fun and this time Coughlan accompanied them on their nocturnal ramblings but the evening was only slightly more successful than the previous one. The men had yet to come to terms with the Spanish custom of quietly drinking and smoking while watching the world go by. They were good at drinking and smoking but 'watching the world go by' was proving somewhat alien to them. They hankered after a game of darts or cribbage and Jack was hankering after a slightly more adult form of entertainment. Ivor for one enjoyed his evening; he discovered a bar with a pinball machine and once armed with a pocketful of low denomination Pesetas, he could not be moved.

The men dribbled back to their hotel in various states of inebriation but not before Coughlan and Jack held a discussion. Both were of the same mind, they had something of an urge. Coughlan promised to question the porter and maybe the sailors the next day with a view to locating the local brothel and the two men slightly appeased by the promise of action followed their colleagues to the their rooms.

ten
13th August, 1944

5.42am. **Sitges.** Maurice and Ivor were in the other men's room stealing a set of Jack's overalls each. As they were leaving, Maurice noticed a flash of pink plastic protruding from beneath Jack's bed. He stooped to investigate and drew out a partially deflated blow-up doll. The brothers examined the sad flesh-coloured article and laughed nervously. They poked and prodded at it but initially neither plucked up the courage to explore the doll's lifeless cavities. Finally Ivor could restrain himself no more and he brutally introduced his index finger into the forbidding clammy cavern in the thing's rubbery nether regions. With a cry of anguished horror, accompanied by a worrying slurp, he whipped it straight out again and brandished a frogspawn coated digit at his sniggering brother:

"Look! Look!" Ivor squealed waving his porridge dripping finger hazardously close to Maurice before rushing headlong for the urine smelling sink unit in the corner of the room. Maurice by now laughing uproariously was quick to take evasive action. Once Ivor was satisfied that his fingers were free of the viscid ooze, which took a considerable amount of time, the brothers rushed to join their work mates at the port, bursting to tell them of their sticky discovery.

The men arrived at the ship and began to kit themselves out in primitive protective clothing. Maurice and Ivor put on Jack's spare overalls; he didn't say anything. The other four wore their own overalls and balaclavas. Jack even smeared Vaseline over any areas of skin not covered by overall or balaclava, so that the paint would not stick. He had to endure the usual gibes about "beware the man with Vaseline" but he had heard it all before.

Skilfully, Keith flipped the lid from the first of the paint cans. He shook his head: "A bit dark don't you think?"

Jack agreed.

Bert took a look: "That colour seems familiar. Reminds me of when I was in the army I think. Can't quite put my finger on it," he mused. "Anyway, let's start bollocking it on the walls."

The morning's work again proceeded without a hitch The Prussian Blue paint went on smoothly and the men downed tools shortly after midday. They were lazing in the warm August sun, munching nervously on some weird fishy stuff provided by the Serbian cook, when a cloud appeared on the horizon.

Konrad/Manuel teetered along the gangplank and angrily stood over them as they ate. They did not move One of the first lessons they had all learnt was never to interrupt a tea break when an employer arrived. They all remained seated and claimed to have just that minute downed tools.

Without thinking, Konrad looked at his watch. The men hooted their derision and Konrad hastily pulled down his shirt cuff but not before Maurice's sharp eyes had made a speedy appraisal of the offending time-piece.

"Nice watch, that," he commented. "Lange & Sohn? German?"

Konrad said nothing but Coughlan rushed to his feet and dragged Konrad away from further scrutiny. "It's going well," Coughlan smiled. "Want to take a look?"

Konrad smiled back. In spite of himself, he rather liked the contractor. He nodded and followed Coughlan to the hold. Coughlan showed the incognito Nazi what progress had been made and explained what was next on the agenda. As they reached the deck Konrad asked Coughlan to join him for dinner. Coughlan stuttered but, for once in his life, could not come up with a plausible excuse. The two men agreed to meet at eight o'clock that evening.

As the somewhat bored Nazi wandered away from the portside, Coughlan roused his men to action. The work proceeded at pace and

Ian Cassidy

Coughlan was able to call time early, leaving the now gleaming Prussian blue walls to dry in the late afternoon sun.

After stopping for an obligatory post-work beer, the men returned to their hotel and cleaned up. Only Maurice and Ivor had to scrub themselves with turpentine. Despite the stolen overalls, they still managed to get paint everywhere. The others were more careful and more liberal with the Vaseline so they were relatively paint- free. There was one area which all six men had been unable to protect from the paint: their eyes. Goggles soon become coated in paint whilst spraying and so, as experienced paint sprayers, the men did not bother to use them. Industrial paint with its heavy lead and aluminium content has a remarkable effect on the eyeball, an effect well known to women in Georgian times, giving the eyes a truly brilliant lustre. Coughlan's evil shark eyes glowed and even Don's black cesspools shone like beacons across the dingy bar, causing considerable concern amongst the Spanish patrons. With some trepidation, Coughlan announced that he was leaving them to their own devices for a couple of hours.

Coughlan told Ivor to behave himself and handed Jack some expenses for the forthcoming evening. He winked at Jack and whispered that he had somewhere in mind for their planned sexual jaunt later on. Coughlan left the men arguing about the venue for their evening meal.

The argument was an omen of the horror that was to follow. Without their employer's guiding hand the men did not fare well. The food was inedible, the beer undrinkable, Maurice upset Don, and Ivor had to be restrained from thumping the waiter.

Coughlan, on the other hand, had a delightful evening. Konrad was a meticulous host and the wine and food flowed with gay abandon. Coughlan was at his most charming. He always found it made very good business sense to get on the right side of the works manager.

Flushed and slightly drunk, Coughlan prepared to take his leave. As he shook hands with Konrad, the German left his hand in Coughlan's for slightly longer than propriety dictated and Coughlan returned the gesture. It had been eleven days and he was getting a little frustrated. Coughlan considered accepting Konrad's offer of another brandy but as much as the possibility of being fellated by the elegant young man currently appealed, he just could not bring himself to make the leap into yet one more depravity. Coughlan made his excuses and with his trousers tightening he went in search of Jack.

Coughlan hurried back in the direction of his hotel and located his men bickering in their newly adopted local. After buying the men yet more lager, Coughlan took Jack aside and the two men were soon off in search of action.

With directions obtained that afternoon from one of the sailors on the Atheling, Coughlan lead Jack through the back streets of Sitges. They traversed the Carrer Major and walked along the Carrer Francesc Guma, taking a note of the magnificent Bartolemeu Carbonelli I Massons House only as a landmark for future reference. Deep in the old town they slowed their pace and concentrated on the tricky navigation. Darkening streets and sailors scrawl proved no obstacle to the two men; they could smell it.

With growing anticipation they traversed the cobbled streets of the old town, reading the street names as they closed on their quarry.

Less than ten minutes after leaving their colleagues, Jack and Coughlan came upon the place they wanted.

"Is this it?" Jack asked eagerly.

Coughlan nodded and knocked on the heavy oak door. He pressed close to shutter in the door anticipating the doorman drawing it aside. Nothing happened, so Coughlan knocked again and again.

Jack sighed and pointed to dark bulb above their heads: "The red light's not on."

Coughlan looked up: "It's bloody Sunday, they're closed."

Long-faced, the two men meandered back to their work mates and grumpily joined them in another round of drinks. The evening had not been a success and not one of the seven men was keen to prolong it. The firm of James Coughlan & Sons turned in early.

eleven
14th August, 1944

6.03am. **Sitges.** The men grumbled towards the harbour, too much beer, upset stomachs and the total impossibility of masturbation in the shared lavatory had only added their usual Monday morning blues.

Once inside the freshly painted hold, the men set to work with reluctant efficiency but not before Ivor had secured the first of many pots of tea from the Serbian cook, who had by now learnt the art of tea-making from the men and could now produce an almost acceptable brew.

The men worked steadily all day without incident. Coughlan took his usual post on the deck and punctuated his anti Ministry of Works vigil with stints of very gentle labour down below.

Much to the men's annoyance, Konrad again checked on their progress but as he spent most of the time with Coughlan or elsewhere on the ship, their annoyance was short-lived.

At five-thirty, Coughlan told his men to down tools. He did not have to tell them twice. Soon they were propping up a harbour-side bar.

Harried along by the eager Jack, the men hurried through their ablutions and soon assembled in the bar opposite their hotel.

Their evening meal was an equally hurried affair, Coughlan achieving the impossible of eating at an even faster rate than usual.

Coughlan and Jack prepared to leave and the others took up their now familiar positions, Ivor happy at the pinball machine, Don and Bert gloomy at the bar, and Maurice somewhere in between but enjoying himself nonetheless as he sniped at Don or accidentally on purpose jogged his brothers' flipper fingers.

Coughlan and Jack, now familiar with the route, made good time and much to their relief noticed that their destination's crimson light was illuminated.

Coughlan rapped on the door and handed a large denomination Peseta note through the grille. The door swung open and a massive Somali doorman with bloodshot, hophead eyes invited them in. He pulled aside a plush red velvet curtain. Blinking, the two men entered the dimly lit room. The room looked surprisingly small despite the mirrors that lined its low walls. Banquettes lined one side of the room and there was space for just two free standing tables between these and the bar. Sitting at one of the banquettes was a swarthy sailor, who may have been from the Atheling, but he was now scrubbed up, without overalls or coating of grease and Coughlan could not be sure if he recognised him. There were no other customers and just two scantily clad, bored girls sat at one of the free standing tables. At the far end of the room was a small dance floor with an exotic mirror ball spinning above it.

Jack was dazzled by the lights. To him it all seemed very sophisticated. By the side of the dance floor stood a clapped-out upright piano unattended by a pianist. Instead, an antiquated gramophone strangled the tones of the Spanish equivalent of Peter Dawson.

Coughlan gulped and pressed towards the bar. He ordered two scotches and looked about him, trying to adopt an air of cosmopolitan unconcern. Inwardly he was feeling anything but. He had never been to a brothel before He had never needed to pay for it. He swigged his whiskey and fidgeted uncomfortably at the bar.

With the advent of new customers, a steady stream of young women wearing just their underwear began to filter into the bar.

Coughlan and Jack eyed the women with longing unwillingness but avoided making eye contact with them as they promenaded around the room, coming ever closer to the two men at the bar.

Coughlan ordered a refill and turned to his employee. "What do you think?" he asked.

Jack muttered something incoherently. He did not know what he thought. It was all a little too much for him, a little too predatory. But the sight of all those legs in black stockings was producing a tingling in his loins.

"I fancy that one." He finally managed to splutter, indicating a petite prostitute of Oriental extraction: "Madame Butterfly." He giggled.

Yeah, very nice," Coughlan said, barely considering the tiny Oriental butterfly. "But I don't think Madame Butterfly was actually a working girl."

"Well, you'd know. Jim, you've read all those books."

"Anyway she's very nice but I'm after something with a little more meat on her bones."

"Guvnor." Jack began, "Is it true what they say about Oriental women?"

"Is what true?"

"That their virginias go the other way?"

Coughlan almost spat his whisky across the bar. He did not enlighten his employee, merely said: "Why don't you go and find out?" Handing Jack a bundle of pesetas: "That's coming out of your bonus. I don't mind paying for food and lager but pussy's a different matter."

Jack did not complain He had always considered the possibility of his employer paying for all of the night's entertainment a long shot. "Let's have another drink first," he said.

Coughlan took another long draught of scotch. His eyes brightened as something more to his taste entered the room.

"There she is," he whispered to Jack "The coloured girl."

Jack turned and was confronted by a tall but chunky teenager with features that betrayed her Amazonian ancestry, with long black hair, unfeasibly large breasts that seemed to almost touch her chin and ample child bearing hips.

"That one?" Jack asked.

"Oh, yes," laughed Coughlan: "I think she could be wearing my bollocks tonight."

The two men laughed, three large scotches making them feel more at ease.

"What do we do?" asked Jack.

"Just go up to the one you fancy."

"Here goes," said Jack, heading towards his first choice. Coughlan gulped down his drink and approached the Amazonian beauty.

The girls led the two men to the first floor. The men eagerly followed, all feelings of unease forgotten. Their libidos had trampled on any qualms they may have felt.

One hour later, Coughlan stumbled down to the bar where he ordered a beer. He was swigging thirstily when Jack joined him.

"How was it?" asked the red faced painter.

Coughlan grinned lasciviously. "Fucking brilliant," he grunted. "What was yours like?"

"Out of this world but funny thing was, she insisted on calling me 'mein herr'. Why would she do that?"

"I don't know," said Coughlan. "Fancy another go?"

"Of course, but …" Jack hesitated, thinking of his diminishing bonus: "But … the money?"

"This one's on me," said Coughlan.

"Right," said Jack and he was gone in a flash, taking his beer with him and picking up a curvy local hooker as he headed for the stairs.

"That's my boy," laughed Coughlan. He had another beer and a leisurely cigarette before making his selection, undoubtedly the most senior of the working girls but Coughlan was drawn to her prettily plump backside and long stocking clad legs.

One hour later Jack was waiting at the bar when Coughlan joined him.

"Well?" he asked as he ordered a beer.

"Better," smiled Jack. "I tell you, back home sex hasn't been invented yet."

Coughlan guffawed and turned back to face the girls on the dance floor.

"You're not going to have another go? Surely …" Jack asked his rampant employer.

"Why not?" said Coughlan offhandedly, then added, "And why are you calling me Shirley?" He just couldn't help cracking the occasional bad joke when an open goal presented itself.

Jack didn't laugh. "Too rich for my blood," he said, preparing to leave.

Coughlan was already off his stool and advancing menacingly on his chosen prey. "See you in the morning and don't be late," he grinned over his shoulder.

"I won't be if you won't," said Jack, shaking his head, but Coughlan did not hear. He had already grabbed the Amazonian Beauty with a view to making a night of it.

twelve
15th August, 1944

6.10am. **Sitges.** The men waited in vain for Coughlan, who, shoes in hand, had crept along the corridor past their rooms only moments before the first of them had stirred. He was sleeping soundly as they whistled and yelled smutty comments at his bedroom window.

Finally Don, the senior charge hand in the absence of Jack, who was present only in body that morning, took charge and dragged the men off to the port.

Jack shambled along at the rear, saying nothing for now. His lips were closed by a monumental hangover and strange conflict in his breast. He was dying to tell his mates about his exploits on the previous evening; yet at the same time he was reluctant to tell them. The fact that he had been paying by the hour somehow embarrassed him. He strolled along smiling to himself despite the thumping going on inside his head.

Once onboard, the serious work of carpentry commenced. The ends of the massive lengths of six-by-two were shaved so that they would fit snugly into the steel girders. Once sprags had been nailed in between the wooden joists, a solid base for the floorboards was created.

Copious tea breaks aside, the men worked competently until lunch time. There was no sign of Coughlan or Konrad. Coughlan still slept soundly but Konrad was in something of a panic.

Over breakfast he had heard a confused and sketchy report on Spanish radio that had alarmed him. Allied troops appeared to be landing on the French Riviera.

He took the milk train to Barcelona and made his way to the German Consulate, only to find that his now former colleagues in the Reich Civil Service had adopted an indolently Latin approach to their labours. The office did not open until ten o'clock.

With almost two hours to kill, Konrad trawled the bars of Barcelona in search of one with the radio news playing. It proved surprisingly difficult. When he did, he was forced to give up on his attempts to glean more information because his rudimentary grasp of Spanish could not cope with the speedy Catalan tones of the news announcer, especially when it was interrupted by the continuous babble of work-bound Barcelona office workers. He went in search of a less frequented bar.

9.21.am.
Sitges.

After a lengthy soak in the bath and a more than acceptable breakfast, Coughlan joined his men on the Atheling. He winked conspiratorially at Jack and picked up a hammer. Like them, he was unaware of the invasion getting underway to the north, although on deck, if one strained one's ears it was just possible to hear the massive naval bombardment providing cover for the landing crafts. Down in the hold, amongst the hammering and the cursing there was no chance.

8.24.am.
Berlin, Office of Reich Marshal Hermann Goering.

Goering tore off the teleprinter message and swore. The damn machine only brought bad news these days. He sat at his desk with a thump and called his new aide on the intercom.

"Get in here!" he barked unceremoniously and sat back and waited. He knew he would have to wait. He always had to wait for the inefficient young man who had replaced Konrad. In fairness to the young man it was fear, not inefficiency, which caused his tardiness. After a call on the intercom, with growing terror he would collect his notepad and pencil and anything else he fumblingly guessed the Reich Marshal might require. He would then button his tunic and straighten his hair before gingerly entering the office of his terrifying employer.

Ian Cassidy

Goering heard the boy knock and testily shouted "Enter." He watched the young man scuttle across the room with none of the immodest thoughts that always came to him when he witnessed Konrad's languid movements. He could not imagine having his buttocks caned by this boy. This boy needed a good kicking and besides the dolt would drop the cane. He missed Konrad.

"The consignments bound for Spain, have they all left?" he demanded.

The boy dropped his pencil. From a crouched position on the floor he replied: "Yes, Herr Reich Marshal. I have Major Soellner's notes and instructions right here."

Goering puffed noisily as the boy fumbled with his bundle of papers.

"Here it is, Herr Reich Marshal," the boy said at last. "As of last week all consignments but one have reached Spain."

"What!" bellowed Goering. "What hasn't gone yet? I ordered that everything be dispatched without delay."

The boy stuttered: "Major Soellner's notes are quite specific, Herr Reich Marshal. They state that the final package is a special consignment that is to be handled personally by yourself. The orders go on, that it is no concern of mine whatsoever. All arrangements are to be overseen by yourself and yourself alone."

The penny dropped. "Yes of course, I know the package or packages to which Konrad … Major Soellner is referring," said Goering, glancing at the photograph of his wife and child that stood on his desk. "You can leave it to me."

"Will that be all, Herr Reich Marshal?" asked the timorous aide.

Goering paused a moment. "See that my private aeroplane is made ready…" He hesitated. "I must attend a meeting with the Führer at Berchtesgaden. You won't be able to contact me on route and I would prefer that you do not attempt to contact me there. The Führer is under a lot of strain at the moment and does not take kindly to unnecessary interruptions," Goering lied.

"Very well, Herr Reich Marshal." The aide saluted.

"I will return on Wednesday," Goering lied again, thinking, *Like hell I will*. "But I have to host a highly confidential meeting here and your presence will not be required, so take the morning off. In fact, give the whole of the staff the morning off." *That will delay the discovery of my flight to freedom*, Goering thought to himself.

The confused aide saluted again and started to leave. Goering bellowed after him, "See that my car is made ready immediately."

He picked up the telephone and asked for a private line to his Berlin residence. As he waited to be connected he had second thoughts. *You never can tell who might be listening.* He replaced the receiver. It would mean a tongue-lashing from Emmy but she would just have to pack in a hurry.

9.59.am.
Barcelona. Imperial German Consulate.

Konrad pushed his way past the surprised commissionaire and surprised the man even more when he asked the way to the Consul's office in fluent German.

The doorman gave him directions with a look betraying his amazement at meeting a fellow countryman in this neutral city and a fellow countryman young enough to be in the services to boot.

Konrad was thankful that the man's astonishment had jolted him back to reality. He was carrying only Portuguese papers and what's more he was dressed in a very Southern Mediterranean style. He would have to carry through the subterfuge and feign only a passing acquaintance with his mother tongue.

He strode down the corridors repenting the haste with which he had embarked on this journey to Barcelona. With his currently assumed identity he had no *locus standi* here. Why should the Consular officials give information about the military situation in Southern France to a Portuguese businessman?

He paused at a dusty water fountain and tried to think of a cover story.

10.03am.
Leipziger Platz, Berlin.

Goering marched up the steps of his Berlin palace and with barely a glance at the saluting sentries, he crashed into the imposing entrance hall.

Ian Cassidy

"Emmy!" he bellowed.

Unaccustomed to her husband returning from his duties before sundown, Emmy Goering rushed to meet him.

"Hermann, whatever is the matter?" she said as she skidded over the marble floor.

Goering took his wife in his arms. "You know the matter we have been discussing? Well, my darling, it is time."

"What, now?" said his wife, sitting on the carved Black Forest chair by the door: "I can't, I'm not ready … Edda … she's still at school."

Goering called for his butler. "Arrange for my daughter to be collected from her school immediately," he ordered. Once the man had left, Goering turned to his wife. "Now, Emmy my sweet, we must make haste." He led her up the magnificent sweeping marble staircase and pointed her in the direction of her boudoir. "Emmy, pack only what is irreplaceable," he said and left her hesitatingly wandering around the room.

Goering plodded down to his study and threw open his roll top desk. He pulled the tin wastepaper bin towards him and began dropping in burning sheets of paper.

As the flames crackled, Goering paced to the cabinet against the far wall. He surveyed the medals and decorations on display there. Which ones were irreplaceable? He fumbled through the many Iron Crosses that he had been awarded and chose the first, from 1916. He threw it into an attaché case and followed it with his Knight's Cross and several other baubles that Hitler had awarded him. He closed the case and sighed. It was a wrench to leave so many behind but he simply did not have room for vast amounts of luggage. He planned to use his own personal aeroplane, a light twin-engine trainer that he always flew himself, just to keep his hand in, for the flight to Spain.

Picking up an album of photographs, mainly of himself at the controls of brand new Fokker tri-planes or ME 109s, he went to his dressing room and hastily packed a small suitcase with civilian clothing that he would need for the journey. He called the footman and gave him instructions to put the bags in the car, before going off in search of his wife.

He found her sitting on a chaise in her boudoir tearfully studying an album of ageing *carte de visites*: "Must we leave these behind?" She asked through her tears.

"I think we can find room for them," he said tenderly, taking the album from her and placing it in the bottom of her case although inwardly he shuddered at the austere countenances of his wife's ancestors.

"Now why don't you leave the packing of the keepsakes to me, while you put some personal things in a case. Enough for a four week cruise, but Emmy, a very informal four week cruise. There'll be no captain's table or cocktail parties, just the three of us and some staff."

Emmy Goering mechanically opened her wardrobe. Goering went in search of his wife's personal jewellery, not the looted royal stuff she wore at Nazi Party functions but the cheap baubles he had given her all those years ago, before Mein Kampf, before the Reichstag was burnt, before all this madness.

He had little trouble finding the poor quality velvet-covered musical box where it lay, treasured but forgotten. It was the only box left on his wife's dressing table. The boxes containing the glittering arrangements that had once graced the crown jewels of so many European states were safely in the hold of rusting tramp steamer berthed at a sleepy Spanish port.

He picked up the box, careful not to set off its tinny mechanism. and put that beside the *cartes de visite* album in his wife's suitcase.

He looked away as his wife transplanted a drawer of lingerie straight into one of the drawers of her Louis Vuitton steamer trunk and was relieved to hear his daughter skipping up the grand staircase.

"Edda, come into your mamma's room," he shouted kindly.

Goering smiled at the gawky pre-teenage girl who stood awkwardly on the threshold of his wife's private apartment.

"Edda, we are going away for a short time, so I want you to go and pack your suitcase, your large suitcase. It may turn into an extended absence. Mamma will be along to help you in a moment." He smiled again. "And why not bring some of your favourite dollies along, too. They will help to pass the time. Now, run along, there really is very little time."

Ian Cassidy

The girl blinked and skipped off, such hasty upheavals were not uncommon. The family of the second most powerful man in Germany was used to decamping at a moment's notice.

Goering called the footman and instructed him to take his wife's trunk to the car. Then he paced the floor of her room impatiently as she continued filling vanity cases and small travel bags. He snorted and went to help his daughter.

Goering stood in the doorway and watched the little girl studiously select her clothes and toys. She looked up and smiled. "Where are we going, Papa?"

"To Karinhall," he lied. "But we will spend some time on the Carin so bring your Wellingtons and waterproofs."

The little girl nodded. "Shall I bring my school books?" she asked studiously.

"Just a few," he said gently. "Shall I give you a hand?"

"Don't fuss, Papa, I can manage," she said seriously.

Your Mama will be along in a moment," Goering said quietly and walked slowed back along the corridor. He hesitated at the top of the stairs and reasoning that he would only get in the way of his wife's packing, he shambled down the stairs to the hallway.

He paced the polished marble floor alternating between feelings of annoyance at the delay and regrets that he allowed himself to completely overlook that his daughter, his beautiful baby daughter had grown up so much. But he had been very busy in the service of the Reich and if things went according to plan, there would be many years ahead of him to put things right.

As he waited, Goering called the butler to him and informed the servant that he planned to take his family to Karinhall for a brief holiday. Relieved, the servant took his leave of his master and made haste to his pantry, where he poured himself a large glass of the Petrus he had secreted there. Regrettably, the last bottle. He had noticed that many of the fine wines from the cellars at Leipziger Platz had vanished over recent weeks. No doubt they had been shipped to Karinhall for the delight of the yes-man Visigoths his master was so keen to entertain. If only he had known the truth.

Goering had been bellowing for less than two minutes when his wife and daughter came to the head of the stairs. Edda skipped obliviously over the carpeted marble treads but Emmy hesitated at the top. For the benefit of her daughter she had cleared up her tears and looked a picture of composure but Goering could tell that her edifice of calm could easily give way. He bounced up the staircase and met her halfway. He ushered his wife and daughter quickly from their home and bundled them into the car. There would be time for explanations later.

"Tempelhof!" he barked at the chauffeur before settling back in his seat.

10.07am.
Barcelona. Imperial German Consulate.

Konrad stood at the counter and tried to catch the desk clerk's eye. There were a few German nationals in the office and the clerk was giving his countrymen priority over the foppishly dressed gentleman who was bobbing around at the counter.

Finally the clerk came to Konrad. "Yes, Signor," he said wearily.

Konrad began in a mixture of his best pidgin German, halting Spanish and Portuguese. "My wife is originally from Germany, Dusseldorf to be exact. Her younger brother, the last we heard from him, was stationed just outside of Cannes."

"Oh, yes," said the clerk suspiciously.

"And I was wondering if you could give me any information about the current situation in the area."

"I'm sorry, Sir, we have only the sketchiest news from France and in any event we are not at liberty to pass on such information to members of the public."

But I'm not a member of the public, Konrad screamed inwardly. *I'm a major in the Lufftwaffe.*

"You cannot tell me how far the British forces have advanced into France?"

"I'm sorry, Sir," replied the clerk, moving on to the next enquirer.

Konrad turned away; he could not risk revealing his true identity. He would just have to hope that Goering's train made it through France ahead of the advancing Allies, or if he was trying to reach Spain by air, that his aeroplane avoided the allied ack-ack batteries.

He left the Consulate and was about to head back to the railway station when he had an idea. He crossed the street and waited for one of his fellow enquirers at the consulate to leave. After a minute or two hiding behind a copy of Spanish newspaper, Konrad spotted an obvious German expat leaving. The man was even wearing a green hunting hat with a feather in the side. He set off in pursuit.

He followed the man through the streets of Barcelona, hesitating before he tackled him. The man went into a bar. Konrad followed, hoping that it would be frequented by German expats. Konrad was in luck, the pseudo bier keller was German-owned and German-run. He ordered a coffee and settled himself behind a newspaper, listening to the conversations going on about him. The talk was of little else but the invasion, although the details were sketchy and exaggerated at best. Beyond learning that the Allied advance over the beaches of the Riviera was meeting lighter resistance than had been the case in Normandy, Konrad learnt little. He finished his coffee and left, resolving to return to the café later in the week and perhaps even strike up a conversation with one of its patrons, that was if Goering had not shown up by then.

11.13am.
Tempelhof Airport.

Goering grunted out of his limousine and without waiting for his wife and daughter. He grabbed a travel bag from the chauffeur and stomped across the tarmac towards the dispatcher's office at the rear of the art deco building.

The short journey from the centre of Berlin had been a nightmare. The tirade of incendiaries dropped by the RAF the previous evening had left many streets blocked and the chauffeur had been forced to make many tortuous detours. To make matters worse, just as Goering's car had reached the outskirts of he city, those madmen in the USAF had carried out one of their famed daylight raids. Goering had watched impotently as the flying fortresses rained down death and destruction in broad daylight. If only his beloved Lufftwaffe had been up to strength, his ME

109s would have knocked the hulking sitting ducks out of the sky. He could only sit back and curse as his car crawled out of the city, every bomb blast screeching "Meier."

Goering handed the surprised air traffic dispatcher his carefully fabricated flight plan to Berchtesgaden and, after checking that his wife and daughter were being taken care of in the outer office, he made his way to a minion's office. He ordered the harassed and nervous clerk out of the room and picked up the telephone. It was risky but he had no choice, he had to inform Konrad that he was en route. He would need a reception committee and crucial landing lights. He asked for an international line. He gave the operator the number of Konrad's hotel in Spain and waited to be connected.

He was confronted by a gabble of incomprehensible Mediterranean gobbledegook, so he barked, "Signor Rodriges," Konrad's assumed Portuguese name. He repeated his request, this time remembering the por favor and waited to be connected to Konrad's room. The telephone rang for what seemed an eternity before the same Spanish voice came back on the line. Goering assumed that Konrad was not in his room and, forsaking an attempt to get the monoglot receptionist to search the public rooms of the hotel for his aide, he put the telephone down. He swore to himself. He would have to try and contact Konrad when he refuelled. He left the office and headed to the washroom.

Once inside he opened his case and took out a set of civilian flying clothes, leather hat and goggles, insignia-less leather jacket, cream jodhpurs and brown boots. He quickly changed out of his uniform and thought of the last time he had performed a quick change in a toilet. The memory of removing his silk lingerie in the filthy lavatory of a Kentish alehouse brought a warming flicker to his loins. He brushed the feeling aside and hastily pulled on his jodhpurs. He had reluctantly decided to abandon his collection of women's underwear. Transporting the trunk that he kept concealed in the attic at Karinhall halfway around the world would have been too risky. He would just have to put his little kink on hold until he could purchase some replacements in Asunción or Montevideo. He would not risk borrowing his wife's underclothes, not again. The potential for embarrassment was too great No matter how carefully you refold and replace them, women always notice that their unmentionables have been tampered with.

Pulling down his leather flying cap, Goering went in search of his wife and daughter. He brushed aside the astonished gaze of the dispatcher's clerk and ushered his family towards the hangar.

Goering strode across the floor of the hangar, leaving the woman and child in his wake. His personal pilot and co-pilot, like the dispatcher amazed to see the Reich Marshal out of his customary white Lufftwaffe uniform, hastily stubbed out their cigarettes and jumped to attention.

With barely a word of explanation, Goering dismissed the two men, announcing that he wished to take the controls himself. He turned to the chief engineer: "Pre-flight checks!" he barked. "Get to it."

"Everything has been done by Major Neumann, Herr Reich Marshal," stuttered the engineer, nodding towards the departing pilots.

"Nevertheless an experienced pilot like myself takes nothing for granted. Get on with it."

"Yes, Herr Reich Marshal," said the man reaching for his clipboard.

Goering gave orders for the junior engineer to see that his wife and daughter were seated comfortably inside the aeroplane and joined the chief engineer with his checks. Very soon he took charge. Goering the pilot was every bit as formidable as Goering the politician. He knew every inch of his beloved Seibel Si 204D and every word of the flying manual. If the chief engineer had thought that he could scrimp on this second unnecessary check, he was wrong. It was over an hour later before Goering was satisfied. He ordered the engineer to pull the chocks away and climbed slowly up the steps to the aircraft's cabin.

He walked past his wife and daughter and went into the two-seater cockpit. He sat at the controls with a satisfied smirk. Everything was going well. He had a full tank of fuel and a beautifully tuned aeroplane. His only concern was that the field outside of Sitges that Konrad had selected as a clandestine landing strip would be adequate. He tapped his jacket pocket to check that he had the strip's coordinates and heaved himself from his seat. He went into the plush cabin and sat next to his wife. His daughter was sleeping peacefully but his wife looked petrified.

"Are you sure about this, Hermann?" she began doubtfully.

"We've come too far to turn back now," he said tenderly.

"But we could just go to Karinhall and you could rest for a few days. No-one need ever know that you planned to flee the country," she pleaded.

"We have to go now, my dear. The Allies will soon have Germany surrounded and our chance will be gone."

"But Hermann, things may not be so bad under the Allies. The Führer is very canny. He may strike a very favourable peace agreement."

"Emmy." Goering puffed. "We've been through this before; the Allies will accept nothing but unconditional surrender. No matter how cunning he is, the Führer can expect nothing but the noose and I do not intend to join him on the gibbet."

"But Hermann … "

"It's too late for buts, Emmy my dear. The time has come to leave." He sighed and went back to the controls.

He pointed the nose of the aircraft towards the hangar door and with a deft pull on the stick, he set the plane in motion.

Once outside the hangar, he switched on the radio and began to call up the tower. His wife's sobs, audible even in the cockpit, pulled him up. "Emmy, please," he shouted. "The radio operator in the tower will hear you. And what if Edda should awake?"

Emmy Goering stifled her tears in her handkerchief. Goering asked for and not surprisingly got clearance for an immediate take-off. The Junkers troop carrier would just have to be a little delayed taking its reinforcements to the beleaguered troops in the carnage of the Falaise Gap.

At twelve twenty-five, Goering gunned the Seibel's 's twin engines down the runway. A minute later they were airborne. He was free, well almost, at least the skies were his territory, and he was in control. He made a pretence of heading for Berchtesgaden and headed directly south. Once over the Bavarian Alps, he would lower his altitude and alter course to the west. He slipped his goggles onto the top of his head and relishing the roar of the Seibel's Argus HI engines. He smiled to himself as the suburbs of Berlin went by beneath.

12. Noon.
Sitges Harbour.

With a spring in his step, Coughlan ran up the gangplank and met the Serbian cook as he was about to deliver yet another tray of tea to the men working below. He relieved the man of the tea things and hollered down to his employees.

They joined him on the deck in seconds. He good naturedly ignored their winking questions about how he spent the previous evening. Once they were settled with mugs of the unspeakable liquid, he took one for himself and with a scowl accompanying every sip, he went to the hold's rail and surveyed the men's morning's work.

The joists were all securely fixed and a good proportion of the tongue and groove floorboards had been laid, giving a solid platform for the remainder of the work.

Once the floor was in place, the men could begin on the studwork partitions. Things were taking shape. Coughlan turned away, quite satisfied that they could finish ahead of schedule.

"What the fuck we doing here boss?" Maurice croaked at his employer.

"What do you mean?" Coughlan said disingenuously.

"Well, all this, it's a bit iffy, isn't it?"

"No, no, everything's fine, it's all straight as a die."

"Come off it, Jim." Jack joined in: "If this was kosher we'd be extending the cabins in the superstructure not building hidden cabins in the hold. The geezer we're working for must be a people smuggler."

"Where'd you get that idea? You've seen the state of the ship. It's quicker and cheaper to start from scratch in the hold." Coughlan lied effortlessly.

"It might be worse than people smuggling," Bert piped up.

Jack and the others turned to their usually taciturn work mate.

"What do you mean?"

"Well, there's a lot of people in Germany and Italy and France who are going to want to leave in a hurry. We could be helping a Nazi to escape."

Coughlan's mind had carried the same suspicion for many weeks but the promised amount of Swiss francs had been enough for him. He betrayed no hint of his suspicions when he answered. "That's bollocks, you met the woman who gave us the job," he said, appealing to Jack and Keith. "She was English and she said her employer was a Londoner."

"But who says she was telling the truth?" asked Maurice.

"She even said we worked on her boss's house in London before the war. So he must be English."

"Why?" asked Maurice again. "Germans could buy houses in London then."

"Just cut all this crap out," snapped Coughlan, his round cheeks getting redder. "I'm telling you everything's okay and besides in ten days time we'll be on our way home with a thick wad of cash each."

"Yours will be thicker than ours," grumbled Don.

Coughlan ignored him.

"Look if it makes you feel any better, I'll have a talk with Manuel, see what I can find out."

"That's another thing," said Bert. "He's a funny coot that Manuel, where did he get that accent from? I fought in the first war and I saw a lot of Germans and I think he's a German."

"What do you know, you silly old bugger," laughed Coughlan. "You were in the pay corps."

"I still saw my fair share of Germans," said Bert sticking to his guns.

"Oh bollocks," said Coughlan losing patience. "Look, anyone who doesn't like it can fuck off home. I'm not stopping them."

"But you won't pay for them either," said Don.

"Course not, anyone who comes home with me at the end of the job comes for free, if you leave early you pay for yourself." Coughlan stood his ground.

The men said nothing but scowled at Coughlan.

"Look, everything's alright, I tell you. Now fuck off back to work," Coughlan said to break the silence.

The men filed silently back to the hold and Coughlan heard the pocket cheering sound nails being hammered into timber as he commenced his siesta.

Coughlan invented a few errands for himself to make sure that he was absent for the men's afternoon tea breaks but he met them at five thirty as they exited the ship and offered to buy them all a pint. The men grudgingly accepted, although they had no choice, Coughlan had the petty cash exclusively under his control.

The men followed their usual evening routine, a mad dash for bathroom, hot showers for the lucky ones, cold ones for the rest, a few liveners in the bar across the road, a meal with Coughlan and then an aimless and disappointing pub crawl. Coughlan added another element to his nightly routine. After a quick postprandial brandy he headed off to the brothel.

4.47pm.
Geneva Airport.

Goering taxied his aircraft towards to the tower at Geneva and prepared himself for the onslaught of red tape and red-faced officials.

He struggled with the tower controllers in a mixture of broken French, English and German. Thanks to a few confidently delivered lies, he had finally obtained permission to land.

Now that he was on the ground, the problems would begin. The airport authorities would undoubtedly find a German speaker and he would no longer be able to dodge awkward questions by feigning ignorance of the language. His explanation for his need to make an unscheduled stop would soon be found wanting. Goering hoped that the Swiss would live up to their reputation and sell him some fuel and get him out of their airspace as soon as they could. Neutral, non-aligned and not interested.

Goering instructed his wife and daughter not to leave the cabin and looked wistfully at his daughter's perplexed expression. His wife would have to take care of it. In the absence of steps he struggled down the aircraft's rickety ladder.

Edda Goering looked plaintively at her mother. "Where are we Mama, this isn't Karinhall."

"No, dear, your father's duties require that we make a short stop in Switzerland but we will continue our journey very shortly."

The little girl picked up her favourite doll and began to play, quite unconcerned. Unscheduled itinerary changes were nothing to new to the family of a politician and statesman.

Emmy Goering looked briefly at her daughter before helping herself to a large schnapps from the aircraft's galley.

The Unsinkable Herr Goering

Goering strode across the runway and towered over the sombre suited immigration officials, who were crossing the tarmac in his direction, and smiled.

"Gentlemen, it is so good to feel terra firma beneath one's feet. My fuel situation had become dangerously low." He lied, he had plenty of fuel, the Seibel's range was approximately fourteen hundred kilometres and they had travelled only nine hundred but Geneva was the only place along the fifteen hundred kilometre route to Barcelona that he felt safe landing at. If the technicians refuelling the aircraft noticed that the tank was half full, Goering planned to blame instrument failure but he was hoping that once the fuel merchant was in possession of price of a full tank he would keep quiet.

"Your passport please," demanded the taller of the two officials, oblivious to Goering's bonhomie.

"Of course, Mein Herr," said Goering, handing over one of the many forged passports that Canaris had produced for him, as he had for all the members of Hitler's cabinet.

The official eyed the passport warily. "You are Austrian?" he asked.

"Yes, from Vienna," smiled Goering.

The official handed the passport back. "That seems to be in order. Have you any passengers on board?"

"My wife and daughter."

"Their passports?" demanded the official.

"They are with my wife's things on board the aircraft, I will get them to you shortly. Now, can you direct my to an aviation fuel merchant?"

"All in good time, Mein Herr." scowled the official: "First we must deal with you attempting to enter Switzerland without permission."

"But your tower gave me permission to land!" Goering puffed out his chest and faced down the petty official.

"Permission was granted only because you claimed it was an emergency."

"And so it was, I was dangerously low on fuel."

"What was your destination?" barked the official.

"My destination was and still is Cologne. We were en route from Vienna to Cologne when I had to change course to avoid a skirmish between aircraft from the opposing powers. I then became disorientated in the poor weather and before I knew it I was lost and short of fuel. It was a great stroke of luck that I recognised the environs of Geneva and was able to make my way to the airport."

"What poor weather?" asked the official suspiciously: "No other pilot has reported bad weather to the east."

"It must have been a freak Alpine storm." Goering grinned ingratiatingly. He brought all his charm to bear. "Now all I need is a tank of fuel and I will be on my way."

The official consulted his colleague. After several minutes he announced, "Follow me!" He turned away and headed for the terminal. Goering had little choice but to follow. He stomped along barely concealing his anger. *Who did this jobsworth think he was?* If circumstances were different he would show him, he would have the man bowing and scraping. He was Hermann Goering and he had many many millions of marks on deposit in this very city.

Once inside the terminal, the official pointed Goering to a seat and left him. He kicked his heels in the clinically tidy office for over an hour.

With mounting frustration Goering lumbered to his feet and knocked on the door through which the officials had passed an hour ago. A young woman came to the door and looked blankly at Goering.

"How much longer am I to be kept waiting?" He demanded.

She paused before she answered: "I'm sorry, Sir, but I am not involved in your case and so I have no knowledge of how it is progressing."

"Well find me someone who can," snapped Goering.

"That is not possible, I am alone in the office at present but as soon as my colleagues return I will inform them of your concerns," she said mechanically.

Defeated by Swiss bureaucracy, Goering took a step back. "Is it possible for me make a telephone call?" He smiled at the young woman.

"We cannot make international calls from this office," she stonewalled. "So I assume that will be of no help to you."

"You assume correctly," snarled Goering: "Who would I want to call in Switzerland? I merely wish to be on my way."

"I'm sure everything will be concluded very soon." The girl smiled as she closed the door.

Goering stalked back to his seat and thumped himself down. He snorted and looked out the window. The pressure of his situation and the tiring flight from Berlin soon took its toll and before long he was snoring violently, his angry demeanour accosting him with belligerent dreams.

Almost an hour passed before the two officials came silently into the anteroom. They coughed politely but Goering did not stir.

Throwing away the protocol manual for dealing with foreign nationals, the more senior of the two men tapped Goering on the shoulder. He awoke with a start. "What! … What! …" he bellowed before he remembered where he was. "Ah, gentlemen, so glad to see you again."

"Everything is in order Herr Krauss," said the official without a hint of a smile. "A tow truck is being sent to your aircraft and once you are at the controls it will take you to the refuelling hangar."

"Thank you gentlemen, thank you very much," said Goering, just a little surprised.

"Safe journey." The junior official spoke for the first time. The two men left and, blinking, Goering went out into the evening sun.

Inside the cabin of the Seibel he quickly appeased his frantic wife and flopped in front of the controls, waving to the impatient tow truck driver that he was ready to proceed.

Once inside the hangar, Goering agreed a price with the fuel merchant and waited while the high octane aviation fuel was pumped aboard.

Once the fuel was on board, he asked the fuel merchant if it was possible to make a telephone call, accompanying the request with a deftly placed large denomination note.

He anxiously dealt with the now familiar babble of speedy Spanish and more anxiously waited as the telephone rang in Konrad's room. He gave a massive sigh of relief when he heard Konrad's voice. He ignored his aide's many enquiries and gave orders that the landing strip be operational from midnight onwards. He replaced the receiver and almost ran to his waiting aeroplane.

After obtaining permission to take off, he taxied onto the runway and pushed the stick to full throttle.

As the wheels left the ground he turned to his wife: "Next stop Spain and freedom," he announced. She did not hear him, she had made copious use of the Seibel's well stocked bar during their extended stopover.

11.34pm.
Madame Ramona's, Sitges.

Coughlan returned the Somali doorman's smile and slipped him a few Pesetas. Without waiting to be shown through the thick velvet curtain, he eased into the bar and ordered a drink. He winced at the sound of Spain's Peter Dawson strangling yet another ballad and took a long slug of his whisky.

Feeling more at ease on his second visit he took his drink over to a banquette and sat down surveying his surroundings and more importantly the girls ringing the dance floor.

There was no sign of the Amazonian beauty who had been so accommodating the previous evening but Coughlan's regrets were somewhat muted. Last night had been truly remarkable, especially when her lithe and powerful thighs had clamped around his back like she was riding a wild pony back in her native Venezuela but Coughlan doubted whether he had the stamina for another all night romp.

He ordered another drink and sat back, spoilt for choice. Two of the working girls in particular caught his eye. After a moment's consideration he made his choice and plumped for the more comely of the two. A tall, dark prostitute with an ample backside and long and beautiful legs encased in black silk stockings.

As the woman teetered between the tables towards him, Coughlan had a thought - *Why not?* He waved at his second choice. She hesitated. Coughlan waved more vigorously and she followed her colleague.

Coughlan introduced himself as 'Keith' – much safer - and asked the ladies to join him. He ordered a round of drinks, scotch for himself and fizzy overpriced pap for the girls. The three began to chat in a strange mixture of Coughlan's beery, mostly forgotten, schoolboy French and the smatterings of many languages the ladies had picked up servicing the multitude of multinational merchant seamen who passed through Barcelona.

Coughlan ran his hands down the stockinged thigh at each side of him as the ladies blew in his ears and ran their fingers through his thinning hair. He sat back, luxuriating in the smoky atmosphere. This is the life! He said to himself and smiled.

After another round of drinks, Coughlan began to have misgivings about his bar tab and so he suggested that they adjourn upstairs.

The ladies led him up the stairs to a deluxe room contrasting greatly to the stark cubicle with a leaky shower he used on his previous visit. This room was lavishly furnished with an enormous round bed, mirrored walls and another mirror ball. Then there were the gadgets, and what gadgets! Coughlan stood back as the ladies demonstrated. His first choice straddled a white porcelain pan, not unlike a drinking fountain. Her colleague turned a tap and sent a bubbling jet of warm water splashing against her friend's clitoris. The lady sighed affectedly and moved rhythmically against the jet. Coughlan came up behind and inserted a finger in her anus, he gently moved her up and down on the jet. The other lady undressed him and began to stroke his already erect penis.

When Coughlan tired of this little diversion, the ladies demonstrated another of the rooms amusing little fixtures, a contraption resembling an obstetrician's stirrups but cunningly modified for cunnilingus by the addition of a suitably placed chin rest.

The first lady placed her legs in the stirrups with her backside against the chin rest, where her colleague was ready and waiting to tongue her clitoris. Coughlan giggled and pushed her aside, he was soon lapping away like a truffle pig.

The rest is history. Suffice it to say that once again James Coughlan was late for work, a little light in the pocket and carrying a vicious friction burn on the side of his penis.

Meanwhile the men gloomily returned to their hotel, the heat, the Spanish beer and the unusual food all adding to their discomfort and forcing them to once again engage in a roughhouse for the lavatory.

After each man had sweated over a period of solitary confinement in the toilet, they gathered in the larger of their two rooms and over Andrew's liver salts they discussed their predicament.

Uncharacteristically, Bert was the most vociferous. "We're in, or should I say Coughlan's got us into a right mess here. We're a thousand miles from home and we're working for some very dodgy people."

Ian Cassidy

The others agreed and Bert continued, "For one, I don't fancy a doing time in a Spanish gaol or getting hauled off to the nick as soon as we get home."

Maurice and Ivor, the voices of experience, were wholehearted in their agreement. Ivor especially - his assigned prison job for much of his last stretch had been to pick up newspaper-wrapped parcels of excrement that prisoners threw from their cell windows rather than spend the night with a foul-smelling slop bucket. Despite the welcome few hours away from the foetid interior of the cell block such a job afforded, it was an experience Ivor was keen not to repeat in a hurry.

Bert continued, "If we are trading with the enemy then we could all be looking at plenty of porridge."

"That's if we're lucky," Jack piped in. "We might not get a long stretch at all, it could be a very short one followed by an appointment with the hangman."

"You're not serious!" said a very worried Keith.

"Damn right I am, it could be treason."

"But do we know for certain that this Manuel bloke is really a German? He could be what he says he is. A Portuguese businessman who sails close to the wind at times," said Don, anxious not to cut short such a lucrative contract without good reason.

Ivor backed Don up. "Look, we've worked for villains in the past, bloody hell half the foundries in West Bromwich are run by gangsters, we're just working blokes doing what we're told."

"We might not get away with it this time," said Bert gloomily.

"Look, if this Manuel is just an ordinary decent criminal," said Ivor, "then we've got no problems."

"But what if he isn't, what if he is a Nazi."

"We'll just have to find out. Won't we" announced Jack: "We'll confront Coughlan first thing tomorrow."

"Why not now?" asked Keith.

"Cos the dirty bastard's at the knocking shop again, that's why."

"That's settled then," said Bert: "We'll have it out with Coughlan at breakfast tomorrow if the randy old bastard manages to drag himself out of bed."

"Whose bed?" Keith asked no-one in particular.

"Let's just get some sleep and sort things out tomorrow."

The men agreed and silently filed back to their rooms, where, Keith and Maurice excepted, they slept badly. Don worried about losing two weeks wages plus overtime and a completion bonus. Jack had similar concerns but also dreaded the thought of breaking the law, as did Bert. Keith could not sleep because of the drizzle of beery urine striking his face every time one the insomniacs used the sink as an improvised lavatory.

thirteen
16th August, 1944

3.32am. **The outskirts of Sitges.** Goering decided to avoid all possibility of encountering other aircraft in the vicinity of Barcelona Airfield and approached Sitges from the sea. He flew low over the north of the town and looked down at the sleeping port. Even at this ungodly hour a few lights still burned in stark contrast to the blackout that cloaked all of his beloved Germany. He re-checked his coordinates and banked further north. Once away from the town, the land below took on a uniform blackness, the peasant farmers not caring to illuminate their hovels throughout the night. With growing trepidation he scanned the horizon for any sign of the makeshift airstrip.

Soon Goering was starting to sweat. He had over flown the map coordinates twice and seen nothing to indicate a landing strip however improvised. He re-checked the directions and banked to the right. He commenced another fly past and tried not to think of his rapidly dwindling supply of fuel.

Something to his left caught his eye. It looked like a row of lights, so he banked steeply and went to investigate.

As he got closer he breathed a sigh of relief and commenced his landing routine. After hearing the satisfying thud of the undercarriage lowering he pointed the Seibel's nose slightly towards the waiting lights.

He shouted to his wife and daughter to fasten their safety belts. *This could be a very bumpy landing*, he said to himself so as not to alarm them and commenced his final approach.

Goering eased the racing engines to their minimum speed, to stall now could be fatal and waited for the crunch as the wheels hit the hard Spanish earth.

With textbook efficiency he brought the aircraft down but still the smash of rubber on sun baked dust was a shock. The stick was nearly wrenched from his grasp and he struggled to control the hurtling Seibel as it careered over the scorched scrubland Konrad had selected as a clandestine landing strip.

With his massive flabby biceps straining, he wrestled the aircraft to a halt and slumped at the controls.

Konrad had watched in growing horror as the frighteningly small aircraft had whistled passed him like a silver bullet. Now he relaxed and sent his two hired hands - disinterested farm labourers - to douse the lines of braziers. Stumbling over the uneven ground, he approached the aeroplane and made for the Seibel's rear door.

He stretched for the handle and with an effort pulled open the door. With just his head and shoulders poking into the fuselage he shouted into the darkened interior, "Herr Reich Marshal."

He received no reply from his exhausted employer but as his eyes became accustomed to the gloom he spied two frightened figures huddled in the rear passenger seats: "Frau Goering!" gasped Konrad. "Is everything alright?"

"Yes, Herr Mayor." Emmy Goering replied tiredly. "We are fine, if a little shaken. My husband has had a very long stint at the controls. You had better go and see if he needs your assistance."

Konrad agreed and, deciding that it would be counterproductive to ask his employer's exhausted wife to struggle with the aircraft's steps, he heaved himself into the body of the aeroplane.

After an unseemly struggle on the cabin floor he regained his feet and saluted the Reich Marshal's wife. With a nod to Edda: "Fraulein." He headed towards the cockpit.

A shambling Goering met him halfway. "Ah, Konrad, good to see you. Now I am anxious to put a very long day behind me. Let us make haste." He yawned. Konrad saluted and without further instruction he began to lower the Seibel's passenger steps.

Ian Cassidy

Goering stooped to pick up his sobbing daughter who was disorientated by the unexpected heat and heavy scent of jacaranda and olive trees in the air. "Papa, where are we, when are we going to Karinhall?" she asked breathlessly between sobs.

"We are going to take a short holiday first, my dear," said her father. "We're in Spain and you will love it here."

Edda Goering looked at him suspiciously. "Spain?" she asked. "Why?"

"We all need a rest and some warm Mediterranean sun. Now you go to sleep." Goering patted his daughter's head as she dozed on his shoulder.

"Now, Konrad, I trust you have some assistance?"

"Yes, Herr Reich Marshall."

"Well, show them where the luggage is kept and then show me to my car."

"It may be better to do that in reverse order, Herr Reich Marshal."

"How so?" snapped Goering.

"My men are still dealing with the braziers, so I will get you settled in the vehicle and deal with the luggage later."

"As you prefer, Konrad, only do it quickly."

"This way, Herr Reich Marshal," said Konrad, thinking *I have a lifetime's exile with this man,* and frowning.

Goering helped his wife from the cabin and the three exhausted figures trudged behind the aide towards the ageing Hispano Suiza that Konrad had purchased from an impecunious Spanish Grandee earlier in the week. Konrad settled the three travellers into the back of the dowdy limousine and went in search of his hired hands. He returned several minutes later followed by two sweating farm labourers, carrying the suite of luggage the Goerings had bought along. Two further trips were necessary. Goering and his wife had joined their daughter at her slumbers when finally an out of breath Konrad climbed behind the jalopy's wheel.

The throaty roar of the Hispano Suiza's straight twelve-engine shook Goering back to consciousness.

"My aircraft?" he demanded: "What arrangements have you made?"

"Regrettably Herr, Reich Marshal, there are no barns in the area large enough to take her, or none that I could rent, that is."

"I trust that you have made other arrangements then?"

"Your temporary residence has a very substantial courtyard surrounded by outbuildings and orchards, we can conceal her there."

"I suppose that will have to suffice," grumbled Goering.

"At first light I shall taxi the Seibel down to the farm and park her in the yard, she will then only be visible from the air."

"Very good Konrad. Now, my temporary residence, it is comfortable I hope?"

"I have rented the farmhouse to which this field belongs. It is basic but adequate for a short stay, with plenty of warm water and comfortable beds."

"A comfortable bed is all that I require at the moment," sighed Goering, "and perhaps a bite to eat."

"The larder and the wine cellar are well stocked, Herr Reich Marshal."

"Good, good," mumbled Goering as he drifted back into unconsciousness.

Konrad bumped the cumbersome limousine along the rutted farm track and at a stately pace covered the half mile to the farmhouse.

He got as close to the front door as the massive car's outlandishly wide turning circle would allow and turned off the engine. Relieved that the ear-shattering roar of the engine had been silenced, he left the driver's seat and held open Goering's door.

Goering struggled from his seat and while Konrad assisted his wife and child. He surveyed his home for the next few days.

How are the mighty fallen, was his first thought. *From the grand facades of Karinhall and Leipziger Platz to this grubby one storey peasant croft, with a wonky red-tiled roof.*

Goering looked at the heavily carved oak front door and the two small, almost arrow slit windows at either side and groaned at the thought of shoehorning himself into the poky rooms they concealed. He stamped his foot and shook away his anger. *It's only for a week or so*, he told himself and strode towards the door.

He grasped the cast iron door handle and noticed that it had been recently cleaned. He silently commended Konrad for his attention to detail and pushed his way inside.

Ian Cassidy

The interior was much as he expected, low and cramped with harsh stone floors that gave a chill to the rooms even in the height of summer.

Goering waited in the doorway as Konrad escorted his family towards the house.

"Emmy," he said quietly so as not to disturb the sleeping child. "Can you take care of Edda? I have things to discuss with Major Soellner."

Emmy Goering nodded and then stopped in her tracks She had no idea where the bedrooms where.

Goering looked at her impatiently. *What did the woman want now?*

Konrad came to her aid. "The most suitable room for Fraulein Goering is the second door on the left." He smiled apologetically: "The facilities are next door and the master bedroom is next to that."

"Thank you, Konrad," Emmy Goering said with a sigh of relief and an exasperated glance at her husband.

Goering called after her, "Join us the drawing room as soon as you've finished."

"Thank you, Hermann, but I think I'll turn in, perhaps Major Soellner could bring me a hot drink."

"Of course, Frau Goering, and can I bring you a night-cap?"

"Thank you, Konrad, just a cup of coffee will suffice." The hangover she was expecting in the morning did not need adding to.

"Very well, Frau Goering." Konrad saluted and, after pointing Goering in the direction of the sitting room and furnishing him with a bottle of Spanish brandy, he went to kitchen and struggled with the ancient range.

After delivering a cup of coffee to the shattered Frau Goering, Konrad went to join his employer in the sitting room.

The now former Reich Marshal was fidgeting in a primitive over-stuffed armchair and wincing with every sip that he took of the rough Spanish brandy. A far cry from the dusty little bottle of 1788 Augier Vielle Fine looted from a French Chateau that he kept for himself alone at Karinhall. Still, a half case, probably the last half case in existence was by this time stored in the hold of his ship. He took a long and painful slug and turned to Konrad.

"How goes the work on … what is she called, The Alething?"

"The Atheling, Herr Reich Marshal. It is proceeding to schedule, slightly ahead of schedule, in fact. But we are still some way from completion."

"As much as I look forward to the pleasures of residing on a Spanish farm," he said sarcastically. "And I'm sure I could learn to stomach the local brew." He waved his brandy glass and poured on the sarcasm. "I am anxious that my stay here be a very short one."

"Of course, Herr Reich Marshal. What would you have me do?"

"Make these Irish navvies work harder."

Arbeit Macht Frei, Konrad said to himself. "I will do my best, Herr Reich Marshal," he said helpfully.

"And do it immediately, Konrad. We must leave here as soon as possible. It will not take Kaltenbrunner and Müller long to track me down, so we must stay one step ahead of their Gestapo bullyboys."

"Should I offer their employer extra funds to cover overtime payments?"

"If you must, Konrad, but only if you must The blasted man is being overpaid already."

"My experience of the man leads me to believe that he will insist on some extra funds, Herr Reich Marshal."

"Agree to meet the overtime payments then, it cannot be a great deal, if the man is so money grabbing then he can only pay his serfs pennies. But Konrad, just the overtime, no more."

"Very well, Herr Reich Marshal. I will tackle the man about it first thing tomorrow morning. Now, Herr Reich Marshal, if you will excuse me, I must attend to your luggage and see that your aircraft is safely concealed."

"Yes, Konrad, that is all, thank you. And Konrad, do not bother to attend on me until lunchtime at least tomorrow. Today has been very trying and I need a proper rest."

Haven't I always known better than to try and get you to do any work before noon? Konrad said to himself. "I have business in Barcelona tomorrow morning in any event, Herr Reich Marshall."

"What business pray?" demanded Goering.

"Our Captain requires some equipment that cannot be obtained locally. Indeed some items are unavailable anywhere in Spain. I have had to arrange for them to be sent here from a ship's chandlers in Marseilles. With luck, they will arrive on the milk train from Perpignan tomorrow."

"Very good Konrad. I will meet the man tomorrow afternoon. Bring him here."

"That was my plan, Herr Reich Marshall. I thought it best that from now on, he lodges in one of the outbuildings. Yet another new arrival at the port may draw unwanted attention."

"As you see fit, Konrad. I'm sure my wife will be reassured to have another strong man around but remind him to behave himself in front of my daughter. I won't stand for his grubby matelot tricks around her."

"However coarsening the years at sea may have been, I'm sure he will remember how to behave in female company, Herr Reich Marshal, but I will remind him."

"Very well, Konrad, good night." Goering yawned and dismissed his aide.

"Good night, Herr Reich Marshal," said Konrad. He saluted and left.

6.30am.
Sitges.

The delegation of uppity painters and decorators lingered over their third cup of coffee: "That randy bastard's not gonna get up again," grumbled Jack, indicating his employer's vacant seat at the breakfast table.

"Better go and do a bit then, he won't pay us for sitting here and we may as well get paid for being here," said Don.

"Yea, the quicker it's done the quicker we can get the hell out of here," agreed Ivor, getting up.

The others concurred and lazily got to their feet. The six worried painters wandered down to the docks and sluggishly commenced the day's labours.

Progress was steady if unspectacular, the studded walls were complete and the carpenters made a start on the ceilings. Bert began the wiring, complaining about the dilapidated state of the ship's generator as he did so. Maurice and Ivor painted what they could and Keith kept himself busy with his trusty broom.

Just before eleven o'clock and far earlier than the men expected, Coughlan breezed into the hold, happy and content after yet another very enjoyable evening, the worsening friction burn on his penis excepted. He rubbed his groin as he greeted his men.

The men downed tools and following closely behind Jack and Bert they confronted their employer.

"Jim we want some answers, is this job kosher?"

"Not this crap again," said Coughlan, his mood changing immediately. "We went through all this yesterday. I told you there's nothing to worry about."

"But we want to know who we're working for and just what they're up to."

"That's none of our fucking business but if you must know, I think the chap's a smuggler and black marketeer."

"Well, that's okay so long as he's not smuggling people, like Nazis."

"Don't talk daft, the bloke's English, I met his secretary and his gaffer over here's Portuguese, what would they be doing smuggling Nazis," Coughlan snarled.

"What's to stop the Portuguese working for the Nazis?" asked Ivor.

"Look, look, I'll have a word with Manuel and see what I can find out." Coughlan turned to Ivor. "You've got the cook straightened, have a word with him and see if he knows who's paying his wages."

"Okey Cokey Boss," smiled Ivor.

"And," Coughlan continued: "I'll see if I can't up the finishing bonus, it'll mean almost no profit for me but I think I can stretch it a bit."

The men hooted derisively. "You're making a fucking mint on this one." Don gave voice to what the others were thinking.

Coughlan scowled and was about to reply when he spotted Konrad peeping over the side of the hold.

"Now shut the fuck up and get back to work, here's Manuel," Coughlan whispered.

"Are you going to have a word with him?" asked Bert.

"Yea, yea," said Coughlan indifferently as he mounted the steps to meet the Nazi in civilian clothes.

"It's coming on well," he announced expansively as he greeted Konrad.

"Yes, very," agreed Konrad. "However, my employer would be happier if the work progressed a little faster."

Ian Cassidy

"Happy enough to pay for it?" Coughlan came back at Konrad instantly.

"My employer is of the opinion that you are being paid handsomely as it is." Konrad said making an attempt at negotiation.

"Being paid adequately for a two week job," said Coughlan. "Not being paid to work double shifts to do it in a week."

"Very well, can you persuade your men to work double shifts if I can arrange to cover their extra wages?"

"I'll have to offer them double time," said Coughlan, already planning to offer them time-and-a-half.

"How much will that be?" asked Konrad.

"Let's see," said Coughlan: "Seven men, double time for shall we say an extra five shifts, five hundred pounds should cover it. Cash!"

Konrad breathed a sigh of relief and rapidly tried not to show it, he had expected Coughlan to ask for far more. He reached for his wallet.

"Forgive me, I'm a little unfamiliar with the exchange rate, how much is five hundred pounds in Pesetas?" he said, fumbling with a wad of Spanish bills.

"About what you've got there," said Coughlan, snatching the money away. He quickly counted it and found that there was the equivalent of almost seven hundred pounds there: "Yes this adds up to about four hundred and ninety five pounds," he. "You can owe me the rest."

Konrad had suddenly lost the will to haggle any longer. He gave an exasperated sign. "And you now guarantee that the ship will be ready for my employer within five days."

"I'm not giving any guarantees," said Coughlan evasively. "But we won't be far away."

"So long as you are." Konrad turned away, defeated. "Good day to you, Mr Coughlan.

"Yes, see you, Manuel." Coughlan smiled and went back down to his men.

They downed tools again on seeing him. They stood silently watching his approach a collective "Well?" unspoken on their lips.

"Good news lads. The geezer wants the job finished pronto, so we can all get home a bit quicker."

"How's that good news?" asked Bert. "We'll have to work longer hours."

"But he'll pay for it. He'll pay time-and-a-quarter for overtime."

The men gave their increasingly cliched hoot of derision.

"Alright," said Coughlan: "I'll make it up to time-and-a-half out of my own pocket, that's the best I can do."

The men formed into a huddle.

"How many extra shifts?" Jack asked after a while.

"Four or five," said Coughlan.

Jack nodded and rejoined his whispering colleagues.

"And we can definitely go home as soon as it's done, there'll be no little extras for us to do?" Jack, the delegated spokesman asked again.

"No, I guarantee that we'll be Blighty bound by next weekend."

The huddle continued.

"And the finishing bonus plus the extra you promised this morning, we still get that, right?"

"Yes the bonus we agreed." Coughlan hesitated: "Plus an extra tenner for everyone."

Jack returned to the huddle. After several moments he popped his head up again. "Make it an extra pony and we're in."

Coughlan shook his head: "I'd pay you twenty-five pounds if I could afford it. Twenty quid's the best I can do."

The men continued their deliberations although their final decision was a foregone conclusion. They all wanted to get home as quickly as possible, they all needed the money and they were all sick and tired of mooching around a sleepy, unfamiliar seaside town each evening eating strange foreign food and drinking unpleasantly cold and fizzy beer. If they worked through the night then they could persuade the Serbian cook to cater for them and they all preferred the sandwiches and the dubious stews that he served to the more exotic fare in the town.

Finally Jack spoke. "Okay Jim, you've got a deal, when do we start?"

"Tonight's as good as any. We'll finish up here about half five as usual, go and get something to eat, have a quiet drink and be back here for the night shift about seven. How's that sound?"

Ian Cassidy

It sounded bloody awful but they were being paid over the odds, so the men agreed.

"Right, I've got to nip off for an hour, so I'll leave you to it," said Coughlan. He was already calculating how many trips to Ramona's the difference between double-time and time-and-a-half would buy him.

The men did not even bother to complain and slowly drifted back to work.

At around one o'clock, when the heat in the hold became unbearable, they filed sweatily onto the deck.

As they sat around sipping sweet, milky tea courtesy of the Serbian cook, Jack observed: "If we cut out this extended dinner break, we'd have to do less on a night."

"No, it's like an oven down there at this time of day," said Bert. "It'd kill us to work down there in this heat. It'll be much cooler at night. That's why the locals have a siesta. Besides, I need a long lunch hour today cos I've got to go into the town."

"Why?" asked Jack.

"I need to buy a few things," replied Bert, without elaborating.

"I'll come with you," said Keith.

Bert hesitated but finally agreed, welcoming the company. He downed his tea and got to his feet. "Come on, then," he said to Keith. The two men left the ship. Once on the quayside Bert began, "I'm going into Barcelona, it's only a few stops on the train, you don't mind do you, Keith?"

Keith did not but he asked, "What you going there for?"

Reluctantly Bert explained: "I need to find a proper chemist, my piles are playing me up something rotten and the haemorrhoid cream I got from the chemist in the town is fucking useless. He didn't speak a lot of English and the stuff he gave me could have been anything. It looked and smelt like wall tile adhesive and was about as much fucking use. So I've got to find a proper chemist."

"Right," said Keith, laughing at his work mate's predicament. "I'm up for the trip, it could be a giggle."

The two men set off in the direction of the railway station.

2.02.pm.
Berlin: Office of ObergruppenFührer
Ernst Kaltenbrunner. Gestapo Headquarters.

The Gestapo agent, looking surprisingly unthreatening without his sinister leather ankle length overcoat, knocked on the door of Kaltenbrunner's office.

"Enter!" bellowed the man within.

The agent approached his superior's desk and saluted.

"Yes, SturmbanFührer , what is it?"

"An interesting little report, Herr Oberst. It appears that the Reich Marshal has gone missing."

"What do you mean, missing?"

"It appears, Herr Oberst, that the Reich Marshal set off for Berchtesgaden but his aircraft never reached its destination."

"Surely this is not a matter for us. It's for the authorities on the ground. Pass it on to the Bavarian police. I suppose you had better inform Lufftwaffe Headquarters, so they can mount an aerial search."

"Yes, of course, Herr Oberst, but the interesting thing is that there was no reason for the Reich Marshal to visit Berchtesgaden. The Führer is not in residence; he is in France."

"Yes I am aware of that." Kaltenbrunner pondered. "Perhaps your informant made an error. Perhaps Goering has gone off on a jaunt to his country house. His passion for hunting, fishing and shooting is well documented."

"My informant is adamant that the Reich Marshal left instructions that he could be contacted at Berchtesgaden not Karinhall."

"And who is your informant?"

"A junior secretary at the air ministry and that is another thing, the Reich Marshal's regular private secretary, Major Soellner, has not been seen for almost a fortnight."

"Soellner?" asked Kaltenbrunner. "Don't we have a file on him?"

"Yes, Herr Oberst, he is suspected of getting up to very questionable things with a veteran of the Russian front."

"Well, that probably explains that then, these pansies are notoriously unreliable."

"If you think so, Herr Oberst."

"Yes. I don't think we need overly concern ourselves but keep an eye on the situation and keep me informed of any developments. Keep me informed personally SturmbanFührer, GruppenFührer Müller is very busy at present. There is no need to bother him with this." Herr Müller is getting a little too big for his boots. Kaltenbrunner mused, he may be head of the Gestapo but I am the Head of Reich Security. It's time I showed the GruppenFührer who's boss.

"Very well, Herr Oberst."

"Just one more thing Major, was Goering piloting the aircraft personally?"

"Yes, Herr Oberst, the flight plan filed at Tempelhof lists just the Reich Marshal as pilot and two passengers."

"Passengers?" asked Kaltenbrunner.

"I understand them to be the Reich Marshal's wife and daughter, Herr Oberst."

"Well, it will be tragic if the woman and little girl are lost as well but it further reinforces my belief that your informant is mistaken. Why would Goering take his family on a business trip to Berchtesgaden?"

"Perhaps the Führer invited the women as company for Fraulein Braun."

"Leaving aside the charming company that the Goerings make, the Führer isn't there to receive them, you dolt, and dearest Eva is currently…" Kaltenbrunner stopped short. The man in front of him did not need to know what their leader's mistress got up to in her free moments. *Caesar's Wife*. he said to himself before continuing: "Fraulein Braun is not in residence at the Eagle's Nest either. Goering must have gone on a family break to Karinhall."

"It would appear so, Herr Oberst" admitted the adjutant reluctantly.

"You'd better pass it to the police in both districts and inform the Lufftwaffe. They will have reports of any activity by the Allied air forces in the areas."

"Very well, Herr Oberst."

"That will be all, Major." said Kaltenbrunner, dismissing the man. Alone in his office, Kaltenbrunner sat back and gave the situation some thought. He could not help smiling at the irony, the fat bastard forever claimed to be the best pilot in the Reich and he had gotten lost on a clear July day. But even the best pilot in the Reich would be no match for a Spitfire when he was at the controls of an unarmed civilian aircraft. Serves the arrogant fool right, the Allies have mastery of the skies although Goering would never admit it.

Kaltenbrunner rang through to his secretary and ordered a pot of coffee. While he waited he turned his thoughts to the vacancy that had possibly arisen. Should he throw his hat in the ring? The possibility of promotion to Reich Marshal appealed to him, he was a little bored with his duties as a glorified policeman. Then again the responsibilities that accompanied such a position were onerous and not a little risky. He decided to monitor the situation closely before showing his hand and impatiently called again for his mid-afternoon coffee.

2.25pm.
Whitehall. MI6.

"Yes, Harrison, what is it?" asked the Section Commander.

"That matter I raised with you some weeks ago, Sir, re the Anglo-Irish paperhanger."

"Come again, Harrison?" interrupted the section commander, "I don't follow you." The Section Commander had got his own way this lunchtime. He and his opposite number in SIS had partaken of the fare at Boodles, so a feeling of deep satisfaction was affecting his powers of recall.

"You remember, Sir, the suspected Nazi sleeper who made an irregular journey to Birmingham to meet with a local house painter."

"Yes I remember now, Harrison, what of it?"

"Well, very soon after the meeting was concluded, the man made a trip to Ulster."

"Is that unusual, Harrison? If the man is Anglo-Irish then the old country's probably chock full of his relatives."

"Well he took a party of his employees with him and our information further suggests that he has very few family contacts in Ulster but a great many business ones."

"There you are then; he was going over there to work."

"Perhaps Sir, but he seems to have disappeared. Our man in Belfast kept him under surveillance but the target and his employees gave our man the slip and skipped over the border into the South. We picked him up again in Dublin and tried to make contact but without success and then they went missing again."

"Does he have business contacts over there?"

"Possibly, Sir, but none we've managed to track down as yet."

"Well that is odd, Harrison. Surely the Nazis have stopped funding the IRA. I mean what would be the point at this late stage in the war?"

"That's what I thought, Sir, and there's another thing. We discovered that the target did some work for the German authorities over here before the war."

"Really, do go on."

"Yes, Sir, it appears that in 193 he carried out a large contract for the German Embassy, refurbishing Von Ribbentrop's country house in Kent."

"Well from what you've told me, it's certainly worth looking into a bit more detail. But Harrison, don't waste too much time on it. I mean the man is probably just working in the Republic without permission to avoid paying tax and excise duties. And I wouldn't worry about having trouble tracking him down, it's such a backward place once you leave Dublin it's like travelling through Darkest Africa."

"Very good, Sir."

"Keep me informed, Harrison. Good day."

Harrison left the office.

3.02pm.
Barcelona. Just off Las Ramblas.

Bert walked gingerly from the Barcelona chemist's clutching a brown paper parcel containing the much needed ointment that he and Keith had, with a mixture of hand signal, broken Spanish and frequent recourse to Black Country slang, finally managed to purchase from a somewhat baffled Catalan pharmacist.

Keith could barely contain his amusement at his colleague's anguished gait: "Come on you old git." He began: "Siesta time's almost over and I've had nothing to eat yet." He smiled as he chivvied his work mate along.

"We'll get a sandwich in here then," said Bert stopping at the first bar they came to. "I need to pay a call anyway."

Inside the taverna, Bert made straight for the lavatory whilst Keith went to the bar and adopted his now foolproof method of ordering. He looked around at the other diners and selected a dish that looked palatable and then pointed vigorously at it, shouting loudly, "I'll have one of them." With a beer in hand and the possibility of food arriving at some point, he adjourned to a table and awaited Bert.

Bert placed his package on the sink in the unspeakable washroom and carefully unwrapped it. He opened the zinc tube and took a sniff. "Bloody tile adhesive again." He said to himself and contemplated the brutal looking applicator. He screwed the long pointed applicator on to the tube and reluctantly entered the cubicle. He closed the door behind him.

Keith would later swear that he could hear Bert's screams outside in the crowded bar.

Several minutes later, after a very unpleasant time in the cubicle and an interminable, halting, pants filled progression across the room a red faced Bert joined his work mate, who was happily tucking into some sort of toasted sandwich, the name of which he would never know.

Bert took an eternity to sit down.

"You want one of these? I can recommend it." said Keith in between guffaws.

"I'll just have a beer," gasped Bert. Keith went into his familiar routine with the barman, waving his glass in the air and raising a victory sign to indicate two were required.

"Can you get me a brandy as well?" asked Bert. "My ring piece is on fire."

"I don't know a signal for brandy. I'll have to go up to the bar and point."

"You definitely will have to go. It would take me half an hour to get there and back." said Bert, fidgeting.

Laughing good naturedly Keith went to the bar.

He returned to the table to find Bert on his feet: "What's up?" He asked placing the drinks down.

"Drink up," said Bert. "We're leaving."

"Why? I've still got half a sandwich left."

"Bring it with you; we've got something to do. Look," he said, pointing out the window.

"What do you think he's up to?" asked Keith as he recognised Konrad aimlessly window shopping on the other side of the street."

"I haven't got a clue but I think we ought to follow him, he might be meeting his boss and we can really find out who's paying our wages."

The two men guzzled their drinks and Keith stuffed the half-eaten sandwich in his pocket before leaving some crumpled notes on the counter.

They left the bar and burst on the street, Keith set off at a trot but Bert pulled him back: "What do you think you're doing?" he whispered for no apparent reason. "You can't follow a man like that, be cool and try and be inconspicuous."

"What do you know about following people, Coughlan said you were in the pay corps not the Secret Service."

"I still saw some action," said Bert creeping stealthily along the street.

"Well even if you did, you wouldn't have learnt how to follow a man, all you'd have done was wallow around in a trench."

"Just shut the fuck up and do what I do. We already stand out like sore thumbs in these overalls as it is, so we'll need to be very bloody slippery."

Bert commenced a seemingly disinterested saunter down the street and Keith followed, aping his movements. They kept a close eye on the slow-moving Konrad on the other side of the street. As they passed a newspaper stand, Keith tapped Bert on the shoulder and pointed. Bert immediately recognised the value of such a prop. The two men stopped and went into the familiar mime they customarily adopted when effecting any purchase in Spain. The confused newsagent offered them a range of wares, including cigarettes, a Nationalist Pamphlet and a rather racy Mediterranean version of Health & Efficiency before the sight of

The **Unsinkable Herr Goering**

Konrad's disappearing back shook Bert back to reality. He plonked down a handful of coins and snatched up a daily, dragging Keith along with him: "Come on, you prat, we're losing him."

Peering over the top of the newspaper, which they had cunningly divided into two, the two men followed Konrad through the back streets of Barcelona. They concealed themselves in doorways and peeped around corners and more by luck than judgement they avoided Konrad's notice but not the notice of many bemused Catalans, who were treated to the spectacle of two scruffy pre-Beckett clowns pratfalling along the side streets.

Konrad sauntered through the sun baked city streets with time on his hands. He had left the Captain at the chandler's negotiating the purchase of a marine compass and gone to the railway station to collect the items they expected on the Perpignan train but his journey had been wasted as he had been informed that the train would be delayed for several hours at least by Allied activity in the area. Konrad suspected that the Captain and the chandler would engage in particularly protracted negotiations. The rum had already been resorted to before he left on his errand to the railway station and so he went in search of a means of killing time while he awaited the delayed train. He hoped that Spitzweg could be trusted to stay out of trouble because there was a place he very much wanted to visit. With the arrival of Goering who knew when he would get another chance.

Konrad meandered through the back streets until he came to the German run bar he had chanced upon on a previous visit. He had an itch and could think of no better way of killing time than scratching it. But first he wanted information about the situation in France and he felt best able to obtain that information using his mother tongue. Also he needed to confirm the sketchy directions he had to the place where he hoped his itch would be scratched.

Bert and Keith positioned themselves in an alcove across the street. They watched Konrad enter the bar and studied its exterior. To a veteran of the First World War, like Bert, the heavily carved Black Forest oak woodwork and predominantly red, gold and black paintwork could mean only one thing.

Ian Cassidy

"That's a bloody German bar," he ejaculated from behind his newspaper. "I told you he was a bloody Jerry."

Keith was having a little difficulty keeping up both mentally and physically. Whether it was the unexpectedly efficacious haemorrhoid ointment or just the Adrenalin rush of the chase, Keith did not know, but he was finding it increasingly difficult to keep up with the ageing jack-of-all-trades now that his rectally-challenged gait was a thing of the past. He cursed his penchant for Capstan Full Strength, or worse still, the foul smelling Ducados he had developed a taste for since his arrival in Spain. He tried to make sense of the situation.

"How do we know that?" he asked haltingly.

"That's a German bar, I tell you." said Bert emphatically. "He must be a Jerry, why else would he be using it?"

Keith hesitated. "There could be hundreds of reasons for him going in there. He could just be thirsty or he needs a shit." Keith smiled mischievously: "Or his piles could be playing him up."

"Bollocks." Bert smiled back. "Alright, we'll wait here until he comes out and see where he goes next."

The two painters waited in the alcove squabbling over their tatty newspaper screen, Bert chugging on his malodorous pipe and Keith chain-smoking strong Spanish cigarettes. Both watched and fidgeted. Keith frequently and anxiously looked at his watch. "What about the others," he worried: "They'll miss us, especially now it's become a rush job."

"They won't mind," replied Bert. "In fact they'll thank us if we get to bottom of this."

Keith reluctantly agreed and returned to his vigil.

Over an hour passed before Konrad emerged with just the hint of a spring in his step. Extracting the information he required had needed a lot of tact but finally he gained the directions he wanted and from the most unlikely source. *Appearances can be deceptive,* he said to himself as his informant rejoined his wife at their table. Once again Konrad had time to kill as the venue to which he had been directed was currently joining in the almost universal siesta. So began another passage of aimless wondering about the streets of the Catalan capital.

Oblivious to the shadowing painters at his rear, Konrad made his way once again to the railway station and, with fingers crossed, renewed his enquiries about the estimated time of arrival of the Perpignan express. He received glad tidings for himself and his planned afternoon's diversions but bad news about the items coming from Marseilles, as the train was now not expected until the evening, perhaps even later. He did not notice the sweating Englishmen with flat caps pulled low straining to overhear his conversation with the guard. Behind the newspaper Keith whispered to Bert, "Did he just say Purplenan?"

"Yeah he asked about the Perpignan train."

"Where's Purplenan then?"

"In France."

"Well he can't be a Jerry can he, there's no Jerries left in France."

"They've still got a bit of it. We'll just have to keep following him."

Konrad thanked the guard and checking his watch. He smiled that his enjoyment was drawing ever nearer. He left the station and headed for the dingiest of Barcelona's back streets.

Bert and Keith, not to be confused with Vladimir and Estragon, were still closely on his tail.

4.06pm.
Berlin: Office of ObergruppenFührer
Ernst Kaltenbrunner. Gestapo Headquarters.

Kaltenbrunner nodded and the adjutant began his report. "I have received no reports from the Bavarian Police or the Lufftwaffe, Herr Oberst, but my own sources have provided me with an unconfirmed report that an aircraft similar to that of the Reich Marshal's landed and refuelled in Geneva. Details are sketchy, Herr Oberst, but a man matching the Reich Marshal's description was at the controls, although the gentleman seems to have been wearing civilian clothing."

"Not like our Hermann to discard his beloved regalia." Kaltenbrunner commented. "If it was Goering then I expect he just had a little private business to conduct with his Swiss bankers." *God knows there's some business of my own I must attend to, as soon as possible*, Kaltenbrunner said to himself.

"But Herr Oberst, surely such transactions would not lead to such a prolonged absence?"

"Well, perhaps he treated Emmy to an evening sampling the delights of Geneva. He'll show up in the morning, mark my words. In the meantime, get back to your man in Geneva and tell him to do a little more digging."

"As you wish, Herr Oberst." The adjutant saluted and left the office.

4.25pm.
Barcelona.

Bert and Keith watched as Konrad took a furtive glance around him before heading through the railings towards the basement door. He quickly gained admittance to the illicit drinking den and was gone from sight.

"What sort of place is that?" Asked Keith

"I've got a pretty fair idea," said Bert: "And I think we'd better follow him inside."

"But he might see us."

"No," said Bert. "If that place is what I think it is, then it will be very dark inside. He won't see us and we'll be able to get close to him and see who he meets."

Keith was becoming confused again: "Will you tell me what sort of place it is?" he pleaded.

"It's a whorehouse."

"How do you know what the inside of a whorehouse looks like?"

"During the last war I spent some time in Paris and I saw some sights in the Pigalle. Just saw, mind, I didn't do anything."

"I believe you," said Keith, "although thousands wouldn't."

"We'll be safer inside anyhow," said Bert, indicating their sordid surroundings. "All we do out here is attract streetwalkers and drunks."

The prospect of attracting a streetwalker did not seem too bad to Keith; nevertheless, he followed his colleague towards the basement door.

Bert pushed open the peeling bar door. Blinking in the near darkness, the two men tried to make their way to the bar. Bert ordered "Dos cervesas." That much Spanish he had picked up and he did not want

Keith's hackneyed dumbshow drawing attention at the bar. He bundled Keith to an out of the way table and looked about him.

The basement room was surprisingly large, with a vaulted ceiling and medieval style wrought iron chandeliers and wall lights. ***Obviously an old wine cellar***, Bert said to himself. He strained his eyes in the gloom trying to locate Konrad.

The bar was the only bright spot in the room, illuminated from behind by a large fish tank, filled with vividly coloured artificial plants and rocks but no fish. Bert continued looking about the room. The dance floor was empty, but then it was still early. Perhaps things livened up later. The few tables were empty. Bert did manage to pick out huddled figures in some of the shaded banquettes but he could not see Konrad.

"Not many women for a whorehouse!" Keith announced loudly.

"Keep your voice down!" Bert whispered, buying time; he too had noticed the dearth of women and he was desperately trying to think of a way of revealing the bar's true nature to Keith without causing uproar.

"There's no women here at all," Keith whispered.

"It's early yet," said Bert. "There'll be more in later." He pointed to a large woman sauntering across the room. "Here's a little sweetie pie now."

"Sweetie pie," choked Keith. "Look at the size of her, she's got shoulders like a hod carrier."

Bert sighed. "Keith, I think there's something you ought to know. Well, you know we thought Manuel was a bit funny."

Keith nodded and Bert continued, "Prepare yourself for a shock. This might be a queer's bar."

Keith spat his beer across the table. "Let's get the fuck out of here," he said, his panicky homophobia instantly taking over.

"We'll be alright and we've got to find out more about Manuel."

"But he won't be meeting his boss in here."

"You never know, a place like this is as good a place as anywhere for a secret meeting. Look, we'll have another drink and play it by ear."

With frightened eyes flicking staccato around the room, Keith sank down in his chair. "Don't look now," he wailed as the huge Spanish transvestite approached their table. Despite his advanced years and Pigalle experiences even Bert gulped as he looked at the looming, cross-dressed, construction worker, with his tight satin skirt, fishnet stockings, enormous calloused feet crushed into wedge sandals and five o'clock shadow.

The man smiled at the shrinking Keith and launched into a flowery Spanish address, the words of which were incomprehensible to the two men, although they were both aware of their implications.

Bert thought fast. He moved closer to Keith and grabbed his hand. Accompanied by many hand signals he cried, "We're together." Keith joined in, gesticulating wildly with his free hand until the man got the hint. As the disappointed transvestite hitched up his false breasts and left, Keith and Bert remained transfixed at their table, their horny navvies' hands still locked together.

They were still in the same position when several minutes later the elegant figure of Konrad returned to the bar. On this occasion he was accompanied by a heavily made-up teenage boy dressed in thick black stockings and frilly French panties.

The sight shocked the watching painters from their panicked reverie.

"Fuck me!" said Keith.

Bert winced. "I don't like it either," he announced, his usual broad-mindedness deserting him.

"Let's wait outside," Keith pleaded. "He's not meeting anyone in here, he's just a randy brown hatter."

"Yeah, why not," said Bert. "There's only one door."

The two men paid for their drinks and slipped out of the bar to blinkingly take up position in the sunlit Barcelona street.

They sat sweating behind their newspaper parts on the kerbstone for twenty minutes before Konrad appeared with the now more discreetly dressed boy at his side. Konrad chatted animatedly to the boy as the painters listened.

"Listen to them," said Bert. "They're speaking German, I knew it, he's a Kraut."

"Could be," agreed Keith, but then he had a rare moment of inspiration. "But he speaks very good English and very good Portuguese, perhaps he can speak lots of languages."

"He's a Jerry I tell you," said Bert and set off in pursuit of Konrad and his catamite.

Keith had his second moment of inspiration. He pulled Bert back. "There's no point following him anymore today. I really don't want to know what they're going to be getting up to. Let's get back and tell the lads."

"Yeah you're right," said Bert. "I tell you what, I'll throw a sickie tomorrow and follow him again. I'm determined to get to the bottom of this."

Keith nodded and the two men set off in the direction of the railway station.

5.47pm.
Berlin: Office of ObergruppenFührer
Ernst Kaltenbrunner. Gestapo Headquarters.

The adjutant stopped Kaltenbrunner just as he was leaving his office for the day. The Head of Reich Security grumbled back to his desk and motioned to the aide to begin.

"I've just received a further report from my contact in Geneva, Herr Oberst. He is by now fairly certain that it was the Reich Marshal. It seems the Reich Marshal did not leave the environs of Geneva Airport. He merely dealt with immigration and then had his aircraft refuelled. He paid the broker an inflated sum for the fuel and informed Geneva Air Traffic Control that he was bound for Cologne."

"Well, we can be sure he was lying, his aircraft would have reached Cologne long ago," Kaltenbrunner interjected, "unless he was brought down en route."

"Information is sketchy, Herr Oberst, but there is as yet no evidence of a light aircraft crash landing anywhere between Geneva and Cologne."

"So he was headed elsewhere?"

"It would appear highly likely, Herr Oberst."

"Any ideas?"

"A full tank of fuel would leave many destinations open to him, Herr Oberst."

"England?" asked Kaltenbrunner.

"You don't think he's attempting to do a Rudolf?"

"Why not?" snapped Kaltenbrunner.

"I think it unlikely, Herr Oberst. The Reich Marshal's aircraft does not have the range to travel from Geneva to England without refuelling and we have no reports of such a stop anywhere in France."

"Perhaps not but he could reach Normandy on a full tank."

"Theoretically, but I think not, Herr Oberst, we would have heard if he was in the hands of the Allies. That man Montgomery could not resist lauding such a high profile capture."

"The same is true of that egomaniac Patton in the south," Kaltenbrunner agreed. "So you believe he is headed elsewhere?"

"Yes, Herr Oberst, to North Africa or perhaps the Middle East."

"Well you had better find out where he is and why he's gone there and do it now, Major. I shall be at the Ministry of Propaganda until about 10pm. After that you can contact me at home." So saying, Kaltenbrunner dismissed the adjutant.

5.58pm.
Sitges Harbour.

"Where the fuck you been?" Maurice announced as he spied his two errant colleagues. Keith and Bert strolled over to their work mate. Maurice was uncharacteristically leaving the ship later than the other men due to his brother mischievously mixing an excessive amount of wallpaper paste that needed to be used up before the shift ended.

"Have we got a story to tell you," said Bert.

"Tell me on the way to the digs," Maurice said, striding up the dock. "I want some dinner and a couple of pints before the bloody night shift starts."

Keith and Bert ran after him. "Slow down," panted Keith. "You'll want to hear this. It's a real cracker."

"It better be," said Maurice. "Coughlan's going fucking potty about you having the afternoon off."

"Don't talk to me about Coughlan. He's pulled some stunts over the years but this takes the biscuit. He's really dropped us in it this time."

Maurice stopped short. "Why?"

"It's Manuel, he's not Manuel at all, he's a fucking Kraut. We overheard him talking German."

"You sure?"

"I am," said Bert. "Keith's not so sure."

"We'd better tell the others and see what they say. Come on," said Maurice, quickening his pace once more.

8.47pm.
Berlin, Wilhelmsplatz, Ministry of Propaganda.

The white-coated orderly showed Kaltenbrunner into an unpopulated office: "Your call has been put through to that telephone, Herr ObergruppenFührer."

Kaltenbrunner returned the man's salute and waited for him to leave before picking up the receiver.

"Kaltenbrunner," he barked into the mouthpiece.

"SturmbanFührer Haller here, Herr Oberst. I have a further report from Geneva."

"Get on with it, man."

"Reports are once again sketchy, Herr Oberst, Swiss radar is somewhat primitive; compared to ours it is little better than a man with a pair of binoculars."

"I can believe that," interrupted Kaltenbrunner: "I'm paraphrasing here but you'll be familiar with the words: what have six hundred years of peace and democracy produced in Switzerland? Whilst in these few troubled years the German Reich has produced such staggering technological advances."

Yes, thought Haller, *we've produced ballistic missiles, a primitive hydrogen bomb and countless widows and orphans.* He kept it to himself and agreed with his superior. "Yes, they have come up with nothing, not even the cuckoo clock, which I believe was a German innovation."

"Your report, Major."

"Yes, Herr Oberst, when the Reich Marshal's aircraft passed out of range of Swiss radar, it appeared to be headed towards Southern France."

"Southern France?" queried Kaltenbrunner. "But the Allies are there."

"I think we must assume that he planned to over fly the war zone."

"So you assume he is heading west?"

"Yes, Herr Oberst."

"To Spain?"

"Yes, Herr Oberst."

"How far into Spain would his fuel take him?"

"Quite a distance, Herr Oberst, but the most likely destination would be Barcelona."

"Right, get on to our man in Barcelona and tell him to find out if Goering's plane has landed there."

"I have already contacted him, Herr Oberst. I am currently awaiting his report."

"Pass it on to me as soon as you get it. Goodnight, Major." Kaltenbrunner replaced the receiver. With a worried expression, he rejoined the babbling freeloaders at their guzzling in the Propaganda Ministry's lobby.

6.24pm.
Sitges. A hotel room.

Maurice, Bert and Keith waited for their three colleagues in one of the hired rooms. The other three awkwardly took their leave of their employer. With much belching and grumbling about their truncated evening meal, they took their seats haphazardly on the unmade beds.

Bert related the day's events and then threw the matter open to the floor. "What we gonna do?" he challenged.

Ivor was first to respond. "Get the fuck out of here PDQ." The memory of parcels of prison excrement came rushing back to him.

"Hold on a minute," said Don. "We can't afford to get home from here."

"True," agreed Jack. "Let's not be hasty. What we need to do is find out for certain that we're working for the Nazis."

"I'm convinced that we are," said Bert: "But why don't I throw a sickie tomorrow and follow Manuel or whatever his name really is and see if he makes contact with anyone."

"That's a good idea," said Jack: "But you can't do it. JC will notice if you miss another day. The wiring's miles behind as it is."

"Get Keith to do it then," suggested Bert.

The men looked at Keith and although he was slightly put out that his skills were considered superfluous, he readily agreed.

"Right," said Jack: "That's agreed then and lads, not a word to Coughlan, we don't know how deeply he's involved."

The men agreed. Bert spoke, "I'm sorry lads but if we are going to properly convince Coughlan that we're not suspicious, we're gonna have to go to work as normal tonight." Bert smiled weakly as he got up and led the men to work.

"What's fucking normal about working two shifts a day?" grumbled Maurice as he followed reluctantly.

10.26pm.
Berlin. Home of ObergruppenFührer
Ernst Kaltenbrunner.

The manservant coughed nervously in front of the armchair in which his master was sleeping. He coughed again and tapped Kaltenbrunner lightly on the shoulder.

"There is a call for you, Herr ObergruppenFührer," he whispered.

Kaltenbrunner rubbed his eyes and snapped his fingers in the direction of the telephone. "Pass it here, man, and bring me some brandy," he snapped. Maybe it would have been better to let Müller handle this. He sulked as he waited for the retainer to leave the room.

As the manservant pulled the ornate Werner Werkstatte double doors to, Kaltenbrunner croaked into the receiver: "Yes, who is it?"

"SturmbanFührer Haller here, Herr Oberst. I have that report you wanted from Barcelona."

"Good, good, major. Let me hear it."

"Our man can find no trace of Goering's aircraft at the main airport or any record of it landing there."

Kaltenbrunner swore. "So the trail has gone cold?"

"Not necessarily, Herr Oberst. While our man has come up with nothing at the airport, he has made an interesting discovery in the city itself. He frequents a little back street bar that is German owned and attracts a lot of German customers."

"Yes," Kaltenbrunner interrupted impatiently.

"While he was in the bar yesterday afternoon, he noticed a man, a German, who resembled Soellner."

"Really, that is interesting. Soellner goes on ahead to clear the way and Goering follows. You had better confirm the sighting immediately. Telex our man an up-to-date photograph of Soellner."

"Immediately, Herr Oberst."

"In meantime Major, I think you had better prepare yourself for a trip to Barcelona. The fat traitor cannot be allowed to escape."

"Very well, Herr Oberst."

"Call me as soon as you have confirmation about Soellner. Good night, Major." Kaltenbrunner hung up.

10.49.pm.
Sitges Harbour.

The six skilled workmen and their less skilled employer, who had surprisingly worked alongside them without once sneaking off since they had commenced the night shift, were disturbed at their labour by the arrival of the Serbian cook with a tray full of his curious one-pot tea. The welcome hiatus caused those men who wore them to look at their watches. A unanimous but unspoken thought reached them all simultaneously: *Last orders!* Coming from Staffordshire, the men were more fortunate than their "townie" peers. Their local public houses stayed open until eleven o'clock so that thirsty farm workers could get a much-needed pint or two after long hours of toil at the harvest.

"We'll just make it. What do you say Jim?" Jack asked his boss.

Coughlan looked at the chipped enamel mugs of greasy liquid that the Serbian cook was handing around and agreed with indecent haste. He threw down his paintbrush and without a word he made his way out of the hold, a crocodile of thirsty painters following behind.

The seven men stopped at the first bar they came to on the quayside and pushed their way inside. They were surprised to find that there was no nervous clock-watching crush at the bar but, with a collective sigh of relief, they ringed the bar and watched as Coughlan ordered thirty-five pints of beer.

The sleepy Spanish bar owner was a little surprised at so large an order but he set about the task regardless. The first seven beers were dispatched before he had scarcely begun. Intrigued, he carried on pouring and his customers continued throwing the beers down their necks. Twenty-one pints into the order, the barman realised what was going on.

"English?" he asked.

Coughlan nodded. The barman proceeded, with great difficulty, to explain Spain's more liberal licensing laws.

"I don't close until you go home." This was music to the men's ears and with many a windy smile they began to drink at a more leisurely pace.

After what he judged to be a generous period for a mid-shift break, Coughlan ordered them all back to work and, accompanied by smiles and handshakes from the bar owner whose takings had been unexpectedly boosted, they trudged back towards the ship.

It was only when they got back into the hold and were once more taking up their tools that they noticed that Coughlan had not joined them for the remainder of the night shift.

"The dirty fucker's gone off shagging again," observed Maurice. As usual, he was right.

11.31pm.
Sitges. A Farmhouse in the hills above.

Goering shifted uneasily in the rickety peasant armchair. He was worrying about just what he was sitting on. The lumpy, antique horsehair seemed to him to be a fertile breeding ground for fleas and other unwelcome bugs.

He grumbled his massive buttocks from side to side and tried close his ears to the true reason for his discomfort. The sound of his daughter's eager, childish footsteps could be heard in the corridor. The little girl was coming for a goodnight kiss, which in other circumstances would have been delightful to the recently retired Nazi statesman. Tonight he knew that his daughter's embraces would be accompanied by a lot of awkward questions.

Edda Goering careered through the door of the Spanish sitting room with her mother, slightly unsteadily, following on behind. She skipped into her father's ample lap and began at once "Papa, before I go to my room, please tell me what we are doing here?"

"We've come here for a sailing holiday," Goering lied.

"But we can sail in Germany."

"Yes but it will be nicer here. The weather is warmer and the sea is so much calmer. You must admit it is lovely to play in this beautiful warm sun."

"Yes, Papa." The little girl nodded uncertainly.

"And you are enjoying yourself, aren't you? We have a lovely rustic farm and it's so much quieter than Berlin."

"Oh, yes, Papa, but I miss Germany."

"Of course you do. We will be back there very soon," Goering said, avoiding eye contact with his wife. He continued, "Now what have you done today?"

"Mama and I walked in the hills and we picked some lovely flowers."

"That's grand," said the Reich Marshal, sitting back in his chair "Now it's very late and I want to talk to your Mama, so run along and we will think of something for you to do tomorrow." Goering kissed his daughter on the cheek and the little girl left.

"I'll come and tuck you in," Emmy Goering called after her daughter, her voice slightly thick with Spanish cooking sherry.

Alone with his wife, Goering took an ambitious slug from his glass of brandy and winced as the rough liquid sent flames rushing up his oesophagus. He rubbed his sternum and commented: "I will send Soellner to get me some milk of magnesia, if the wretched man ever returns from Barcelona."

His wife said nothing. Reluctantly, Goering got up to refill his glass. As he poured the noxious, deep brown liquid from the bottle, he noticed that it was almost empty. *I'm drinking too much,* he said to himself and retook his chair.

"Is everything alright?" he asked his wife.

"Yes, Hermann," she replied distractedly. "In the circumstance things are going fine."

"Good, good." said Goering, keen not to prolong the conversation.

The Unsinkable Herr Goering

He stubbed out his cigar and, steeling himself against the acid burn, he drained his brandy glass.

"Are you coming to bed, Edda dear?" he asked as he struggled from his chair.

"In a moment," she replied. Goering left her sitting motionless on the other rickety peasant chair. Edda Goering followed her husband about fifteen minutes later, just after she drained the brandy bottle.

fourteen
17th August, 1944

2.54am. **Berlin. Home of ObergruppenFührer Ernst Kaltenbrunner.** The manservant gingerly pushed Kaltenbrunner's shoulder. "Herr ObergruppenFührer," he whispered. "That call you were expecting."

The manservant tried again and eventually his master coughed his way to consciousness. He took the receiver from the servant's outstretched hand and motioned for the man to refill his bedside pitcher of water.

"Kaltenbrunner," he croaked.

"Herr Oberst, Haller here. Good news, our man is convinced it is Soellner and he is sure that he is not alone. He has been seen with another man who our man believes is a naval officer, with a beard and heavy coat and sweater."

"That doesn't sound like Goering" snapped Kaltenbrunner.

"No, Herr Oberst, I do not believe it was the Reich Marshall, even heavily disguised."

"There's no way you could disguise his enormous gut," spat Kaltenbrunner.

Haller laughed hollowly and continued, "Our man followed them to the railway station and observed them buy two single tickets to Sitges."

"Where the hell's that?"

"It's a fishing port in the Greater Barcelona area."

"So you think Goering plans to escape by sea."

"It is a distinct possibility, Herr Oberst. Our man did some further snooping and it seems that Soellner has been buying building materials and having them delivered to the port."

"So it appears that Soellner is preparing a vessel for a journey. This naval man is going to do the steering and the principle passenger is to be Goering. That sound plausible to you?" asked Kaltenbrunner.

"That is my theory, Herr Oberst."

"We'll have to test your theory, Major. Get to Spain as soon as you can. If you leave immediately you should be able to dodge the Allied advance."

"Of course, Herr Oberst."

"And take Gunther with you. He should be just the man if things get a little rough."

"Gunther!" said Haller panicking at the thought of such a long trip with one of the Gestapo's more bloodthirsty operatives.

"Yes. You may need him. We don't know the strength of Goering's contingent. I would have suggested Skorzeny but he's otherwise engaged so Gunther will have to do."

"We'll leave at dawn, Herr Oberst."

"Excellent. And Haller, don't foul this up. Goering must be returned to Berlin at all costs."

"Alive?" asked the major.

"If possible, but I leave that to Gunther's discretion."

That's as good as signing his death warrant, thought Haller. "What if the Allies should have cut off Spain by the time our task is completed?" he asked instead.

"Leave that with me. I'll speak to Doenitz, he must have a U-Boat that is still operational. We will arrange for you to be picked up off the Spanish coast and if the fat bastard won't fit through the submarine's hatch then tow his traitorous carcass behind you."

"Very well, Herr Oberst, I'll make contact through our consulate in Barcelona."

"Haller, you have my permission to sign the Mercedes 600K from the motor pool. I had been saving her for myself but you need to make great haste and it has a top speed of 190 kilometres per hour."

"Really, Herr Oberst, it seems a shame to leave such a fine machine to rot in a Spanish fishing village. I understand that there are only twelve such beauties in the whole of the Fatherland."

"There is no other way. Goering must not be allowed to escape."

"Very well, Herr Oberst, I will report as soon as I am able."

"Yes, and I must inform the Führer," Kaltenbrunner said prissily. "Goodnight, Major." He replaced the receiver and belched loudly. The ersatz tit-bits from Goebbels' reception were sitting leadenly on his chest. He rang for his man and pulled the silken bed sheets around him. *I'll take something for this dyspepsia before I disturb the Führer,* he said to himself peevishly. *This would have been a job best left to Müller,* he grouched, *but think of the good it will do me when I bring that fat bastard home in chains. But what if I don't?* Reluctantly, he picked up the receiver.

3.02am.
Sitges Harbour.

Coughlan gave the order to down tools and the men filed from the ship into the cool Spanish night. They grumbled behind him through the quiet streets of Sitges. Coughlan had only joined them for the last hour of the night shift, being otherwise engaged at the brothel for the rest of the time. The men, on the other hand, had worked non-stop, copious tea breaks and the memorable beer break excepted, since seven-thirty.

The seven weary men came to a halt outside their darkened hotel and Coughlan produced the latch key that he had secured from the landlady at the beginning of their stay. He had intended to use it after late nights of horizontal activities with the local ladies of the night, not to gain entry after a night shift on the boat. But he was getting well paid. He fumbled in the darkness with the lock and eventually pushed the door open, trying to make as little noise as possible. The following men tried to do similar with disastrous results. They clumped and clodhopped through the lobby producing a frightening din. Coughlan's whispered admonishments went unheeded and all he could do was rush his employees to their rooms.

Before he retreated to the sanctuary of his own room, Coughlan whispered to his men, "Be down for breakfast at seven tomorrow, we'll have a bit of a lie in."

They whistled back and he hastily closed his door.

The Unsinkable Herr Goering

6.58am.
Barcelona. Seaman's Mission.

Konrad awoke with a start and tried to familiarise himself with his surroundings. Before his eyes had a chance to register anything, his nostrils were assaulted by a foul odour, a mixture of rotting fish, sweaty bodies and fetid breath. He lit a cigarette to try to mask the smell and gingerly sat up on the lumpy mattress that had been his bed for the night. Konrad looked about him. The dingy grey room was bare of all furniture except six rusty iron framed beds. Mercifully, four were unoccupied; his only companion in the room was the seaman who was to take charge of Goering's escape vessel.

He looked down at the mattress and decided not to spend a moment longer on the foul smelling, bug infested horsehair.

Konrad swung his legs to the floor and looked at the snoring seaman in the next bed. Herr Captain Richard Spitzweg, Iron Cross First Class, late of the Imperial German Navy, was sleeping soundly, reeking of rum and oblivious to his less than salubrious surroundings. If anything, he seemed to find them rather luxurious. Konrad hesitated before waking the formidable matelot and looked around for his shoes.

He found them where he had left them, on the captain's advice under the feet of the iron bedstead. The captain had recommended such an arrangement as it meant that any would-be thief would have to lift the bed and thus disturb the sleeper in order to carry out a successful act of larceny. Konrad gave a silent prayer of thanks for the Captain's long experience of Seamen's Missions, without which he would probably have been stripped down to his last possession in this unspeakable place.

Then again if he had not been with Spitzweg, he would not have been in such a godforsaken place at all. The Perpignan to Barcelona train, which bore the items that Spitzweg insisted upon before sailing, had not reached its destination until almost midnight, by which time all through trains from Barcelona had departed. Konrad had searched in vain for a taxi to convey them to Sitges. Finally they had been compelled to spend a terrible and terrifying night in this hellish place.

Konrad coughed and nervously prodded the great blond hulk in the next bed. Spitzweg was instantly awake. He blew his nose violently into his hand and wiping it on the heavily-stained blankets, he heaved his legs to floor.

"Good morning, Major. Did you sleep alright?"

"Not especially," mumbled Konrad. "And I think it would be wise if we dropped our military appellations for the time being. We don't know who is listening."

"As you wish, Soellner," smiled Spitzweg. "But I did a little checking before I turned in and I'm sure there isn't a German speaker in the building. Now I'm off for breakfast, they usually rustle up something quite palatable in these places. Coming?"

Konrad shuddered at the thought of the mouse-turd infested porridge or greasy slabs of Catalan hog that he was likely to be presented with in whatever passed for a dining room below but agreed anyway. He looked at the four empty beds and decided that braving the refectory was a safer option than being alone in the room, should anyone be sent to fill the vacant places.

He nodded and hurried after Spitzweg.

Once inside the slimy refectory, Spitzweg greeted the aged cook like an old friend and surprisingly in very passable Spanish. He took his plate of food and jostled his way onto a crammed table, where he was soon munching away with gusto and mixing it with the bleary eyed matelots at his side.

Konrad approached nervously, his enamel tray of lukewarm slop held rigidly at port. He took a seat at the edge of the table and pushed the grey comestibles around his plate.

Much to his relief, years at sea had taught Spitzweg to eat speedily. Before long he was on his feet, smacking his lips and bidding his new found friends a hearty farewell. He took a pipe from his pocket and filling it with the roughest of rough shag he strode towards the door.

Konrad followed gratefully and found his companion in a cloud of noxious smoke on the steps of the mission.

Without speaking, Spitzweg offered him his tobacco pouch. Konrad declined and suggested that if it was alright with the Captain he would settle their bill and they would head to the railway station.

Spitzweg agreed. After Konrad had gratefully handed over a few coins to the mission manager, the two men set off for the railway station.

Konrad led the way and tried to engage his charge in conversation. The man puffed away at his pipe and gave only monosyllabic replies. Konrad soon tired of this one-way traffic and was relieved when the railway station came into view.

Konrad presented the two single tickets he had purchased the day before and the two men boarded the train for the short journey to Sitges.

In the quiet of their first class carriage, Spitzweg stretched out with his filthy Wellingtons on the seat opposite. After re-igniting his offensive briar, he took out a small volume and began to read.

Konrad sat opposite, wincing through the smoke and trying to make out what was written on the spine of Spitzweg's book. He struggled to decipher the faded embossed gold lettering as he was anxious that the Captain did not notice his interest. Finally he made it out: "***Almansor.***" "***Heinrich Heine.***"

Konrad was a little taken aback and nervously asked, "How do you find the works of Herr Heine?"

"I find them the works of a truly great man," Replied Spitzweg. "And now that I am away from Germany I find that I am more comfortable reading them."

"Really, why's that?" asked Konrad, who had studied aeronautical engineering at Heidelberg and had subsequently limited his literary endeavours to those authors favoured by the Party thought police.

"Any man who can write: "Dort, wo man Bucher Verbrennt, Verbrennt man auch am ende menschen." cannot be overly popular with our leadership."

"I should think not. I remember his works were among the first on the bonfires in the thirties but that was extremism when the party was young. I have never heard the Führer express any deeply felt opinions about poetry. Art, yes, he has strong views on that."

"Some of us have never had the pleasure of a discussion on aesthetics with the Führer," Spitzweg said gruffly and returned to his reading.

Konrad pressed him again: "I am a little surprised Herr Captain, I would not have thought that long service on the high seas and a love of fine writing were natural bedfellows."

"You are tactfully suggesting that you think I am too rough-arsed to appreciate the finer things in life," Spitzweg smiled menacingly.

"Not at all, not at all," said Konrad defensively, struggling to extricate himself from the awkward situation that had been all of his own making.

Spitzweg did it for him. "Es bildet ein talent sich in der stille, Sich ein charakter in dem strom der welt."

Konrad smiled blankly.

"Goethe," Spitzweg explained and once again returned to his reading.

Konrad was happy that he did not have to pursue the discussion and looked out of the window for the remainder of the journey.

7.45am.
Sitges.

Keith perched on a low wall at the roadside opposite Konrad's hotel and waited. He struggled with a freshly bought Spanish newspaper and fought the urge to doze off.

He only had to endure the curious glances of sluggish Spanish artisans as they pushed past his swinging legs on their weary way to work for a few minutes before he was jolted back to full consciousness by the sound of an approaching taxi.

Shortly before eight o'clock, the roar of an antique diesel engine shook the quiet side street. Keith rubbed his eyes and watched as the ageing taxi-cab limped to a halt at the hotel steps. Two men climbed stiffly from its rear door.

Keith recognised the slimmer of the two as Konrad but the other man, the great hulk of a man in oilskins and turned-over Wellingtons was a stranger to him.

Keith sank down behind his newspaper and watched as Konrad paid off the taxi driver and went up the hotel steps.

He strained to listen to the two men as they exchanged words in the Hotel's entrance. He was not sure but they could have been speaking German. The plethora of different tongues that he had encountered over the last few weeks had by now formed a murky alphabet soup in his brain. It was getting too much for him so he went back to watching. He watched as Konrad left the oilskinned man on the hotel terrace and went inside. He studied the man, who he assumed to be a sailor, as he sat disinterestedly kicking his heels on the flimsy patio furniture. *A right hard bastard,* Keith said to himself. Even Ivor with all his very special talent

The Unsinkable Herr Goering

as a street fighter would be hard pressed to put that one away. Keith looked on nervously, worried that the man would notice the special attention he was receiving from across the street. *That type develops a sixth sense where things like this are concerned.* Keith said to himself. *And if he spots me, I don't fancy my chances.* He huddled behind the newspaper and limited his furtive glances hotel-wards.

A few minutes later, Konrad reappeared and called the other man to him. They hailed another taxi of similar vintage to the one that had deposited them at the hotel and slowly pulled away into the light Spanish rush hour.

Keith panicked He could not afford to hire the next taxi on the rank. He looked around. In the alleyway at his rear he spied a bicycle, a great rusty grey sit up and beg machine with primitive gears. Without giving it a second thought, Keith hopped aboard and pedalled frantically after the sluggish taxi.

He had little trouble keeping up. The bulky car was unsuited to Sitges's narrow back streets, although with his cap pulled down low as a precaution against Konrad recognising his unlikely pursuer, he struggled to avoid potholes and pedestrians.

The perilous journey continued with Keith frequently apologising in a broad Black Country accent as he dodged sleepy, school bound children and angry but bemused Spanish matrons as they commenced their daily chores.

Even on the outskirts of the town and in the hills above, Keith did not lose the taxi. Like the narrow back streets, the winding hillside roads were difficult for the cumbersome boat-like car to negotiate. With his stubby legs pumping ten to the dozen, Keith was able to maintain eye-contact with his quarry.

Keith was still pedalling furiously when, one hundred yards up ahead of him, the taxi slowed and turned right onto a dirt track. Keith stopped and mopped his brow. He watched as the taxi bounced over the unmade track. *What would Bert do in this situation?* he asked himself. It would be too dangerous to follow along the track, so he would have to go cross-country. He tossed the bicycle into the undergrowth and set off.

He guessed the car was heading to a farmhouse he could just see at the end of the track. He headed in the same direction, clambering through the thick locust trees that lined the highway and dropping down onto one of the farm's fallow fields.

Keeping low, he struck out across the scorched and dusty field, making slow progress. He had one awkward moment when he failed to realise that the approaching cloud of dust was the taxi returning after dropping off its fare. Just in time, he dived down into the brown reedy grass and covered his balding head as it passed.

Suitably warned about taking a slapdash approach to surveillance, he crawled the rest of way. After several long and dusty minutes he pulled himself up onto a ridge overlooking the farmhouse. He rubbed the red soil from his eyes and scanned the scene. There was no sign of life. The front door was closed and the windows were dark. Wearily he flopped down to the dry soil and crab-crawled around to the rear of the building.

From a vantage point behind an olive tree, he looked out at the rear lawns of the property. Konrad and the sailor were standing at a wrought iron table drinking lemonade, while a young girl and a very large man were playing tennis on a makeshift court. The large man seemed vaguely familiar so Keith crept closer.

From behind another olive tree, Keith watched as the large man called a halt to his game. He watched as the girl solemnly shook hands with her opponent and the large man patted her affectionately on the head. The man then marched across the lawn where he nodded to Konrad and shook hands with sailor.

With the large man now stationary, Keith was able to study him more closely.

He slammed back against the olive tree in shock. "Fuck me! It's Goering." He said aloud, "Fuck me, old Hermann himself."

Keith sat against the knotty bark of the tree and shook his head. "Fuck me!" he said again, this time more quietly. He mopped his brow to remove the new layer of sweat that had formed just in the last few seconds, superseding that already put in place by his cycling and creeping activities. "Fuck me!" he said again.

We're not working for any old gang of people smugglers; we're working for the big guns. "Fuck me!" he said aloud once more.

He got to his feet and slipping and sliding over the hard, dusty pathway he ran as fast as his short, hairy legs would carry him in the direction of his discarded bicycle. "Wait till the lads hear this," he said to himself as he struggled to pedal the slightly buckled bicycle along the steaming road back to town. "Fuck me!" he said yet again.

Sitges Harbour.
10.23am.

Keith crept up the gangplank and over the deck until he came to the lip of the hold. He peered over like some a balding but furry Chad with a Woodbine in the corner of its mouth and looked around for his employer.

Fortunately for Keith, Coughlan had left for a mid morning snack, toilet break and appointment in the town. Once Keith had satisfied himself that this indeed was the case, he stomped down the aluminium stairs and went to join his workmates amid the flurry of construction that was transforming the floor of the hold.

Keith poked his head through an uncompleted doorway in one of the growing apartment walls and whispered to Maurice, who was hanging a strip of hand painted wallpaper, "Psst, JC's not here, is he?"

"No, he pissed off about an hour ago, said he had to meet someone in the town."

"A hooker? At this time in the morning?" Keith shook his head.

"He said not but I don't believe the randy bastard. He said he was seeing an estate agent."

"Is he buying somewhere out here then?"

"Could be but I think it's probably a lady estate agent and he's boffing her," smiled Maurice.

"That sounds more like it. Did he swallow the story about me being ill?"

"Yes, he thinks you've got a bad case of the shits."

"He ain't far wrong, this fucking dago beer goes through me like a V12 Bentley."

"It's doing the same to all of us but more important, what have you found out?"

"You won't believe it."

Ian Cassidy

"I'll get the rest of the lads and you can try us," said Maurice as he began hallooing the remainder of the workers.

They rushed to a half-completed room, eager to hear Keith's news and sitting on upturned buckets and fizzy pop crates used by the diminutive paperhanger to reach the ceiling, they waited for the unlikely spy to begin.

Keith obliged. "Hold onto your hats, lads, cos we're working for Goering. Hermann fucking Goering."

"Bollocks," the other five said in unison.

"It's true, I tell you, I saw him with my own eyes. Hermann bloody Goering."

"You gotta be wrong," said Bert: "He's one of Hitler's disciples, a true believer in all the Nazi claptrap. He'd never leave Germany."

"He might be a true believer," said Keith, "but I bet he believes more in saving his own neck. And when Churchill and Roosevelt get hold of him, they'll see that the fat bastard swings for certain."

"Alright," said Jack: "Now, Keith, are you sure it's Goering?"

"It's him, I'm telling you. I've seen the fat bastard on the newsreels enough times. I'd recognise him anywhere."

"It makes sense," said Don: "The amount of money that's been spent getting us here and doing up the boat. Someone big would have to be behind it."

"Right then," said Jack: "If it is Goering who wants the boat to escape in, what we gonna do about it?"

"Tell Coughlan and get the hell out of here," suggested Ivor.

"I think it's best to leave Coughlan out of this," Bert interjected. "We don't know how deep he's involved with the Nazis and it wouldn't be the first time the slippery bastard's lied to us."

"But we can't afford to get home without him," said Don.

"Let's worry about that later. First thing we've got to do is stop Goering escaping. Agreed?"

Bert's work mates agreed with him, even Don, if somewhat reluctantly and yet again he raised the possibility of it being expensive.

"How?" asked Ivor.

"Set the boat on fire," suggested his brother. "There's plenty of white spirit and gloss paint, it will make a lovely blaze."

"No way," said Jack. "I don't fancy setting things on fire. I can't see the Spanish Harbour Master liking it if we start an inferno in his port. Like Don says, we ain't got the money to get away from here, so we could end up being nicked for arson."

"What about just opening up the scuppers and letting the boat sink where it is?"

"That's almost as fucking dangerous as setting it on fire. What if we didn't make it to the dockside in time?" said Bert.

"And," said Jack, "we'd have just as much trouble with the harbour master. He won't like it if we block up his port with a sunken ship."

"We could say it was an accident. The fucking wreck looks like it's on its last legs as it is."

"They wouldn't believe us. It could take months to sort out. Out here they lock you up first and ask questions later. I don't want to spend months in a Spanish nick. Grady and Paddy saw the inside of a few Spanish lock-ups when they were here with the International Brigade and we've all heard the horror stories they have to tell." said Jack, referring to the two painters who had been left behind in Brownhills because of their service in the Spanish Civil War.

"Let's pinch the ship then."

"And do what with it?"

"I dunno, sail it down to Gibraltar - anywhere - if it ain't here, then Goering can't use it."

"Why get involved at all?" asked Don. "Let's just fuck off out of here. We can hitchhike or work our passage home on a tramp steamer." Don scowled at his work mates. The affair sounded to him like it could get very costly indeed. "I don't like it, starting our own private war, could cost us all the money we've made on this trip."

"Will you shut up about the fucking money."

"Well I don't like it, I tell you, we shouldn't be financing the war against the Third Reich, that's what the American's are for."

"Whatever it costs we can't let a murdering bastard like Herman Fatso Goering get away."

"Why not? He's done nothing wrong according to German law. Putting him on trial will be nothing more than victor's justice."

"Bollocks!" said Bert. "It's fucking Goering. We can't let him escape."

"He's only done what Hitler told him."

"That's no excuse and besides, I reckon he volunteered. He's enjoyed every murder and every dirty trick that he's ordered."

"I don't see it like that."

"Well I fucking do," snapped Bert. "All this 'I'm only obeying my orders' business is a load of crap. I met plenty of Germans in the last lot, even a few officers. Very honourable, the lot of 'em. They lived and breathed the traditions of the Wehrmarkte. Real officer class, the Prussian Junkers. They would never have ordered one of their men to commit murder. They would have asked for volunteers and if no one volunteered they'd have done it themselves. This stuff about only obeying orders is all a blind because there's been so many volunteers."

"Alright you two, calm down," said Jack: "We'll pinch the boat then and sail it somewhere that Goering can't find it."

"Can we sail a ship that size?" asked Keith.

"It can't be that difficult and we could get the crew to help us."

"I don't think they'll do that. Goering's paying their wages, don't forget, and he won't pay them if the ship's in Gibraltar."

"So we gotta chuck the crew off the ship before we nick it then," said Maurice.

"No problem," said Ivor, rubbing his hands.

"Why don't we knock out the crew and then wait until Goering comes on board and kidnap him and take him with us to Gibraltar. That way we can be sure the bastard won't get away."

"But he'll probably have some Panzer stormtroopers with him."

"I didn't see any," Keith piped in.

"Well you wouldn't, would you," Bert scoffed: "They wouldn't be on the lawn drinking fucking lemonade with him, they'd be out of sight on guard duty."

"But if they were on guard duty, then Keith wouldn't have got close to Goering. They'd have spotted him and probably shot him."

Keith gulped and Bert smiled at him, "You're a very lucky boy, barging in there without thinking."

"So we're fairly sure that he ain't got any guards with him."

"Yeah, but even if he ain't got a platoon of infantry with him, you can bet he's got a gun and so will the people Keith saw with him."

"He was with Manuel and a real rough looking fucker," Keith piped in again.

"There you are then, that's three armed men and even Ivor can't put a man with a gun away."

"Give me first punch and he'd never get a chance to use it," Ivor said confidently.

"Don't talk stupid," said his brother, "You'd never get close enough to land one, you twat."

Ivor was about to protest when Jack interrupted, "Right, we'll forget the kidnap plan, we'll just sail the ship to Gibraltar and tell the Navy where Goering is and they can send some marines to get him."

"When we gonna do the deed?" asked Keith.

"As soon as we get the chance. We'll wait until Coughlan and most of the crew are in town and then we'll strike. We'll make some detailed plans later when Coughlan fucks off to the knocking shop."

"And lads, we better get back to work. We don't want Coughlan suspecting anything."

"I don't feel like working for the fucking Nazis," grumbled Maurice.

"We've got to. If JC or Manuel suspect that we're onto them, they could tip Goering off and he could do another midnight flit."

"Still don't like it," Maurice mumbled peevishly.

"Look, we'll just go through the motions."

"Alright," replied Ivor and reluctantly the men returned to the work of building a suite of rooms that they hoped would never be used.

2.56pm.
Stuttgart.

Haller brought the steaming Mercedes to a halt and looked warily at the heat haze, caused by the sizzling Hungarian fuel oil, rising from beneath the bonnet.

He shook his head and peered over at the sleeping killer in the passenger seat. He reminded himself that he was a Sturmbanführer in the Gestapo while Gunther was a mere lieutenant, albeit a particularly psychotic lieutenant. He shook his passenger by the arm. "Lieutenant, it is time for you to take over at the wheel," he commanded. "I must rest but we cannot afford a moment's delay."

Gunther blinked back to consciousness and heaved his heavy murderer's frame through the passenger door.

Haller waited for his subordinate to open the door for him and then climbed out rubbing his aching back. He walked quickly around the nose of the simmering sports car, trying not to inhale the noxious nut-flavoured fumes emanating from the overworked engine.

They had covered almost three hundred and fifty miles since setting off shortly before five o'clock that morning — a remarkable rate of progress, aided by the use they had made of the newly constructed autobahns. Herr Todt was to be congratulated but only just. There had been some very hairy moments as they gunned the Mercedes at breakneck speeds over the uncompleted sections and some frustratingly slow interludes when they encountered areas not yet reached by the smooth two-lane highways.

Progress would not be so swift on the primitive road system that awaited them in rural France.

Haller looked out over the great industrial expanse of Stuttgart and fumbled in the glove compartment for his flask of lukewarm coffee. . He poured out the last of the sweet greasy liquid and, screwing up his nose, he passed it to the driver, "Here, Lieutenant, take this. It will revive you after your long sleep."

Gunther shook his head. "No, thank you, Major. You have it. I am in full control."

Haller looked at the huge, threatening agent with his still perfectly pressed suit, crisply laundered shirt and unruffled blonde hair as he clutched the steering wheel with unwavering concentration. *Yes, he is in full control*, Haller said to himself. *The man is a fanatic, a zealot. Efficient, methodical, driven and deadly. A true believer even at this late stage in the life of the Reich.*

"Very well, Lieutenant." He sipped gingerly at the unctuous liquid. "We still have a very long way to go. Almost a thousand kilometres by my calculation and that does not take account of any diversions that may be forced on us by the Allied advance. I estimate another twenty-four hours on the road." He reluctantly continued, "Any reduction in that time would be of immense use." He was duty bound to carry out Kaltenbrunner's instructions.

Gunther nodded and performed the calculations for himself. With the sums worked out, he efficiently pushed his foot flat to the floor and made best use of the rapidly dwindling miles of autobahn.

Haller sipped uncomfortably at the revolting coffee as the great Mercedes roared over the tarmac as fast as its twelve straining cylinders would propel it. He slept badly.

4.30pm.
Brownhills.

Bernard Fisher poked his head around the door of the secretary's office. Mary Hilton looked up, startled, "I didn't realise you were still here, Bernie. You can't have much to do."

"Not a lot," he sighed, "but it's either this or go home. How are the weirdoes doing?"

"Oh, fine, I told them to knock off about half an hour ago."

"Good." Fisher hesitated. "I tell you what, why don't you knock off early as well. I'll lock up."

Mary Hilton was happy to oblige. She quickly packed up her things and left the office.

Fisher watched her walk up the drive and waited until he heard the sound of the gate closing behind her and then went straight to the safe. He knew the combination by heart, thanks to years of looking over Coughlan's shoulder. He spun the dials expertly and soon pulled open the heavy iron door. He sniffed greedily at the interior and looked inside.

On the top shelf, he rummaged through reams of untidy and long forgotten contracts and certificates. He decided there was nothing of interest there and moved on to the middle shelf.

The first item that caught his eye was Coughlan's VIP membership card for a back street Birmingham strip club. The card bore Coughlan's name in embossed letters. Fisher reasoned that Coughlan would be well known there, making his own chances of using the card virtually nil. He laid it to one side. Next he picked up a large Manila envelope stuffed with glossy magazines, illegally imported French porn. He flicked through them cursorily before selecting one and stuffing it in his jacket pocket.

He opened up another much smaller envelope and pulled out a scruffy but official looking little piece of paper. He read it quickly. It was an official letter from the Spitfire works at Castle Bromwich. Fisher recognised it as one of Coughlan's blackmail projects. The letter detailed a fault discovered during a test flight of one of the Mark 111 spitfires caused by a poorly designed control cable. The unfortunate member of the ground crew who had absentmindedly pocketed the report rather than consign it the brazier had stupidly shown it to Coughlan. Coughlan had somehow got hold of the report and was now holding the threat of an espionage charge over the none too bright fellow's head. In return for his silence, Coughlan received a steady supply of petrol coupons from the works motor pool.

Fisher considered burning the papers to spare the hapless engineer further pressure from Coughlan but he could not be bothered. *If God didn't want them sheared he wouldn't have made them sheep,* he said to himself and moved on to the bottom shelf.

This was more like it. He gleefully helped himself to a handful of white fivers. With these safely inside his wallet, he pulled out an antique wooden strong box, like the small metal one that held petty cash but much larger and sturdier, bound with brass at each corner, which stood next to the piles of notes. He gave it a shake and heard an encouragingly metallic rattle coming from the inside. He pulled at the lid and swore when it did not move. He grabbed the paper knife on Coughlan's desk and jammed it between box and lid. The lid gave way with an embarrassing crack and Fisher looked at the ruptured timber above the brass lock plate. He shook his head. *That will take some explaining*, he said to himself. Undeterred, he smiled and said aloud, "But I'll think of something." He surveyed the contents of the box. It was stacked with gold and silver coins from all corners of the globe, squirreled away by Coughlan as insurance against those reckless men on Wall Street getting it wrong again. Fisher noticed the newly arrived bag of sovereigns. "Those are new." He said, licking his lips. He took a handful of the sovereigns and packed them into his jacket pocket. Feeling a little lopsided he took another handful and put those into his other pocket.

He forced the box lid closed, struggling with the strained metal lock and then, with a delicate application of spit and pressure to the splintered wood, he satisfied himself that the damage was deniable. Noticeable but still deniable.

Fisher put the box back and was about to close the safe when a small bronze statuette caught his eye. He picked it up and examined the sensitively modelled study of two greyhound-like European hunting dogs at the point for game. He ran his hands over the shiny patinated metal and struggled to make out the signature. "P J Mene," he read aloud. "Never heard of him but you can tell its pucker, not like those monstrosities Garth knocks up." Thinking that it might make a timely present for his big wife and, more importantly, that such a gift would make going home slightly more bearable, he put the maquette under his arm. He locked the office and headed, slightly less reluctantly than usual, for home.

5.30pm
Sitges.

Under the unforgiving Spanish sun the men had worked steadily if unenthusiastically all day. Coughlan had accompanied them for a time but had to leave to attend yet another meeting in the town.

The six weary painters were now using the two hours or so between shifts to rest and shower. Or rather some of them were. Bert was not one to waste water and Maurice and Ivor were well known for getting black and staying that way.

Washed or unwashed as they preferred, the men bolted down their landlady's grisly evening offering and left a bemused Coughlan lingering over his coffee, trying to pull the waitress despite the communication difficulties.

Coughlan considered that his employees were up to no good but reasoned that they were involved in their habitual petty pilfering and doing nothing that could be of any moment to him. He ordered another large

Fundador and when the girl brought it over, he launched into a strange smiling mixture of halting Spanish and schoolboy French that always sounded a little better when oiled by alcohol.

He was confidently into his "Bishop of Bollocks" routine as the men plotted above him.

Of course Ivor and Maurice would lead the assault on the crew. Jack had calculated that at any given time, of the twelve men who made up the ship's compliment, never more than six were aboard. The captain had been dismissed and in the absence of a higher authority the first mate was entertaining himself with a young lady in the port.

Several other members of the crew were doing likewise. They seemed to continually avail themselves of the fleshpots of Sitges and nearby Barcelona. Most of the others could be relied on to be drunk and sleeping it off, either in their dingy quarters or the local police station. That left only five or six who were likely to be of able body and mind to put up any resistance. Two of these, the Serbian cook and the ship's boy, would present no problems even to a lover, not a fighter like himself. The chief stoker and his mate were permanently on board, engaged in repairs to the boiler or periodically running the engine to prevent premature seizures among its rusting parts. They were tough-looking bastards. Knocking them out would be a job for Ivor and Maurice. Keith, Don and Bert were detailed to take care of the remainder.

With their plans now tenuously in place and without waiting for Coughlan the men set off for the nightshift.

7.30pm.
Sitges.

The six men assembled in, if their plan was successful, Goering's never-to-be-completed stateroom and grumbled as Jack allocated their tasks for the evening.

"Look it's just for one more shift," he pleaded. "Tomorrow we'll be on our way out of here."

"Why don't we do it now?" suggested Ivor, spoiling for a fight: "JC's not here and nearly all the crew are on the piss in the town."

"I don't fancy trying to sail something this fucking big in the dark," Said Jack. "I've only ever been on the boating lake in the Arboretum. So we'll just have to wait until we've got plenty of daylight ahead of us."

Ivor reluctantly unclenched his fists and agreed. He joined his work mates in doing what was necessary to put their employer off the scent.

They need not have bothered. Coughlan and his new-found friend, the town's only estate agent, were at the time closing their business inside Coughlan's favourite Sitges haunt.

Despite the large commission cheque that his wife had already spent, the estate agent was sitting uncomfortably at Coughlan's usual table, looking in horror on the long line of painted tarts who seemed so pleased to see his client. A lifelong resident of Sitges, he had had no idea that such a place sullied the back-streets of his beloved home town. Now that he knew that he had no wish to become better acquainted with the dubious pleasures it had to offer.

Coughlan, on the other hand, was having a rip roaring time. He had just secured at an embarrassingly knockdown price, a farmhouse and several acres of land just outside of the town. He had a quadruple brandy in front of him and a large tart on each knee. He could not have been happier.

Unusually, the pianist had chosen that night to make one of his rare guest appearances and, lacking practice, he proceeded to badly tinkle the out of tune ivories. The tone deaf Coughlan did not seem to notice the pianist's lack of skill and gleefully took to the floor with the tart on his right knee. For the sake of equality, the tart on his left knee was chosen to accompany him on his second ham-fisted visit to floor. Both accompanied him on his third visit, which soon degenerated into a Bacchanalian display of stockinged thighs, Coughlan's hairy chest and whipping feather boas. Soon Coughlan was stripped to the waist with a feather boa tied around his neck. The tart on the left, who had taken to the floor sans boa, deftly removed the belt from his trousers - he had stopped wearing braces in the Spanish heat and taken to wearing a newly purchased leather belt - and after whipping his buttocks several times, she looped the belt around his neck and pulled him gently towards her vinegary, whalebone trussed breasts. Coughlan nuzzled between them and gave up all pretence of moving in time to the music. The erethitic entertainment continued. Suitably aroused - if there was ever a waking moment when he was not - Coughlan headed for the rooms upstairs. His guest, the now forgotten estate agent, thought this a good time to make his excuses. He stopped Coughlan on the stairs and heartily thanked Mr James for his business. His thanks for the subsequent hospitality were somewhat less enthusiastic.

Coughlan was shocked that anyone could consider taking an early bath, especially if not accompanied in the tub by one of the working girls. "It's on me," he shouted over the strangled music and offered the estate agent the tart on the right.

The estate agent made a series of very hasty apologies and scurried between the tables towards the door. Coughlan shook his head. *Another dago shirt lifter*. He said to himself, before ushering his latest brace of hourly purchases up the stairs.

fifteen
18th August, 1944

3.00am. **Sitges harbour.** The men were wearily washing their paint-encrusted hands in white spirit when Coughlan made his most belated appearance yet. After a typically animated round of horizontal activities, toys included, Coughlan had slept in the room unconcerned about his rapidly rising tab.

He smiled at his exhausted employees. "Just doing half a shift then?"

The men took no notice of Coughlan's hackneyed gibe and continued packing up for the night. Despite themselves, they were unable to feel any deep seated dislike for the generally good natured crook even though he had put them in such an invidious position. The seven men strolled through the cool, deserted streets to their lodgings engaging in harmless, tired banter.

Once inside the hotel, Coughlan turned in immediately but the men held yet another conference in the cramped communal washroom.

Bert took charge. "Right, it's on for tomorrow. As soon as Coughlan fucks off, we overpower the crew and steal the ship."

Jack and Keith gulped The prospect of a violent confrontation did not appeal to them. Don shook his head and grumbled. The prospect of no more wages did not appeal to him.

Only Maurice and Ivor went to bed happy. The prospect of a punch-up was immensely appealing to them. Quietly confident, Maurice announced, "We haven't had a good rumble since we smashed up the

Leathern Bottle." Ivor smiled at the memory and was positively upbeat. "Tomorrow's D-Day then," he said animatedly to his brother.

"What's D-Day mean?" asked Maurice.

"Duffing up Day," Ivor answered enthusiastically as he climbed under the moth-eaten covers.

4.00am.
Clermont Ferrand.

The two Gestapo agents and their top-of-the-range Mercedes had made good progress. By driving in shifts, the car had rarely been still but now, in the heart of rural France, they pulled the over to the side of the road.

Haller sniffed cautiously at his sleeping passenger. The man snored like an asthmatic warthog and broke wind like a bilious hippo. He would down the window before shaking Gunther awake.

"Lieutenant, we must refuel."

Silently Gunther obeyed.

"And while you're getting the drums from the boot," Haller continued, "break out the Primus and I'll brew some coffee."

Haller stood at the rear of the car watching his subordinate and breathing in the fresh morning air. He looked on but did not offer to help, as Gunther struggled with the drums of Swiss petrol that Haller had purchased in Geneva, anticipating the paucity of filling stations in the turmoil that was now southern France.

Haller had brewed a pot of passable coffee by the time a sweating Gunther joined him on completion of his refuelling duties. Haller passed the lieutenant a steaming enamel mug of faintly hazel nut flavoured liquid and began, "Drink up, we cannot dally. There are almost three hundred kilometres still to negotiate between here and Andorra. I estimate that will take the best part of eight hours."

"Ah, but not with me at the wheel," Gunther announced confidently and guzzled down the piping hot coffee. "Let me have the keys, Major, you take a break."

Haller reluctantly complied. Against his better judgement he even said, "Step on it, Lieutenant," as he lowered himself into the passenger seat. Gunther needed no second bidding and the two Gestapo agents were soon hurtling towards another border.

8.00am.
Sitges.

The six distracted craftsmen began work aboard the Atheling as normal. Unfortunately, their employer joined them. The men worked in a wall of white noise, of banging hammers and hissing welders. They accompanied all this with an array of stupid songs guaranteed to annoy their employer and speed his exit. Keith struck, "Daddy wouldn't buy me a bow-wow." As each verse progressed his repetition of "bow-wow" became increasingly more strangled and coyote like. The others chipped in and Bert even gave his now famous rendition of "Que Sera Sera," mischievously replacing the chorus with "Kiss me arse."

Coughlan called a halt to this unpleasant glee club. "Shut the fuck up," he commanded. But he did not leave.

Jack and Bert fitted piping, conduit and cable with one eye on their employer. Don grumbled his way through the construction of a banquette for Goering's salon. He would have kept an eye on his employer if he had not been preoccupied by the imminent plunge in his earning potential.

Maurice hung paper with his usual aplomb whilst watching Coughlan's every move. The sharpest of all the men, he could do both things at once without detriment to either. Ivor tossed paint around and left it to his brother to do the watching. Keith nursed a hangover and tried not to watch anything; the bright Spanish sun was hurting his eyes.

Coughlan flitted from man to man, helping out wherever required. He showed no signs of doing one of his famous disappearing acts.

Up until mid-morning, the men were not unduly concerned by their employer's annoying presence. Coughlan was in the habit of going missing around the time that the Serbian cook arrived with his pot of by now almost palatable tea. Coughlan was very territorial about where he opened his bowels, preferring to retire to the solitary comforts of his en suite rather than share the porcelain in the reeking ship's washroom that had been insulted on so many occasions by both the crew and his employees.

Unfortunately for the plotters, Coughlan had been before he left the hotel that morning and the unusually strenuous - for him at least- morning's work had brought on no unscheduled stirrings in the lower stomach area. He joined the men for their tea break and to their surprise and horror he took a grimy enamel mug from the cook and reclined on the deck. He even took out a packet of cigarettes and passed them around. Despite their unease at his continued presence each man took one, or two in Maurice's case.

They slurped their tea and chivvied Coughlan about the dangers of burnout caused by overwork. He took it all in good part but still showed no sign of preparing to leave.

After a quarter of an hour, Jack jumped to his feet and amazed Coughlan by truncating the tea break.

"Let's go and do a bit," he declared. His colleagues began to protest but quickly got the message. The harder they worked, the quicker Coughlan would find an excuse to slip away.

With Jack leading, the men filed down to the hold. Coughlan ambled along at the rear grumbling, "The bonus must be too fucking big if you're cutting short tea breaks."

Once in the hold, the men set to work with gusto. Ivor painted everything that was stationary and several moving objects as well. Maurice slapped paper on the walls as fast as his short hairy arms could hang it. Jack and Bert were constantly engulfed in a blaze of brazing wire. Even Keith was busy - busy doing nothing, but working hard at it. And still Coughlan did not leave.

The men's frustration mounted. Ivor tried accidentally on purpose splashing Coughlan with paint. From a great height, Jack dropped his monkey wrench dangerously close to his unmoving employer. But still he would not leave.

Noon approached and the men took a smoke break. Coughlan joined them but this time his Woodbines were reserved solely for his own personal consumption.

Ian Cassidy

Jack took Maurice to one side. "We've got to think of something," he said to the man most likely to come up with a cunning scheme to send their employer in search of a few hours rest and recuperation. "Or the bastard will never go."

Maurice gave the matter a few moments thought. "Get him to work with me and I'll see that a full bucket of paste lands on his head. He'll have to go to the hotel and change."

"But can we knock out the crew and get the ship out of the port while he's changing?" asked Jack.

"We won't need to be that quick. He can't keep away from the knocking shop, I think he's bought himself a season ticket. Once he's away he won't be back for hours." Maurice knew his employer well.

"That's true," agreed Jack. "We'll give it a go." The two men rejoined the other five smokers.

Jack pointedly and rather too loudly began, "How's the paper hanging going, Moz?"

Maurice got the message: "Bit slow and there's some tricky bits coming up, so I could use a hand."

Ivor started to volunteer but Jack discreetly nudged him on the backside and jumped in: "Me and Bert are too busy and so's Keith." He looked expectantly at Coughlan: "Why don't you do it, Jim?"

"Yeah, why not." Coughlan smiled. "Show you how it's done, you idle little bastard."

"Let's get at it then." said Maurice. The men threw their cigarette butts over the side. All except Ivor, that is. After years of sporadic incarceration he valued tobacco more highly. He stubbed out his filthy reefer between thumb and forefinger and put the tiny stogie in a battered tin, ready for future re-use.

Once inside the decreasing chaos that was the mutating hold, Maurice began to mix an outsize bucket of paste while Coughlan surveyed the so-called tricky bits. Fortunately for Maurice, the section of the salon that he was working on tending was indeed troublesome. Intricate cuts to the thick hand-made paper needed to be made around a light fitting, the radio speaker and the top of the curved banquette that Don had just finished assembling.

Coughlan sucked his teeth. "Looks a piece of piss. What are you worrying about?"

Maurice ignored him and carried on stirring the very watery concoction in his paste bucket.

"You can do all that standing on your head," Coughlan continued. "And you'll have to cos I've just remembered that I've got to meet some geezer in the town, so I haven't got time to help."

"Another fucking whore more like," Maurice said under his breath. He smiled at his employer, "Yeah, I can manage. You piss off."

Coughlan needed no second bidding and bounded up the stairs to the deck. Maurice gave him a minute's start and then crept out of the partially completed room. He was rounding up his colleagues before Coughlan had made it to the gangplank.

1.15pm.
Andorra.

Sweating and unshaven, Haller slowed the exhausted Mercedes as the border between France and Andorra came into view. The Vichy guards had long deserted their post and, fortunately for Haller, their Andorran counterparts had adopted a similarly lax immigration policy. It was lunchtime after all.

Once through the unmanned checkpoint, he speeded up again and pointed the huge car in the direction of Spain. Gunther spluttered to life, belching and farting simultaneously. "Shall I take over, Major?" he asked. Once again he had shaken off the effects of his uncomfortable slumbers almost instantaneously.

"That will not be necessary Lieutenant, I can cope with the final leg of our trek. We are less that one hundred kilometres from Barcelona. We should get there around three o'clock."

"Then we have to find this Sitges place."

"Yes that may be tricky. I just hope that we are in time."

Gunther did not reply, merely rubbed his clean shaven chin. Every time the two agents had stopped for coffee, Gunther had performed a series of hasty ablutions. It was the duty of a German officer to take scrupulous care of his appearance. He had made no direct comment about his superior's somewhat lax approach to personal hygiene but it had been noted for future reference. Gunther went back to sleep as Haller negotiated the unfamiliar mountain roads.

1.30pm.
Sitges Harbour.

The men stood around nervously, waiting for their employer to get clear of the ship. He was not halfway down the gangplank when the Atheling's rusting flanks shuddered as the great lazy steam engines came haltingly to life. The stoker had chosen now to give the engines their daily turnover.

Maurice was first to spot the implications. "We've got to take control of the engine room now, while the engines are still running. If we don't and the crew turn them off, it could take us hours to find out how to switch them back on."

"Right," said Ivor, nothing more. With jaw set and fists clenched, he headed for the ladder to the lower decks. Maurice followed. With chimpanzee-like agility, the two monkey-men slid down the ship's iron ladders to the booming engine room.

The stokers were used to seeing the contractors in places where strictly they had no business. Ivor in particular was forever mooching about. It was not just the cook he had ingratiated himself with. He was on friendly terms with most of the crew; acquaintances based on a mixture of slowly shouted Black Country English and shared roll-up cigarettes.

The chief stoker was thus not surprised to see the squat street fighter walking over the greasy engine room floor towards him. He was surprised by the merciless kick to his groin and sickened by the plopping noise as Ivor's steel toe-cap crushed his testicles. He doubled up clutching his exploding genitalia and the swift one two delivered by Ivor's short powerful arms was almost unnecessary as he went out like a light.

Although decidedly useful in the street fighting arena when compared to ordinary mortals, Maurice lacked his brother's exceptional abilities. He compensated with an extraordinary degree of guile. As the chief stoker was efficiently dispatched, Maurice positioned himself behind the rumbling boiler and waited. As the stoker's mate came uncertainly to his chief's aid, the unseen paperhanger dealt him a perfectly timed blow with a monkey-wrench. Poleaxed, the mate fell to the floor beside the petty officer.

Ivor glanced around triumphantly. "Let's get 'em up to the deck. Then we'll see how the others are getting on."

The two violent labourers struggled with first the unconscious chief-stoker and manhandled the dead weight up the ladder, Maurice at the top, desultorily pulling at the man's shoulders, leaving his brother at the bottom shouldering most of the burden. They repeated the exercise going up the remaining ladders to the deck before sliding back down to the engine room and dragging out the stoker's mate. Struggling to the deck they left the bruised and unconscious seamen at the gap in the ship's rail next to the gangplank.

The two painters doubled up, hands on knees, panting violently. They were not used to having to clear up the result of their brutal efficiency. More often they beat a hasty retreat, leaving their bloodied victim in the gutter and the darkened Bloxwich streets ringing to the shrill sound of police whistles.

Ivor straightened up first and, patting his brother on the backside, said: "Come on, the others will need a hand."

"What if they wake up?" asked his panting sibling.

"After the pasting they've just had, they won't move for a week," replied Ivor. "But just to make sure." He walked over to the sleeping men and with practised economy of effort planted another hefty blow on each.

"That ought to do it," he snarled and bounced along the deck in search of more action.

The other men were having mixed results. Bert had discovered a drunken deck hand noisily sleeping it off. He had fought his way through the beery fumes and smacked the man firmly on the jaw. The blow had sent the sleeper more heavily into his alcohol-induced coma. Bert heaved the drunkard over his shoulder before making his way to the deck and depositing his victim with his sleeping shipmates.

Keith came across the ship's boy as he tipped a bucket-load of potato peelings over the side. He caught the boy by his shirttails and deftly sent him after the kitchen waste. As the frightened boy spluttered in the oily waters of the port, Keith had gone to help Don, who faced a slightly more troublesome opponent. On the deck below, Don had a not so drunken sailor in a headlock but despite the immense pressure exerted by Don's spindly arms, the man would not go quietly. He bit at Don's forearms and swung his elbows into the body of his gangly Black Country assailant. The repeated blows to his torso were weakening Don's vice-like grip. He was pleased to see Keith running through the bulkhead door. Keith was also pleased with the two-to-one odds in his favour. He rushed forward and let loose an ambitious roundhouse blow. Unfortunately, the sailor spotted Keith's telegraphed punch and rather unsportingly ducked. Keith caught Don full on the nose, which immediately poured blood. Far from making Don loosen his grip, it had the opposite effect. The enraged carpenter tightened his hold on the sailor's swelling neck and, using his giraffe-like legs for leverage, he swung the man violently around and smashed his head into the unforgiving steel walls of the corridor. His resistance at an end, the deckhand's knees buckled and he slumped to the floor. Don turned angrily to Keith and spitting blood he commanded, "You can carry the fucker to the deck. You dozy bleeder. About as much use as a one legged man at an arse kicking contest." Giggling, Keith picked up the sailor and followed his grumbling workmate to the deck.

Jack was experiencing the most trouble and from the most unlikely source. The diminutive Serbian cook would cede no ground in his galley. He was brandishing a vicious looking meat cleaver and pelting the cautiously advancing Jack with wilting vegetables and meat by-products. Jack was chasing the screaming chef around the preparation table as Ivor and Maurice entered the cacophonous galley. Ivor quickly sized up the situation and speedily grabbed the cook's meat cleaver arm with his iron left hand. Next he delivered a stinging right hander that broke the cook's jaw. Ivor's knee caught the falling man in the throat and his resistance was stilled.

"What the fuck did you do that for?" asked Jack stunned by the unnecessary viciousness.

Ivor just shrugged.

"I was trying to get him to come with us. It could take a few days to reach Gibraltar and we'll need someone to do the cooking."

"I don't give anyone a second chance," sniffed the experienced street fighter. Ivor thought about one of his rare adulterous episodes in some godforsaken terrace in Whiteheath. He had been literally caught with his trousers down. The enraged husband had launched an outraged assault on Ivor as his unfaithful wife screamed from the bed. The cuckold never stood a chance. Ivor had efficiently and brutally dealt with the attack. He had momentarily felt bad about cuckolding the innocent man and then beating him up but he had his reputation to think of.

Jack's complaints brought him back from his reverie. "Well, you put the cook out of action, so you can take over. You're in charge of the cookhouse."

Ivor smiled. "I don't mind, always fancied myself as a cook." He went on but quietly, "You might though, when you see what damage I can do with a frying pan."

Jack did not hear. He turned to Maurice. "Right, let's get the crew off the boat and then we'll work out to sail this fucking rust bucket."

The six painters relayed the sparked-out crew down the gangplank and dumped them unceremoniously behind the tarpaulined pallets that littered the dock.

Satisfied that they were the only six on board, Jack assembled the men on the deck. He detailed Don and Bert to raise the anchor and untie the boat, but not until they were given the order. He took the other men with him to the engine room. They passed through to the bowels of the ship, pleased to still hear the reassuring murmur of the engines.

On the floor of the engine room, Jack continued, "Right, the engine's still running. We've got to make sure it doesn't cut out and then work out how we get the turbines or screws or whatever they're called to move."

The four men stood in front of the baffling array of pipes and pistons, scratching their heads. But not for long. Years of working in the technologically advanced foundries of Birmingham and the Black Country had not been wasted. They quickly sized up the situation. Maurice studied one of the gauges closely. "This is the steam pressure gauge. It's more or less at the right level now to keep the engine ticking over, so all we have to do is keep it at this level and the ship should move."

"How do we do that?" asked Keith.

"By shovelling plenty of coal into that," said Maurice, indicating the flaming open mouth of the boiler. "And I've just appointed you chief fire stoker."

Keith smiled at the thought of being chief anything. He stopped smiling when Maurice passed him a shovel, a piecework shovel if ever he saw one. He was about to protest when Maurice continued, "You'd better go see where they keep the rest of the coal. We won't get very far on that lot." He pointed to the small pile of gleaming anthracite in the hopper next to the boiler and Keith set off to scour the oily expanse of the engine room. Maurice rejoined Jack and Ivor, who were puzzling over a large brass lever with bright enamel letters spelling out the legends: "Stop", "Ahead", "Slow", "Full", and "Stop".

Jack thought he had got the measure of the instrument and started to explain. "You just push the lever to the speed you want. Then someone does the same on the bridge and off we go. Like they did in that Noel Coward film, you know, "In Which we Serve."

"Right. Looks simple enough," agreed Ivor. "You'd better get to the bridge and give it a try."

Before he left, Jack put Maurice in charge of the engine room. After all, Maurice had once worked for a Walsall trolley bus and tram company and was thus the only one of the amateur sailors with experience of large modes of transport. What Jack did not know was that Maurice had only been a conductor and for a very short time at that. He lost his job following a typically crafty stunt. On one of the busiest routes between Walsall and Darlaston and at rush hour to boot, Maurice had plied his trade as a conductor, taking the fares from every passenger who got aboard. He did not however issue more than hand full of tickets, explaining that his machine was malfunctioning. He continued in this mode until the end of the shift, taking fares but only issuing sporadic tickets. On arrival at the terminus, he handed over just a few pennies and explained that it had been a very quiet afternoon and that only a dozen or so people had got onto the bus. If they did not believe him, then they only had to look at his ticket machine, which was miraculously back in full working order, and they would see that very few tickets had been issued. The inspector did not believe him but the driver, who was on a percentage, confirmed Maurice's story. A search of Maurice's person failed to turn up the missing fares. Ivor was at that moment safely at home in Bloxwich counting the money. He had gotten off the bus at the last stop before the terminus, his pockets clanking with small change. In the absence of any direct evidence of theft and without the remotest possibility of getting a confession from Maurice, the bus company was unable to prosecute the tight-lipped conductor. They did, however, terminate his employment forthwith.

Jack was met at the ladder to the upper deck by Keith. "I can't find any more coal," he whined.

"What do you mean? It's a steamship; there has to be coal."

"There isn't," insisted Keith. "Just what's by the boiler."

Keith and Jack walked back to the boiler where Maurice and Ivor were concentrating on the dials.

"No coal," announced Keith.

"I suppose they don't stock up until just before they're ready to sail," said Maurice with uncanny prescience. Konrad had not yet ordered the coal or in fact any of the major supplies that would be needed for the journey to South America. He had reasoned that placing an order to supply the ship with a large amount of fuel and provisions would draw unwanted attention. He planned to visit the ship's chandlers at the very last possible moment before the off.

"We can't stop now," said Jack. "We've got to get out of here before the crew wake up or they'll round up their mates and possibly the police and come and sort us out." He was panicking.

"Calm down," said Maurice. "When that bit of coal runs out, we'll just have to burn something else."

"Will the boiler take it?" asked Ivor.

"Yeah, that fucker will burn anything," said Maurice.

"Okay," said Jack. "There's plenty of stuff to burn. There's the wood we haven't used and there's all those packing cases in the front section of the hold, you know, behind that locked door."

Maurice and Ivor nodded and Jack went on.

"Right, well smash the door open and everything that'll burn can go into the boiler. And when that's gone, we'll chuck bits of the ship on, like they do in 'Around the World in Eighty Days'".

"In what?"

"I thought we were only going to Gibraltar, not around the world."

"It's a book, dummy," sighed Jack. "They're on a paddle steamer or something and it runs out of coal, so they put all the wooden parts of the ship into the furnace, like the bunk-beds, and the chairs and tables."

"Yeah we can do that," said Ivor enthusiastically. He brightened up no end at the thought of a little mindless destruction and he was a dab hand with a lump hammer.

"Right then, Ivor, you and Keith get as much burnable stuff in here as you can."

"I thought I was chief cook and bottle washer on this trip," Ivor smiled facetiously.

"You are and you can make the tea as soon as we're underway," said Jack, adopting a nautical air.

"Aye aye, Sir," Ivor answered facetiously.

"And you can cut all that crap out," Jack turned to Maurice. "Moz, I'm going up to the bridge. I suppose I talk to you through one of those tubes on the wall."

"I'll be listening Cap'n," said Maurice, picking up on his brother's nautical puns.

Jack ignored him; he knew when he was backing a loser. He started climbing the ladders to the decks above.

On the deck, Jack met Bert and Don idly smoking and looking suspiciously at the cables and hawsers that secured the rusting hulk to the quay: "You haven't untied it yet have you?" he asked panicking.

"No we're waiting for you to give the go ahead but we've worked out how it's done, we think. Don thinks he can work the anchor."

"Get in position then. I'm going to the bridge. I'll give you the nod when we're ready to go."

Jack left the two apprentice sailors and headed to the bridge. He pushed open the door and looked about. The room was sparsely furnished with a helmsman's chair, a rudimentary control panel, a deal table full of maps and charts, which he ignored. Dominating the scene were a brass and oak wheel. He went straight to the wheel and pushed it from side to side. Looks simple enough, he said to himself and started to study the control panel. The unpolished brass lever was, much to Jack's relief, the same as the one he had just seen in the engine room. Satisfied that he could at least make a stab at getting the ship moving, he poked his head out of the salt-stained window and shouted to Don to get the anchor up. He gave Bert the thumbs up and the ageing electrician starting tugging at the ropes.

Jack waited nervously as his two irregularly press-ganged helpers went clumsily about their tasks. Finally, he felt the hulk move more freely as she floated free of her tethers.

"Here goes nothing," he said aloud and pushed the lever to "Slow". Nothing happened. He tried several times before realising that the lever had to be pushed all the way around the dial and then back to the required speed. That's what Noel Coward did anyway, he mused before giving it a try. Somewhere a bell rang and Jack smiled. He called down the nearest tube to Maurice in the Engine room: "Moz, push your lever to "Slow" and keep your fingers crossed."

In his best pirate's accent Maurice gave a hearty "Aye aye, Sir!" and did as he was told.

The great steam engine roared into action and Jack felt a slow jolt as the twin screws began to turn. "Anymore for the Skylark?" he said to himself as he heaved frantically at the wheel, turning it this way and that. The rusting bulk of the Atheling limped away from the breakwater. Slowly, the Atheling and her oddball crew floated away into the still waters of the marina. Clutching the wheel, Jack felt the clanking propellers push the ship through the water and realised he had to do something fast. The other harbour wall was looming straight ahead. He swung the wheel all the way to the right and said a silent prayer. The Atheling hung dangerously to one side and slowly ploughed into the narrow dog-leg. Jack breathed a sigh of relief as the ship cleared the harbour walls and entered the channel leading to the wide blue waters of the Mediterranean. The ship snaked from side to side. Jack struggled to find the right weight on the wheel and sluggishly slipped up the channel between the two breakwaters before finally meeting the heavier rollers of the open sea. He waited an over-cautious amount of time for the ship to clear the concrete groynes. Then he heaved the wheel to the left. The Atheling plunged through the waves. After what he judged to be a safe distance from the harbour, Jack slung the wheel to the left, before straightening it up and pointing the stern parallel to the baking beaches of Sitges. He hoped that the inshore waters hereabout were not too shallow. His only plan was to follow the coastline to Gibraltar. He closed his mind to the difficulties of pursuing such a clumsy navigational strategy at night and thought instead about increasing the ship's speed. He pushed the lever to "Half" and shouted down to Maurice, "Let's give half speed a go."

Down in the engine room Maurice pushed his lever to the instructed position and listened with satisfaction as the engines changed up a gear. He shouted up the tube, "We've got half speed, Skipper. How's it look up there?"

"So far so good," Jack replied uncertainly.

"It'll be a piece of piss," giggled Maurice, returning to his gauges.

"Throw a bit more coal on." he shouted to Keith over the up-tempo noise of the speeding engines. "We're losing pressure." He turned to Ivor, "Start smashing up those cases, the rate this thing eats fuel, we're gonna need all the wood we can get."

Ivor did not reply. He happily smashed a huge and newly constructed wooden packing case onto its side and started kicking at the lid. The tightly screwed lid resisted initially but eventually gave way under the body blows rained down on it by Ivor's swift moving pit boots. Ivor tossed the splintered lid into the gaping boiler's mouth and looked at the shaken contents of the crate.

"What you found?" asked Maurice as his brother weeded through the priceless collection of Renaissance canvases and painted altar panel.

"Just some old rags and some battered old door panels."

"Chuck 'em on then," said Maurice.

Ivor did so and works by Tintoretto, Titian, and Tiepolo vanished into the flames.

The Unsinkable Herr Goering

Ivor deftly put his boot through the sides of the now empty packing case and that followed the canvases into the boiler. He moved to the next case and repeated his efficient demolition job on the lid.

"More of the same," he said in reply to his brother's unspoken enquiry about the case's contents. He emptied another consignment of priceless European art into the fire. This time works by Durer, Davide, Freidrich and Bosch vaporised as they hit the flames.

The third packing case also fell beneath Ivor's heavy boots: "Nothing but a load of scruffy old papers," he announced: "Who's paying to ship this load of crap around the world?"

"More money than sense," shrugged Maurice. "Chuck it on."

Ivor did so and, along with the Ruebens and the Poussin Arcadian landscape at the bottom of the box, Goering's looted collection of drawings and sketches by Michelangelo, Leonardo, Giotto and Raphael began to smoulder in the conflagration.

The fourth box was heavier and the gorilla-like power of Ivor was stretched to the limit. He called Keith to his aid. The combined gorilla and Staffordshire bull terrier qualities of the two painters proved too much even for the stoutly constructed German built packing case. Soon the engine room floor was littered with splintered wood and a bewildering array of orange coloured stone-like panels.

The three sweating boiler room men looked at the lumps of black flecked semi-precious rock.

"What the fuck is it?"

"God knows, some sort of resin."

"Will it burn?"

"Only one way to find out," said Ivor slinging the first panel of Peter the Great's celebrated Amber Room into the flames.

The three men stood back and watched as the flames took hold.

"Seems to be burning."

"Anything will burn in that heat."

"Good," said Maurice. "There's boxes of that stuff, so just keep a nice steady flow of it on the fire and we're easy on."

Keith nodded and added a second panel to the fire.

As the time approached 2.20 pm. and with a highly dubious and highly colourful smoke trail in its wake, the Atheling's unauthorised journey had well and truly begun.

2.30pm.
Sitges Harbour.

An elated and even more ruddy-faced Coughlan turned out of the town and started to stroll along the breakwater.

His business successfully concluded with his estate agent, he was flushed with the imported brandy that they had consumed to close the deal. He was a little disappointed that he had been unable to persuade the agent to join him at the brothel for some proper post-negotiation celebrations, but overall he thought things were going well. So he was a little surprised to see the Atheling's usual berth at the end of the breakwater unoccupied. He looked out to sea and saw the great grey hulk of the ship pounding through the waves in a cloud of smoky pollution caused by the priceless fuel stoking the flames in her boilers.

The crew must be doing sea trials, he said to himself. *And I hope the lads are still on board. We haven't got time to knock off for any old excuse.* He turned away, chuckling at the thought of his land lubber employees struggling with seasickness as they tried to carry out their duties on the moving vessel.

Coughlan was considering making a lone trip to the brothel when something caught his eye. A greasy lump of seemingly occupied boiler suit slumped behind a pallet on the dock. He approached the sleeping man with care and recognised him as the chief stoker. He scanned the scene and jumped back in amazement. Most of the crew were lying in a haphazard pile on the quayside.

"What the fuck's going on?" he blurted.

It dawned on him. The bastards have pinched the boat. They must have found something valuable in that locked room in the hold and done a runner with the ship. Coughlan stood with his hands on his hips, shaking his head. *The crafty bastards*. He smiled. *I bet Maurice is behind it, he was always the crafty one. You could not help but smile at the audacity of it all.*

He wandered off along the breakwater. He stopped dead in his tracks and definitely stopped smiling. My five grand! I've got to get the ship back here or I won't get paid. He swore to himself. Thinking quickly he ran into the town.

The estate agent, full of an unaccustomed liquid lunch, was about to begin his siesta a little earlier than normal. Unfortunately for him, he had not locked the office door and so all he could do was panic as he saw Coughlan come bustling into the office. *Won't the man take no for an answer?* he asked himself before summoning up his best customer-friendly smile.

When he got his breath back, Coughlan greeted the agent heartily. He put on his most charming smile and asked, "Can you do me a favour?"

"Perhaps," replied the agent warily.

"The other day, you mentioned that you owned a motor cruiser."

"Yes, it's in the harbour."

"Do you think I could take it for a spin?"

"I'm sorry, Mr James, but I haven't got time to leave the office."

"That's okay," said Coughlan. "I can drive it myself."

The estate agent hesitated, so Coughlan took out a wad of money. "I'll pay for the fuel and everything."

The estate agent hesitated but finally agreed. His head was beginning to ache and he just wanted to get rid of this red faced, tumescent, unwanted client. *He's probably got a bevy of tarts out there that he wishes to impress*, he said to himself as he handed Coughlan the keys.

"It's in the Aigualdoc, at berth A16. The fuel tank is almost full. All I ask is that you don't do anything reckless with it."

"You can trust me," lied Coughlan. "I'm just going to take a turn around the headland. See my new property from the sea."

The estate agent smiled and did not believe a word but he was happy to get Coughlan out of the office.

With the keys in his hand, Coughlan raced back to the marina. He ran over the planked jetties and soon located berth A16. He gulped as he looked at the sleek, clean lines of the highly polished teak motor cruiser. He climbed aboard anyway.

He sat in the expensive leather pilot's chair and looked for the key-hole. He located it and with a swift turn the cruiser's powerful engines roared into life. Coughlan looked out over the speedboat's long varnished prow and hesitated before squeezing the throttle. His record behind the wheel of his Armstrong Siddely was poor and it got positively disastrous behind the wheel of any borrowed vehicle. He had lost count of the number of times he had pranged his wife's little runabout. Nothing serious but numerous scraped and dents and plenty of paint spillages in the unsuitable boot.

He inched the throttle forward and slowly the craft nosed from its berth into the calm waters of the harbour. He dodged around the fishing trawlers tied to the jetty. Without looking at the fishermen as they cleaned up after their night's work, he increased his speed and headed towards the open sea.

He was gaining in confidence as he scooted the nippy little plaything around the harbour's doglegged opening. The transition between the mill pond and the open sea set that back a little. He panicked and had to wrestle with the half steering wheel as the small but powerful craft received the first buffeting from the heavier waves. With an increase in power, he got the speedboat back under control. Shortly after three o'clock he slipped the throttle to full and attempted to make up the ten mile start his fleeing employees had on him.

3.15pm.
Sitges Harbour.

The wake from Coughlan's borrowed speedboat was still visible on the static, fuel stained harbour waters when three men, a woman and a young girl, in a lumbering black Hispano Suiza rolled along to the end of the breakwater.

The once again soberly suited Konrad jumped from the car, followed by a powerful man in Wellingtons and a thick nautical polo neck sweater. They gesticulated wildly on the quay before returning to the car where the third man, a very angry third man, had remained in his seat. Konrad leaned into the car and smiled apologetically at the large and irate passenger, who was dressed in an unseasonable hat pulled low and a scarf pulled high up around his face.

"It was here yesterday, Herr Reich Marshal," he stuttered.

The Unsinkable Herr Goering

The fat man demanded angrily, "Where is my vessel, Soellner? If you have taken my money and done nothing I will skin you alive."

"There must be an explanation, Herr Reich Marshal. I shall find out immediately." Konrad looked around for Spitzweg, desperate for assistance.

After weeks of inactivity, either sulking around in Berlin in disgrace or kicking his heels in a primitive Spanish backwater, the sea captain was happy to swing into action. He had quickly spotted the laid-out seamen. Before Konrad could ask for assistance, he grabbed one of the stricken crew by the lapels of his boiler suit and violently slapped him back to consciousness. After a brief and disjointed conversation, Spitzweg obtained a staccato explanation. He efficiently informed Goering that his contractor had betrayed him.

Still skulking in the backseat of the limousine, Goering pondered for a moment. "We must stop them. I need that ship. There is no time to find a replacement," he barked. "Get a boat, we'll go after them."

"A boat? Where from?" asked Konrad, panicking.

"We're in a fucking harbour, Major," bellowed Goering. "Use your initiative."

Konrad dithered on the quay but Goering took the initiative. He pointed at the nearest fishing smack.

"Spitzweg, can you sail that?"

"Yes of course, Herr Reich Marshal."

Goering took a Luger from his pocket. "You know what to do,." he said, handing it to the sailor. He turned to Konrad: "Major, you are armed also?"

Konrad nodded.

"Then help the captain."

Spitzweg and Konrad ran along the jetty, pistols at the ready. They climbed aboard the ramshackle trawler. The last two members of the Spanish crew aboard were surprised to be confronted by two Luger wielding hijackers. Surprised and terrified. Spitzweg with a pistol was a formidable sight and the fishermen's resistance was short-lived. Slightly bruised and befuddled, they were soon standing on the dock looking down the barrel of Konrad's gun. They remained there long enough to witness a large man, hauntingly familiar yet obscure, swathed in scarves as if it were midwinter, usher a woman and a girl along the jetty towards them. Spitzweg helped the enormous man and his family struggle down the short ladder to the trawler's deck. Once they were aboard, Konrad told the fishermen to fuck off and if they knew what was good for them to refrain from reporting this act of piracy for several hours. The men scuttled along the breakwater. Konrad climbed down to the trawler's deck. He left the Goerings standing uneasily at the stern and went to help Spitzweg. The sea captain had already opened the hatch leading to the fishing boat's engine. He ordered Konrad to follow him as he jumped through it. The expensively suited Lufftwaffe officer reluctantly followed. Once inside the cramped and greasy engine pit, Spitzweg immediately started the engine. He gave Konrad some rudimentary instructions in its maintenance and climbed back to the deck, leaving the uncomfortable pen-pusher limply holding a monkey wrench. Spitzweg checked that his illustrious leader was okay and then untied the trawler before running speedily to the bridge.

Inside the cramped wheelhouse, Spitzweg closed his nostrils to the smell of sweat and rotting shrimps and purposefully seized the wheel. He engaged the propellers. At 3.41pm, the recently retired Reich Marshal of Germany, his family, two crew and a commandeered craft joined the pursuit of the Atheling.

3.44pm.
Sitges Harbour

The two bleary-eyed Gestapo agents spun the wheels of the steaming Mercedes over the dusty breakwater and brought the over-heating car to halt at the end of the harbour wall.

Haller stumbled out and immediately scanned the bobbing vessels in the marina.

"Do you see a likely craft?" he asked Gunther as the killer joined him at the water's edge.

"All these trawlers are oceangoing," replied Gunther. "But would the Reich Marshal choose such a slow and uncomfortable means of escape?"

"Beggars can't be choosers," shrugged Haller. "We will check as many boats as we can from the quay and then I suppose we will have to hire a launch to get a better look at those boats at anchor."

"That won't be necessary," replied the sharp-eyed Gunther. "I believe that I see the Reich Marshal on the deck of that trawler." Gunther pointed to the swiftly departing trawler that was passing through the channel at their rear.

Haller's gaze followed his junior officer's outstretched arm. "Fuck me! I think you're right!" he exclaimed.

"There's no mistaking that massive frame."

"We're still in time to stop him, Gunther. Get us a boat," commanded Haller.

Gunther quickly retreated to the boot of the cooling Mercedes and began to sort through the small travelling armoury he had bought with him. He surveyed the highly-oiled weapons lovingly before selecting a broom-handled Mauser pistol and a pair of stick grenades. He cocked the rifle and put the grenades in the pocket of his leather overcoat before striding across the jetty to the nearest rusting trawler.

In just a few very, very violent seconds, another crew of Spanish fishermen were persuaded to give up the most important tool of their trade. By 3.55pm, the two Gestapo agents had hamfistedly joined the pursuit.

4.11pm.
The Mediterranean; off Tarragona.

With the Atheling steaming safely through the calm inshore waters and the boiler pressure satisfactory if a little variable - the unusually expensive fuel delivered an erratic supply of horsepower - Maurice decided it was time for refreshment. With typical economy, he turned to his brother who was happily maiming yet another pile of packing cases and priceless canvases.

"Kettle," he announced.

Ivor stopped what he was doing and breezed through the gently tumbling corridors to the galley where he soon began banging pots with gusto.

With a worrying pop he put a light to the gas under a huge pot of potatoes that the cook had been about to boil when he was so rudely interrupted by Ivor's strong right hand.

Ian Cassidy

He set another pot of water to boil for the tea. Then he looked about for something to add to the lukewarm potatoes. He found an open catering-size tin of grey corned beef that displayed only slight evidence of rodent attention and with the decorator's scraper that he kept in the pocket of his overalls he began shovelling the unwholesome meat into the simmering potatoes. With the same scraper he nipped the tops off a few dirty carrots and bunged them unwashed into the pot. Satisfied that the stew was coming along nicely he turned to the tea.

He sniffed at the unfamiliar leaves that appeared to be of the Serbian Cook's own secret recipe. With a shrug of the shoulders, he began spooning them into the massive teapot whose grimy appearance bore witness to its years of idleness prior to the arrival of the Staffordshire tea-bellies.

We want a good strong brew, he said to himself and carried on piling in the tea leaves. With the pot half full of soggy flavourless floor scrapings, he stood back and waited for the water to boil.

Several minutes later, Ivor banged onto the bridge with a tray of mugs filled with an unctuous, sweet liquid with only one redeeming feature, it was hot.

Jack, Bert and Don were busily and somewhat apprehensively studying the indecipherable sea charts and getting more and more worried. Their plan had seemed easy when hatched the previous day but now, faced with the enormity of the Mediterranean and the rolling obstructive hulk of the Atheling, they were not so confident.

Each of the three men thirstily took a mug of tea and all three instantly regretted it. In relays they rushed outside and spat mouthfuls of the filthy liquid over the bridge's viewing platform.

They grumbled back to the wheelhouse ready to give Ivor a piece of their minds but the inept tea boy had already set off for the engine room.

The reception he received below was little better and so the men had to resort to quenching their thirst with water. All except Maurice, who had craftily secured a crate of beer from the wardroom for his refreshment.

4.14pm.
Sitges. Office of Garda Civil.

The desk sergeant sucked manfully on a Ducados and smiled at his good fortune. He could expect a very peaceful couple of hours as the town took its midday nap. Who bothers the police at siesta time? He put his feet on the desk and thought of his son's impending marriage. He was finally getting rid of the wastrel.

His feelings of content deserted him as four bruised and disorientated trawlermen banged on the counter. After much violent fist waving, a lot of bad language and the total devastation of his paperwork, the sergeant was able to ascertain that both crews had been assaulted and their boats stolen at gunpoint.

Distressed that piracy had invaded his sleepy beat, he ran to his captain's office, only to find it empty. Like almost everyone else in the town the senior officer was taking his siesta. Panicking at having to act on his own initiative, he picked up the telephone and cursed as he waited for the operator to pick up. After an interminable wait the operator answered and the sergeant asked to be connected to the coast guard in Barcelona. There followed another lengthy delay but finally a sleepy voice answered. After some persuasion the dispatcher was prevailed upon to scramble a launch to investigate. Although scramble was hardly the word as the dispatcher explained that he would have to raise the coast guards from their slumbers, prepare the vessel for sea and then get the whole sleepy shebang down the coast to Sitges.

The sergeant thanked the man for his honesty and worried about how he would break the news of such a tardy start to the criminal investigation to the victims, he returned to the foyer only to find it deserted.

The trawlermen had decided to make their own arrangements and were at that moment rousing their colleagues from the fishing fleet with a view to raising a posse to track down their purloined boats.

At 5.25pm, the sturdy coast guard launch nosed from its mooring and, braced by the sea air, the crew shook off their annoyance at their interrupted siesta and pushed the fast sloop to top speed in pursuit of the stolen fishing boats.

At the same time, two rusty fishing boats made an unaccustomed entry into the afternoon waters off Sitges. Each had a pair of dispossessed fishermen on its prow, waving encouragement to their helpful helmsmen colleagues as they too joined the chase.

Ian Cassidy

6.47pm.
Gibraltar. Admiralty HQ.

A white shorted ensign rushed through the corridors of the Navy offices and bumped into the duty officer who was just sneaking off to the wardroom for a gin and it.

The ensign panted an apology and excitedly began his report.

"There may be some hostile activity along the Spanish coast, Sir," he panted.

"Don't be ridiculous Hazel," snapped the thirsty Commander. "There isn't an enemy vessel left in the Med."

Ensign Hazel handed over a radar report. "Look at that, Sir. Radar shows a flotilla of small vessels heading this way."

"Spanish trawlers, you dolt."

"I don't believe so, Sir. It's the wrong time of the day for the Spanish to be putting to sea. Also the blip from the lead vessel is far too big to be coming from a trawler."

"Alright, Hazel, I'll trust your judgement. We'd better investigate. Have we got anything in the area?"

"Yes Sir, HMS Thunder is returning from that shindig on the Riviera. By my calculations she must right on them."

"Get her to divert and have a shufti. But I'm sure it's nothing."

"Aye, aye, Sir."

Storm in a tea-cup, the commander said to himself as the ensign sprinted to the radio room. *But I'll go and have that gin anyway, just in case I'm needed later.*

7.36pm.
Off Castellon De La Plana.

With the late evening sunlight beating down on his balding pate, Coughlan pushed his launch closer to the Atheling as she lumbered through the cooling Mediterranean waters.

He had noticed the two trawlers bearing down on him from behind. He was unsure whether they were just fishing boats or further pursuers of the Atheling, he decided now was the time to act.

The Unsinkable Herr Goering

Had he been aware of the other two trawlers and the coast guard launch also to the north, he would have acted sooner.

Coughlan bounced the speedboat through the waves and came within shouting distance of his quarry. He screeched over the screaming engines and gently lapping waves to Don who was standing gaunt on the prow of the Atheling.

"Slow down you ugly twat. I want a word."

Don pretended not to hear and Coughlan screamed his request again. This time Don waved to his employer and slowly ambled to the bridge to pass the message on.

Jack was struggling with the controls and worried by the fact that the ship was making very heavy going of its progress down the Spanish coast. Despite Maurice's vigilance in the engine room, the Atheling had been steadily losing steam pressure The unusual fuel had not been to the boiler's taste.

Don informed the harassed helmsman that they had a visitor wishing to come aboard. Jack, who was running out of ideas, considered the proposal and quickly decided that Coughlan's financial clout and sharp brain would be very useful to them in the trying hours to come.

As he went to adjust the ship's speed, Jack spotted the low threatening shape of a destroyer through the dirty window of the bridge. If he had ever entertained doubts about enlisting his employer's aid, they deserted him now. He pushed the brass leaver to stop and shouted a similar command to Maurice down below.

With the might of HMS Thunder approaching from the south, Jack turned to Don and said, "Throw him a ladder or something. Let's see what the bastard's got to say."

The lunging cargo ship changed down a gear and finally came to a stop. Coughlan smiled at the swiftness with which his request had been met and waited expectantly as the powerless cargo boat rolled in the calm waters.

Don unrolled a rope ladder and threw it over the rusty flank of the Atheling. Coughlan spotted the dangling ropes and displaying surprising proficiency at the tiller he skilfully manoeuvred the sleek launch to the side of the ship.

He tied the motor cruiser to the ladder and confidently climbed up the swinging ladder.

From his position to the north of the Atheling, Coughlan had been blindsided but once Don had grudgingly helped up on to the deck, he immediately spotted the British destroyer as it crashed at high speed towards them.

"Fuck me," he said. "Now that's a serious piece of hardware. We better get this sorted out fast or we could be on the wrong end of a torpedo." He grabbed hold of Don: "Come on, take me to the others."

Five minutes later Coughlan convened a hasty council of war on the bridge.

"Whatever you were trying to pinch in the hold, you can forget about it now. That's a British warship out there, we can't out run it. And even if we could, there's nowhere to go cos there's two boats chasing us from the north."

"What do you mean, two?" asked Maurice. "I can see five of the fuckers."

"Whatever," said Coughlan indifferently. "Two ships or five ships, you're not going to get away. So you better just hand back what you've nicked and hope the Spanish don't hang you for committing piracy on the high seas."

"We're not trying to pinch anything," protested Jack: "We're trying to stop your fucking Nazi friends from escaping."

"What the fuck are you talking about?"

"Look we haven't got much time," said Bert, taking over. "So let me explain."

"I'm all ears," Coughlan scoffed.

Bert quickly went over the main points and Coughlan stood there silent and astonished.

"Fuck me! Goering, you say." Coughlan looked sheepishly at his assembled employees. "Look, lads, I had no idea."

The six painters hooted in disapproval but Coughlan waved them back to order.

"Right, lads, we need a cover story."

"And a bloody good one," said Don gloomily.

Coughlan pondered for a minute.

"First off, let me do all the talking. I'll tell 'em that we were all working on my place over here."

"But you haven't got a place over here."

"I have now. I bought one this morning."

"We thought you kept on sneaking off to the knocking shop."

"Not every day." The stress of the situation brought out uncharacteristic frankness. "Anyway, that's the story. I got you all over here to do up my holiday home. No permits or forms filled in cos I didn't want to pay Spanish tax or to use Spanish workers."

"Be daft to when you've got builders of your own on the payroll," Maurice grinned.

"Precisely. And then last night, when we were having a drink in the port, we spotted Goering and the Jerries on the boat. We guessed what he was trying to do and this morning we stole the boat so that he couldn't use it."

"Might work."

"It'll fucking have to. Otherwise we're looking at plenty of porridge. Treason, trading with the enemy, you name it," Bert pointed out unnecessarily.

"Okay." said Coughlan. "That's agreed then. We better get a flag of St George flying. We don't want that destroyer shooting first and asking questions later."

The men dithered on the bridge. "Where do we get a flag?" Bert asked.

"Make one." Coughlan ordered. "There's buckets of paint in the hold." He turned to Maurice and Ivor: "You two, you're the fastest painters in the fucking west. Start bollocking red and white crosses on the sides of the ship."

The brothers grim raced off to the hold Coughlan continued, "And the rest of you, take a sledgehammer to the partitions in the hold and chuck everything on the boiler. The less everybody knows about what we've been up to down there the better."

The other four men started to leave the bridge. As he went through the door Jack stopped. "What you gonna do?" he asked his employer.

Ian Cassidy

"I think I'm going to have word with Herr Goering. He still owes me a lot of money."

"You're joking."

"If you don't ask, you don't get," shrugged Coughlan. "I'd take Ivor with me to make sure but he's more use here."

"I don't think he'll pay up, with or without a kicking from Ivor," smiled Jack as he left the bridge.

Coughlan called him back.

"If I'm not back before that destroyer gets here and she starts shelling Goering's boat, try and get her gunners to aim away from me."

You should be so lucky, Jack said under his breath as he ran to join his sledgehammer-wielding colleagues in the hold.

Coughlan vaulted over the rail and scaled down the dancing rope ladder. He untied the motor cruiser and confidently headed off in the direction of Goering's rapidly closing trawler. He steered the quick-moving craft alongside the slower working boat. Bouncing on the gently undulating waves, he made a grab for one of the buoys hanging from the trawlers' sides. On the second attempt, he grabbed it and tied his speedboat to it. Judging the tide perfectly, he caught the upswing and used the momentum to spring onto the deck of the trawler, only to find himself looking down the barrel of a Luger.

Konrad stood in front of him, no longer the diffident, effete Portuguese secretary but every inch an officer in the Lufftwaffe. Coughlan put his hands above his head and smiled resignedly.

"Ah, Mr Coughlan, what a pleasant surprise. Do come into the wheelhouse and meet your employer," he commanded.

As he turned away, Coughlan could have sworn he saw a woman and child hiding among the flapping fishing nets. He shook his head. *Must be the stress of the situation*, he said to himself.

Coughlan stumbled in front of his now less than friendly acquaintance. He blinked in the gloom of the rancid wheelhouse and briefly noticed a large man struggling with the trawlers' controls before his eyes came to rest on the figure of an even larger man sitting uncomfortably on an improvised stool.

"Fuck me! It really is Goering," he exclaimed.

"That is correct, Coughlan," snapped Goering. "And if you've made your reckless jaunt in the hope of bringing me in and claiming a reward, then I'm afraid you are going to be sadly disappointed." He took out his own Luger, personally presented to him by the Führer, and pointed it at Coughlan.

"Turn you in? No, not me." said Coughlan breezily. "I've come to help," he lied, frantically trying to think of an explanation.

"Why would you do that?" Goering demanded.

"Take my boat; it's a lot faster than this." Coughlan said, relieved to have come up with something.

"Alas, even it is not fast enough to outrun the guns on that destroyer. Besides, Coughlan, I do not believe you," sighed Goering. "So I think I'm going to have to shoot you."

Back on the Atheling, the Thunder's contingent of highly-trained marines swarmed up the cargo ship's rusting sides. With Sten guns at the ready, they took control of the deck. First they surrounded Jack on the bridge and rounded up Maurice and Ivor, who were still toshing red and white paint onto every exposed piece of the ship's superstructure. They silently and menacingly frog marched the two painters to the bridge and, despite his precarious position, Ivor could not help craftily splashing paint onto the pristinely camouflaged back of the lieutenant of marines.

Beneath the tarpaulins covering the hold, the other employees of James Coughlan & Sons were burning the last evidence of the firm's contractual arrangement with Hitler's erstwhile deputy.

On the bridge, the interrogation began. A terrified Jack gulped every time he looked at the host of surrounding machine pistols before he completed a stuttering explanation. The marines listened with growing astonishment.

"So you're telling me Goering was planning to desert Germany and get away aboard this cargo ship. And that you stole the ship to stop him," asked the astounded Lieutenant.

"Incredible isn't it?" said Maurice with deliberate irony.

"I'll say. And that Goering is now on one of those fishing boats and your boss has gone after him."

"That's about the size of it," said Maurice.

"Your boss is a very brave man."

"Not the words I'd have chosen." said Maurice under his breath.

The lieutenant continued, "Which fishing boat is Goering on? We must get him if we can."

"The one with the speedboat tied to it," said Jack, pointing.

"Who's in the others then?"

Jack shrugged. "The Spanish, I think, trying to get their trawler back."

"Right," said the lieutenant turning to his sergeant: "Signal to the Captain that all is secure here. Inform him that Herman Goering is aboard the lead fishing boat. Advise that he concentrate his fire on that position."

The sergeant went to the ship's rail and began signalling with his light. The huge brooding gun turrets on HMS Thunder swung slowly to their firing positions.

Coughlan gulped again as he looked at the angry incandescent Reich Marshal.

"Let's not be hasty," he stuttered.

"And why should I not be hasty?" barked Goering. "You have put my family and myself in grave danger." Goering cocked the Luger but never had chance to pull the trigger. The sixteen inch guns on HMS Thunder expertly landed a brace of high explosive shells just metres from the trawler. The explosions shook Goering from his stool. Coughlan steadied himself ready to try and make a run for it, only to find the barrel of Konrad's gun pressed into his back. "Stay where you are, Mr Coughlan," Konrad quietly ordered the Black Country painting contractor.

Spitzweg, who was not noticeably disturbed by the shelling, helped Goering back to his stool, where the Nazi quickly recovered himself. "Get us out of here, Captain!" He shouted.

"We can't outrun it, Herr Reich Marshal."

"Just do what you can," Goering barked before turning to face Coughlan again. He cocked the gun again.

Coughlan thought fast. "Look, my men are with the Navy by now. They're probably telling the gunners which of the boats to shoot at. They won't shoot at me so I can take your wife and child with me, they'll be safe."

Goering thought for a moment: "And in return for this service to my wife and child I won't shoot you. Is that correct?"

"Yes," said Coughlan quickly. "Although if you've got some Reich gold knocking about I could…"

Goering interrupted and despite himself he smiled: "For sheer brass neck Coughlan, I almost…"

Another two high explosive shells once again detonated just to the front of the trawler but much closer than the first salvo. The trawler rocked violently and even Spitzweg had trouble maintaining his balance.

As he shambled to his feet, still holding his trusty Luger, Goering shouted at Coughlan, "Your offer is accepted, Mr Coughlan. You will have two very important passengers on your return journey. Now I suggest you get out of here, before I lose my patience." Coughlan stumbled onto the trawler's bucking deck only to be knocked out of the way by the speeding bulk of Goering as he rushed to take his leave of his wife and daughter.

The Reich Marshal located Emmy and Edda among the tattered nets and hugged them both: "Now the two of you are to go with this gentleman," he scoffed. "Go with him, he will take you to the mainland, where I will join you very shortly."

"But Hermann," pleaded his wife. "Aren't you in danger from that British warship?"

"No, not at all, nothing we cannot handle. It's just that this man's vessel is much swifter than ours, so he can get you out of harm's way so much faster."

"Then why don't you come with us, Hermann?"

"I must remain with my men," Goering replied pompously: "You would not have me abandon these two loyal German warriors to the British?"

His wife nodded and Goering hugged them both closely to him. He kissed the woman and child briefly. "I will be with you again before you know it. Now go with Major Soellner; he will help you aboard."

Konrad led the woman and child away and a slightly tearful Goering turned to Coughlan who was still hovering on the deck, the hope of some financial benefit not entirely extinguished.

The head of the Lufftwaffe towered menacingly over the greedy building contractor and grabbed him roughly by the collar.

"Now, Coughlan, I know all about you, my agent did a very thorough job. I am aware of your unsavoury proclivities. If you lay one finger on either of them you will wish you had never been born."

To drive home the point Goering slammed Coughlan violently into the wheelhouse wall before rushing inside. He returned several seconds later with a briefcase in his hands. Coughlan was dusting himself off when Goering slammed the briefcase into his chest.

"Inside you'll find a little payment. They're bonds and securities, perhaps studying them will make you forget your libido. Now get out of here."

Coughlan jumped aboard his rocking speedboat and checked that his passengers were safely seated on the comfortable double back seat, more suited to sipping champagne than sheltering from exploding munitions. He stashed the briefcase safely at his feet and struggled frantically with the ignition. On the third attempt the engine fired, Coughlan pushed the throttle flat and whipped the speedy cruiser through the cordite-scented air towards the melee of small boats that now surrounded the Atheling.

Goering looked wistfully at his departing family before racing back to the wheelhouse.

"How goes it, Captain?"

"Not promising," Spitzweg growled through clenched teeth.

"Do what you can," commanded Goering.

Spitzweg manfully took hold of the controls and, with the outgunned trawler's puny Diesel engine stretched to breaking point, he flung the sluggish craft into a zigzag series of evasive manoeuvres.

Without the encumbrance of Coughlan's motor cruiser tied to its side, the shabby but powerful trawler responded deftly to Spitzweg's expert touch. Briefly, he succeeded in putting some distance between them and the looming destroyer. It was a false dawn. Spitzweg was good but the gunners were better.

Another expertly directed salvo straddled the fleeing trawler, rattling the fleeing vessel to its core and blowing out the smoke-stained glass in the wheelhouse.

"All is lost, Herr Reich Marshal," panted the exhausted sailor.

"Nonsense, man," scowled Goering. "This small vessel can go where they can't. Take us into the shallows where they can't follow us."

"Their guns would cut us off before we got close."

"Just head for the nearest beach We'll try and get away on land."

"We will never make it. I recognise the pattern of their firing. The Englander gunnery officer is offering us the chance to surrender."

As Spitzweg looked expectantly at his superior officer, two more shells exploded each side of the trawler, sending it rocking like a child's toy in a bubble bath. The experienced sailor clung desperately to the ship's wheel but Goering was flung dangerously into the wheelhouse wall. Visibly shaken, he heard Spitzweg scream.

"And that offer will not be on the table much longer."

Goering sat on the floor of the wheelhouse a broken man.

"I thought you were the pride of the German navy," he said peevishly.

"In my own vessel I am. The Englanders would not have stood a chance. But in this unarmed trawler my hands are tied behind my back. Give the order, Herr Reich Marshal, and I will cut the engines."

Goering hesitated and from his position on the floor looked through the door of the battered wheelhouse. "But the beach looks so close."

"We will never make it and even if we did, the British already have a party of marines in the water. They would soon catch up with us on the shore."

Goering hesitated again.

"Give the order, Herr Reich Marshal."

"Oh, very well, switch her o…" These were the last words spoken by Reich Marshall Hermann Goering, as at that minute the gunnery officer on board HMS Thunder, his patience exhausted, had altered his target co-ordinates just enough and given the order to administer the coup de grace.

Four high explosive shells tore through the flimsy, worm-infested wooden hull of the trawler before detonating and reducing the boat and everyone aboard to splinters. So Hermann Goering, Reich Marshal of

Ian Cassidy

Germany, Commander-in-Chief of the Lufftwaffe, Adolf Hitler's nominated successor, Interior Minister of Prussia, Plenipotentiary of the Four Year Plan, President of the Reichstag, winner of the Knight's Cross (first class) and Architect of the Nuremberg Laws, died.

Seconds before the fatal explosion, Konrad jumped into the cool waters of the Mediterranean and struck out in the direction of the Spanish trawlers, looking forward to peaceful internment in a Catalan prison until the cessation of hostilities. The huge displacement of water caused by the exploding shells and the flying debris from Goering's devastated boat made swimming difficult. Eventually he achieved his aim and, spitting seawater, he clung onto a buoy tied to the side of a one of the pursuing Spanish trawlers.

Imagine his surprise when he was unceremoniously tugged from the water by an angry Teutonic arm. Gunther tossed him onto the deck and Sturmbanführer Haller of the Gestapo welcomed him aboard.

The Secret Policemen treated Konrad in a manner befitting a senior officer of the Lufftwaffe High Command, if a trifle roughly. Their begrudging courtesy did not improve Konrad's mood as he sat slumped and dripping under the trawler's foul-smelling nets, contemplating a brief, brutal, in camera trial in a filthy dungeon beneath Kaltenbrunner's headquarters.

He need not have worried. The three Nazis successfully evaded the wrath of HMS Thunder, as she was currently otherwise engaged in negotiations with an irate officer from the Barcelona Coastguard. Later that evening, as they attempted to slink unnoticed into Tarragona, they were arrested on suspicion of theft and smuggling.

There followed a period of internment before all three were handed over to the Allies.

The looming grey threat of HMS Thunder ploughed through the diesel and debris-strewn waters where moments before had been a fishing smack.

"No survivors, Sir," reported the first mate.

"Very good, number one. Now let's get to the bottom of all this." The captain pointed towards the lumbering Atheling. "Send out the launch with a party to sail that bloody death trap and bring everybody else back here. And make sure you get the three people in that motorboat. I want some answers."

"Aye, aye, Sir."

"And I don't want to hear any more nonsense about Hermann bloody Goering. I want the truth."

Back aboard the Atheling, the lieutenant of marines supervised as his men threw a ladder down to Coughlan, whose overworked pleasure craft was banging into the sides of its much larger sister.

Coughlan took hold of the ladder but did not attempt to climb. He gestured helplessly towards the newly widowed German woman and her daughter. The lieutenant got the message: "Get those two women up here!" He ordered two of his men and two burley marines skipped down the rope ladder and using a mixture of fireman's carries and sheer brute force they succeeded in getting the woman and child to the deck. Coughlan followed unaided by the navy.

The platoon of marines, seven Black Country builders and two terrified German females stood on the deck of the Atheling, unsure what to do next.

"Like spare pricks at a wedding," observed Ivor before the Lieutenant spotted the approaching launch and gave the order to get aboard. Everyone was happy that the embarrassing period of indecision had been brought to an end, except the two marines who were detailed to carry the remainder of the Goering family down the rope ladder to the launch.

The overloaded craft made its way back to HMS Thunder and after a considerable amount of shouting and swearing, climbing up and down ladders and some precarious moments. As the evening waters became choppy, the Captain began his inquisition.

Coughlan explained, backed up by his men and in the absence of other evidence the captain was forced to accept it.

Exasperated he turned to the frightened woman on his deck, "So you really are Frau Goering."

"That is correct," said Emmy Goering, trying to maintain her dignity.

The Captain was a little embarrassed. The skill of his gunners had made the woman a widow. He called to the first mate, "Get the MO to these women immediately and see that they are made comfortable."

Ian Cassidy

He turned to Coughlan. "Now, Mr Coughlan, what are we going to do with you?"

Coughlan shrugged and the captain continued. "Do you wish to return to Sitges?"

With an eye to the main chance and a free trip home, Coughlan replied, "Nothing to go back for, just get us home. I think we've seen enough of Spain for a while."

"But the building work on your holiday home?" asked the captain.

"Nothing that won't keep until after the war." He regretted leaving the money hidden in the hotel's lavatory cistern, knowing that the landlady or more likely her aged handy-man husband would find it. But after the way they had been getting through it, what with his trips to the brothel and the men's services to the Spanish brewing industry, it was probably amounted to little more than he owed her anyway. He turned back to captain, who had not finished speaking.

"Very well Mr Coughlan, we'll get you to Gibraltar and take it from there. You will, of course, dine with me this evening. I am anxious to learn why you acted in such a courageous manner."

Coughlan stuttered, "Oh, heat of the moment, you know."

The six painters guffawed in the background.

"You as well." The captain said, looking at the six dishevelled men.

The men readily agreed.

"Until dinner time then." The captain said, already regretting being so free with the invitations. "And now if you will excuse me I must deal with the Spanish."

Coughlan and his men each took a bottle of brown ale from a steward as he came up from the galley and sat drinking them in the fading Mediterranean sunlight. Coughlan inched away and once at a safe distance began to examine the contents of the briefcase handed to him by the recently deceased Reich Marshal of Germany. He smiled contentedly to himself and sipped his brown ale.

So HMS Thunder started on the short coastal hop to Gibraltar, followed by the under arrest Atheling, and for the firm of James Coughlan & Sons, as they drank and smoked in the evening breeze, the long journey home had begun.

afterword

Emmy and Edda Goering were repatriated to Germany, where Emmy retired into obscurity, taking her daughter with her. On reaching majority, Edda emerged as a vociferous Nazi propagandist and apologist. Although she was never vociferous about the true circumstances of her father's demise.

Major Konrad Soellner, late of the Lufftwaffe, was tried as a war criminal. As a senior member of the Air Ministry he was suspected of complicity in the murders of the fifty escaped Allied airmen from Stalag Luft 111 in the days following March 25th 1944. His indirect involvement saved him from the rope but not a thirteen year sentence. From which he emerged nine years later, older and wiser but otherwise unscathed, to take up a position as head of recruitment at Lufthansa. We have him to thank for the scores of handsome if slightly effete young men who pushed trolleys up and down the aisles - aisles that lack a row 'thirteen' - of the German national carrier's fledging jet liner service in the fifties and sixties.

Haller and Gunther were also tried as war criminals but as their guilt was never in doubt, both made trips to the gallows in the spring of 1947. Their superior officer Gruppenführer Heinrich Müller, Head of the Gestapo, evaded the noose. He vanished from Hitler's bunker and was variously reported to be working in a hardware store in Buenos Aires, as a car salesman in Asunción and as a police officer in Albania. Kaltenbrunner never managed to show him who was really in charge.

ObergruppenFührer Ernst Kaltenbrunner, Head of Reich Security was hanged in Nuremberg on October 16th 1946 along with Von Ribbentrop and the other leading Nazis who did not manage to evade the Allies. Alongside Kaltenbrunner and Von Ribbentrop in the Nuremberg dock was a large blond man who answered to the name of Hermann Goering. The former Reichsmarshall's resurrection was not a miracle; it was the result of frantic activity by British Intelligence.

The Allies were faced with a problem They were resigned to the fact that Hitler would take his own life before they could get their hands on him and allowing for the likelihood that several of the other senior Nazis would slip through the net, the planned war crimes trials lacked a really big name. Hess was a bumbling wreck, Schnacht was a banker and who had ever heard of Von Neurath?

Almost before Goering's body had settled on the seabed, orders were given that his death would go unreported. After all, the Nazis were hardly likely to broadcast the treachery of Hitler's number two. A look-a-like was sought out and quickly found. Soon after, blurred photographs of a large blonde man in Lufftwaffe uniform, wearing handcuffs on the deck of HMS Thunder, were circulated among the World's press agencies.

Private 617493, Timothy Price of the British Army Entertainment Corps, put on a bravura performance while in custody. The pinnacle of his acting career came at Nuremberg. Admittedly he had been kept away from the sharper of the indicted Nazis and deliberately seated by the already barking Hess, who would not have noticed had he been sharing a bench with a hat stand let alone a stand-in Reich Marshal. He even gave an impressive speech, in faultless German, drafted for him by Airey Neave and, rumour has it, an up and coming young novelist with an interest in political skulduggery and espionage who went by the name of Ian Fleming.

After the speech, which many commentators believe sealed the fate, if it was ever in doubt, of the defendants and despite opposition from the Russian Judges who had no doubt read Zweig's masterpiece, "The Case of Sergeant Grischa" the occupying powers thought it churlish to hang him. On the night that the senior Nazis met their maker, a report was circulated that Reich Marshal Hermann Goering cheated the hangman and died by his own hand. However the man who had filled Goering's jackboots for all those weeks following the debacle off the Spanish coast did not die.

The story of Goering's suicide by use of a cyanide capsule concealed in the heel of his shoe was concocted. The Allies claimed the body was cremated and no one was any the wiser. Ashes are after all ashes.

The overweight actor was allowed to quietly slip away with an inadequate pension, to take up a series of undemanding roles in local theatre and several very bitty bit parts on BBC radio. In the mid fifties, his heart could stand the strain of lugging such a massive frame around no longer and he succumbed to a ruptured aorta on the set of *Z-Cars* as he waited to give yet another forgettable performance as a large and unruly drunk.

Diana Coughlan was, of course, traded in for a newer model and while it came as no surprise to their friends and relations that such a virulent sexual warrior as her husband would respond to his increasing baldness, widening girth and wilting penis in such a time honoured fashion, it did to Diana. She endured many painful months coming to terms with the fact that for all those lonely but never dull years, she had been married to a bastard.

She finally emerged from these doldrums of her own making and settled into a peaceful retirement, pottering in her beloved garden and enjoying the company of a new group of friends. She also had the satisfaction of living to see her replacement, the rather ugly and un-trophy-like second wife, recklessly spend her way through her ex-husband's ill-gotten fortune.

James Coughlan and his six employees returned to England in triumph to a series of civic receptions and awards. Coughlan milked the publicity for all it was worth and did not even mind the hefty fine he received for his flagrant breach of wartime travel restrictions.

The acclaim culminated in a trip to the palace, where the young Princess Elizabeth, deputising for her infirm father, pinned a George Cross to Coughlan's chest and presented the six scrubbed and uncomfortably suited work men with an MBE each.

Once the adulation had died down, the six men went back to work in the hellhole of the Black Country's foundry belt. The MBEs went back and forth to the pawnbrokers and one by one the men succumbed

The Unsinkable Herr Goering

to heart attacks and strokes, silicosis caused by the grime and dust, or cancer from the compulsory cigarettes. All except Ivor, who was spared a lingering, coughing death by a tragic and unexpected industrial accident. The man who would hang upside down from the steel trusses of steepling steelworks like a grimy Birmingham bat was a victim of his own total confidence and total lack of fear. He slipped on a vertiginous foundry roof and fell through the brittle asbestos sheeting to the unyielding concrete below. Typically, Coughlan came out of the affair smelling of roses. No verdict of death caused by an unsafe system of work. No fine from the Department of Work and not even a lawsuit from the unlucky painter's dependants to defend. The coroner's verdict of accidental death came about after the telling evidence of Ivor's brother. Maurice explained that no matter what safety measures were put in place, no matter what investment was made in boson's chairs and harnesses, Ivor had his own way of doing things. Typically Maurice put it quite succinctly. "Ivor simply would not be told."

Coughlan continued to find work for his men and to find time for hundreds of slutty office girls from Birmingham's then thriving heavy industries and to plan for the day when he could realise Goering's legacy and retire to doing what he did best: crosswords, reading badly written crime novels and bedding the admin staff, although not necessarily in that order.

That day never properly came. Coughlan slipped slowly into alcoholism, never managing to fully retire although the passage of time and a clever accountant allowed him to gradually launder the earnings from Goering's gilt-edged portfolio into and ultimately straight through his profligate second wife's avaricious hands. She spent at such a phenomenal rate that he was forever forced to supplement his unearned income by constant returns to the fumes of the Black Country's foundries. Although unlike his decorated decorators he was never forced to pawn his George Cross. I still have it. It formed the sum total of his legacy to me, if you discount premature baldness and dodgy skin.

Finally, like his first wife, he too was traded in for a wealthier model an indecently short time after the money ran out. The end came quickly. Anne Cole was arrested at her desk in the sleepy Soho publisher's office

Ian Cassidy

and interrogated by MI6. What had begun as a routine investigation quickly escalated into a full-blown espionage enquiry when a search of her flat turned up the transmitter and other evidence of Anne's work for German Intelligence. English wartime regulations regarding the treatment of enemy agents were harsh, lethally harsh and Anne's fate was never in doubt. She revealed that her true name was Katherine Baatjer but nothing more. She had only done that so that her personal effects could be returned to her family in Germany following her appointment with the firing squad. An appointment she duly kept on a hazy September morning in 1944. No one, not even Anne knew that the forgettable night she had spent with James Coughlan had left her pregnant.

selected bibliography

Butler. Evan & Young. Gordon. The Life and Death of Hermann Goering. David & Charles. Newton Abbot. 1989.

Montgomery Hyde. H. Norman Birkett. Penguin 1989.

Moseley. Leonard. The Reich Marshal. Doubleday, New York, 1974.

Overy. R. Goering. Barns & Noble. New York. 2003.

Shirer. William. The Rise and Fall of the Third Reich. Simon & Schuster, New York, 1960.

Speer Albert. Inside the Third Reich. Weidendeld & Nicolson. London 1970.

Tusa. Ann, Tusa. John. The Nuremberg Trial. BBC Books, London 1995.

Walters Guy. Hunting Evil. Bantam. London 2009.

acknowledgements

My thanks go to Nate Gray for all his hard work and for tracking me down in the first place. Thanks for the music go to Robert Russell and posthumously to Graeme Lily. And to the three Johns; Harris, Moore and Cassidy, thanks for an anecdote I just couldn't leave out to the first two and thanks of a dermatological and tonsurial kind to the third. Most of all thanks to Ken Mercer, James Parry, Michael Parry, John Pettiford, 'Bob' Roberts and Ron Walker, if only more of you were still around.